# SEVEN THOUSAND IN ISRAEL

# SEVEN THOUSAND IN ISRAEL

## A Novel

by

## S. FOWLER WRIGHT

## THE BORGO PRESS

*An Imprint of Wildside Press LLC*

MMX

www.wildsidebooks.com

FIRST WILDSIDE EDITION

# CHAPTER ONE

JOHN OAKLEY sat at the desk in his bedroom window. It was opened widely, for the August afternoon was bright and warm. It gave a view of sloping lawn, flanked with rhododendrons, and then of a short flight of stone steps that led to a tennis-lawn from which a sound of voices came gay and clear on the windless air. Below that was a small paddock, and then the orchard, and then the hollow of Carford brook. The kitchen garden and the glass-houses lay to the left, and on the right the ground rose to the level at which he sat, and there, behind the rising bank, was a little hidden lawn, closed about with rhododendrons and lilac, laburnum and syringas, and with a little group of pines dividing it from the farther field.

They had made that lawn, Frida and he, when he had bought the place nearly thirty years ago. He had planted most of the trees with his own hands. But the choice had been hers. There had always been tea ready there on the fine afternoons when he had been able to get back from the works in time, and at the weekends. That was before the War. It had not been much used since Frida died.

Now his daughter Nina sat there with the friend she had brought down with her from London. He could hear their voices at times, just a few words, clear and distinct as though they were in the room beside him, and then they would be broken off as though by a dis-connecting switch.

It was a peculiarity of that lawn, which was known to all the family, though it was not always remembered. Small as it was, and shadowed by bush and tree, with the falling laurel-crowded bank between it and the larger lawn, it seemed a very quiet and secret place, but it was a curious acoustic fact that the voices of those who sat on its rustic bench would be carried erratically to the windows of the bedroom, which was on the same level, and not so distant as it might seem to be.

John Oakley did not listen. He was occupied with the estimate which he had brought home to complete during the weekend, but for which he would have been outside with the livestock, or in the rose-garden. Neither was he one to listen deliberately to that which he was not intended to hear. Beyond that, he was not greatly interested. He was fond of Nina, as she of him. But she belonged to another world. The world of the youth that had grown up since there had been peace in Europe. The youth that smoked and drank and danced and motored, that talked familiarly of nightclubs and cocktails, and of its right to have a good time. It was particularly clear on that point. A youth which seemed to him at times to be without shame, as it would profess to be without honour. That took its views of life, and its principles of morality, from the harlots of Hollywood. To whom duty was a forgotten word. Probably he was unfair. He was not old in years, but he had been friendless since Frida died. He had lived somewhat apart. He had held his business together through some difficult years. There were the birds, and the roses. Yet he was conscious of falling apart—and behind. He was acquiring the fatal habit of thinking much of the past. Perhaps the first sign of age. Age, not of the body, but of the mind. He was falling out of the ranks. As Nina had said to him at breakfast, not unkindly, but in contemptuous rejection of an opinion he had expressed: "Oh, Father, you're too unsophisticated to be alive." Was her judgement really sounder than his, her experiences more valuable? They were certainly different. He thought again that he might be unfair. Probably every generation has such thoughts, as hope is changed for an ended thing, and the vigour of life recedes. Customs fail and recur. We are at home in youth, but we spend our age in the tolerant kindliness of a foreign land. He had to remind himself again that he was not old in years. Only very lonely since Frida died, and tired with the ceaseless effort to hold the business together in these difficult times of high taxation and shortened hours. There was no forty-four-hour week for him. Day and night his mind must be on urgent problems which must be solved successfully if the works were to be kept going, and the weekly wages paid.

He believed that the commercial supremacy of England was failing, if it were not already gone. And those in his position were the leaders of an army that they could no longer control; that had been taught that it must fight without overexertion, or the risk of wounds; that victory did not matter overmuch. There was always the dole. How great might have been the future of the British Commonwealth of Nations, with its vast resources and its empty lands! But, when the battle was at its height, was not every new law passed to restrain activity, to reduce responsibility, to encourage slackness of living? The battle was at its height, and the captains of industry must lead an army that only fought by the clock. He knew that he was becoming unfair again. That this was not all the truth, perhaps not half.

And, after all, he believed in his own race, and his own land. Cannot a nation be tired at times, as a man tires? Will it always be foolish, because it falls to a foolish mood? That which is fundamental in character will reassert itself with a gathered strength. If he felt at discord with surrounding circumstance, even with those of his own family, must not the real fault lie in his lack of sympathy, or adaptability? At worst, it was the common lot. If he should fail, even with his own children, in understanding or tolerant sympathy, it would be no cause for satisfaction, but a plain fault. Nina, too, would grow old into an alien world that would contemn the outlook of her own youth.

Now her voice came clearly through the screening trees: "Oh, my dear! You should take no notice of that. Men are...." The voice broke off abruptly as it had begun. He scarcely heard, regarding it no more than the frequent call of the tennis-score that came from the lower lawn, and it was five minutes later, when he had completed his calculation of the amount of material that would be needed, and was putting the papers aside for a final revision tomorrow afternoon, that Nina's voice came again, as clearly as though she were standing beside him: "...my dear, you don't suppose mother *wanted* us, do you? Father made her, of course. Why, Aunt Muriel says that Dr. Wilson told him off after Elsie was born, and they had an awful row, and Dr. Wilson refused to come into the...." The voice died again.

For a moment John Oakley sat motionless, listening for the further words that did not come. Then he reached forward, and drew in and fastened the casement-window.

## CHAPTER TWO

"NINA, I want to speak to you."

Nina knew that tone, which she did not like. It reminded her too much of long-distant times when she had been brought into the library, at the door of which she now stood, for admonition, or rebuke of some infant delinquency. Not that she had ever been seriously punished. But she was sensitive at atmosphere. She had always liked to be popular and approved. As a child, a word of displeasure from either parent would make her miserable till the cloud lifted. And she had not often experienced such an incident. She had been obedient to her parents, and a good elder sister to the younger children, in a careless, good-humoured way. If she had done things of which her parents disapproved, she had always been considerate enough to do them quietly, so that their feelings should not be hurt. At least, that had been while her mother lived. Laterly among her London friends—well, her father had to know, more or less, and he didn't make as much trouble as you might have supposed he would. But, really, he was so unobservant, so *unsophisticated*, that it was always difficult to know how much he did know. Anyway, he was a back number. The modern world's different, and you have to do what others to round you. You simply have to.

"Yes, Father," she said, with a hand still on the door, in the half-affectionate, half-flippant tone which was her defensive armour against such emergencies. "I hope it won't take long. The car's...."

"It won't take long, but the car will have to wait a few minutes. Come and sit down. I want to talk to you about your mother. I accidentally overheard something that you were saying to Pauline this afternoon on the lawn."

Nina Oakley flushed easily. She had had a noticeably fair and beautiful complexion as a child, and now that she was twenty-seven, though her skin was somewhat damaged by cosmetics, and slightly coarsened by alcohol, it still reflected her feelings with an honesty which did not always please her. She looked uncomfortable enough as she took the chair opposite her father before the empty fireplace without further protest.

"What did your aunt really say?"

Nina felt slightly relieved by this question. If it were only a matter of having repeated what someone else had said. And probably father hadn't heard more than a few words. And, after all, Aunt Muriel *had* said it, and a good deal more, too, which she hadn't repeated to Pauline, for no particular reason, except that it hadn't occurred to her to do so. Nina's confidential or confessional moods were not frequent, but when they came over her they were without limit or restraint, and the one who was with her at the time would get the benefit of the lot.

"Aunt Muriel? She didn't mean anything really. I told her that I didn't suppose you could afford it. Mother often told me how little money you had about the time when Alwyn was born."

Joan Oakley saw that he was hooking something for which he had not cast his line. He said: "Couldn't afford what?" Nina realized that she was giving the wrong answer also. Unfortunately, she had gone too far to retreat. To invent a plausible alternative to the truth at this urgency was beyond her power. "Auntie said that Mother was in agony all night while you drove an old pony into Hunnerton for Dr. Wilson, because you wouldn't pay for a taxi."

"That is the kind of thing your aunt would say. Did you believe it?"

"I knew it was true about the pony, because Mother'd told me about that. But I said I knew you'd done the best you could. I told Auntie that I knew you hadn't got much money then."

"What did she say to that?"

"She said then…Mother oughtn't to have had Alwyn at all."

"I see. I don't really mind about that tale. If you'd thought for a moment, you'd have seen how silly it was. If I'd waited for a taxi, I should have had to wait five or ten years. But I was not asking you about that. What is the tale about Dr. Wilson when Elsie was born?"

"If you heard it, it's no use saying it over again. It's only what Aunt Muriel said…. I'm sorry I told Pauline. Of course, I know people look on those things differently from how they did then."

"Then you believed your aunt's tale?"

"I only know what she said. I daresay Auntie said more than was true."

"It was not a case of saying more than was true. It was an utter malicious imagination. No such quarrel or conversation ever occurred. It is a lie of a particularly poisonous kind, because Dr. Wilson is dead, and it would be impossible to disprove it, except for one fact that your aunt has overlooked. At the time that Elsie was born, Dr. Wilson was in Italy recovering from a long illness, and neither then nor later did your mother have her at all."

"Well, I'm sorry, Father. I think Auntie ought to be more careful. I only repeated what she'd told me that she knew herself. I know I say things I shouldn't when I get talking. I'll tell Pauline it isn't true."

She spoke with regret, but was not seriously troubled. It was bad luck that her father had overheard, but it was not anything that mattered much, one way or other. Old-fashioned people *did* do old-fashioned things before the years of modern enlightenment, and, except for something to talk about, what did they matter now? People hadn't understood then that they oughtn't to have children unless they were sure that they'd be able to send them to the best schools, and even then they ought to think of whether they wanted to travel or whether it might do their looks any harm. And she had a rather vague idea that they hadn't known how to stop them coming, even if they hadn't wanted them (as, of course, they didn't really) except in crude or dangerous ways. She had no doubt that she was more "sophisticated"—a word to which she attached a curiously narrow meaning—than her mother had been at her age. But it was bad luck that her father had heard.

"Well, if that's all, Father, I'll be getting off. I can't say more than I'm sorry. I'll tell Pauline. I'll tell Auntie, too, when I see her. She ought to be more careful of what she says."

"I don't *think* it will be much good saying anything to your aunt. But that isn't all. I don't really mind these things that are said about myself. It is the slander about your mother...."

Nina Oakley stared at her father in a bewildered astonishment. She was conscious that she would never willingly have said anything detrimental to her mother's memory, and she was absolutely unaware of having done anything of the kind. More than that, she was quite sure she had not.

"About Mother? Father! You know I wouldn't. Besides I don't *think* anything. There's nothing I *could* say. You must have thought you heard something that wasn't said."

"I heard you say that your mother did not want her children."

"Oh, *that*." She answered with a mingling of surprise and relief in her voice. "Well, of course, I didn't mean anything. I didn't mean after we were born. I know what a good mother she was. I only meant she couldn't have wanted us beforehand. There's nothing in that. I don't suppose most mothers do. I know I shouldn't. You couldn't go anywhere."

John Oakley looked at his daughter. She had been a good; affectionate child. He had been a good father to her. They had had their times of confidence, of close understanding, in earlier years. There was real love on both sides, which might show a hidden strength if a test should come. But he saw that there was a gulf of misunderstanding which he could not bridge. There were things that he could say, but were they worth saying? It might be no better than if he spoke in a foreign tongue. But Nina was showing signs again that she was impatient to go. If he did not speak now, he might never do so again.

He said: "I don't think you could easily understand how your mother would have felt if she had heard what you said. There is probably nothing of which you could accuse her in the whole category of crime which would have surprised or hurt her more. Thinking it over, I was almost glad she was dead."

"Well, Father, I'm sorry. I can't say more."

Nina was out of the room at last. It was a beastly mess, father overhearing like that. And all about nothing, too. Of course, she wouldn't say anything against her mother. Tears almost rose to her eyes at the thought. But Father *was* so sentimental. It had been quite uncomfortable. She had a half-articulate, half-resentful feeling that he had acted indecently. Old people must have feelings, of course, but they shouldn't show them to embarrass the young. The ones who really matter.

"I say, you folk, I've been hindered. I'm coming now. You were sports to wait."

## CHAPTER THREE

THE routines of life dominate the mind as the years pass, though not equally so with all, and it changes gear with an increasing smoothness to adjust itself to their requirements. It was three days later before John Oakley found himself with the leisure and in the mood of mind to give further thought to the conversation which he had overheard.

He was home somewhat earlier than usual, intending to have some time in his garden before dinner. He came to the quiet loneliness of a house from which his daughter, and the week-end guests had departed, the smooth service of which seemed to him at times to isolate him more utterly than had he waited upon himself in a more literal solitude.

Nina had caught an early train on Monday morning to resume her secretarial duties in London, where she earned, as she told her father, three guineas weekly for dealing with the correspondence and arranging the interviews of a nerve-specialist in Hanover Square. She was in good spirits, having (as she told Pauline when they parted on the Euston platform) "touched Father for a tenner"— A cheque given with an inward reluctance, from a bank account which was sufficiently strained already, and upon which his other children might have equal or greater claims which they were less quick to urge; and yet with an outward willingness, for it was natural to him to give when he was asked, and he knew well enough that Nina would make no effort to live at the scale of the salary that she earned. Even with the money she had from him, he was puzzled at times to understand how she could spend so freely.

There were two letters by the afternoon post when he got home that day; one from his son Alwyn, and one from his daughter Frida—now Frida Lawson, married at eighteen to journalist of twice her age, and with two children at twenty-four, and a hope of a third which was, as yet, too indefinite for advertisement.

Alwyn's letter was opened first, for he was not one to write to that address without some exceptional occasion. His business letters were addressed to the works, and Frida wrote every week, with a woman's facility. It said:

39a Addison Road,
W.6
(Early Wednesday morning)

Dear Father,

I promised you I'd let you know when I thought
I'd met the right girl, and I think I have, and I hope
you'll be pleased, though I know there are one or two
things that you'd wish had been different. I suppose
we can't expect to have everything.

I'm sure you'll like her herself, and that's the
most important thing, isn't it? Her name's Joy Carfix.
It's a queer name, and she says it was once French,
and has got altered. She isn't French herself, of
course. But she's been at a Convent in Normandy for
the last seven years, and has just come home to live
with her uncle at Treswick. I went there last weekend, and met her first in the train before we knew we
were going to the same place. I haven't told her yet
how I feel, because it did seem a bit quick, and I'd
half-promised to tell you first, but I've got a feeling
that it will come right when I do. It isn't conceit. But
I feel differently about her from what I've ever done
about anyone else, and I think she feels the same.

It's no good trying to tell you what she's like,
but can I bring her next Sunday or the Sunday after? I
don't think her uncle would refuse, if you wrote to
him, but you'll know how we ought to go about that.
He's Richard Corchester, Esq., The Grange,
Treswick. (They call it Cawster. I expect you know
that). But I want you to see her, and I don't want to
lose any time. I don't want anyone to get first. You'll
understand when you see her.

I know you won't like her religion being what it
is, but she can't help that, can she? We can't have
everything. You've always told me that.

Please write when you get this, and fix it up this
Saturday if you can. There isn't overmuch time, but a
wire or two might help. Don't stop to write back to
me first, because we can't talk till you've seen what
she's like, and she seems to think I ought to get your

consent before we begin to fix anything up, and of course I want to know that you like her. But I know that's a sure thing, because everyone does.

Affec.

Alwyn.

P.S. Please send me a line tonight if you get this in time, or wire in the morning, to let me know what you're doing. I'm ringing her up at one, and I can get it fixed if I know.

It was evident to John Oakley that if Alwyn hadn't "told her yet," he had arrived at a very intimate understanding with this week-end acquaintance, whom he was so sure to like, and who had some qualities which her attractions were to be sufficient to overcome. Of course, she must be asked. There was plenty of time before the evening post. He put the letter aside, his mind mildly but pleasantly excited by the shadow of romance, the approach of unexpected incident that it brought. He opened the other letter.

Birchett's Wood End,
Bucks.

My dear Father,

If you can do with us so soon after last month, I'm coming on Friday morning, bringing the children. Of course, I know you can, and we can't afford to go to Westgate again, but I know Mrs. Case likes to know first. Please tell her that we shall be in time for lunch. We shall come on the train that gets in at 12:42. Chester won't come till the evening, as he's gone to Liverpool till then, something about a shipping company that's winding up, and there's to be a meeting, and they are expecting a row, and Dixon wants a special report. That's really why he's away now, but it's about the usual thing that he doesn't want to come back. It's Field & Fletcher again. We may be able to come back by the next Friday. The man's coming this afternoon, and then I shall find out. Chester says if he can dish them this time it will carry it over the vacation, and Berryman's can have the money. I mean, if it comes in. He's sold a serial to a weekly paper for £120, but he doesn't know when they pay. But, anyway, he doesn't mean Field & Fletcher to have it. It's something they call a J.S., and he doesn't want to be in.

Christine is well, and so is Peter, though I thought she'd have caught a cold yesterday. Chester was up at four to catch the early train, and he saw her in the garden with nothing on. She'd gone down to find one of her cardboard dollies that she'd left out; or, at least, that was what she told Chester. You know what Peter is. I think it was because she heard Chester say that the loganberries were best picked in the early morning. But it may have been both.

I shall be rather glad for them to come because Mrs. Potter says that the children have got measles in the cottages in Richett's Lane, and you can't go to the wood without passing them, unless you go nearly two miles round and it's too far for anyone pushing the pram on a hot day....

The letter went on for three pages, but we need not follow it further. It showed Frida in her usual cheerful, practical, matter-of-course attitude to the events of life, adjusting herself with a minimum of friction even to the needless financial embarrassments of the last two years, and Chester's unconventional method of facing them—or, perhaps, facing is not quite the word, though a contrary one would be equally inappropriate. He made strategic moves to the rear.

Well, her father was glad that they were coming again. He was always glad to have Frida, and the children brightened the house. He smiled in recollection of an incident of the visit of a month ago, when Peter had forbidden him the use of his own bed, where her twenty-seven dolls, cardboard and other, had been put to rest in two long rows at head and foot. He liked talking to Chester also— listening to him for the most part. Yes, of course, they could come. It scarcely needed to be said, but he wrote that the house would be vacant, except that Alwyn would be coming, and probably a girl friend. He wrote briefly to Alwyn also, to let him know that he was "fixing it up", in his son's phrase. He must see Miss Carfix first. There could be little to say till then. He wrote more ceremoniously to Mr. Corchester, pausing first in a brief doubt as to whether he would not do better to write to the girl herself. These are not ceremonious days. But Alwyn had met the people, and should be best able to judge. It should be as he asked.

But when the letters were written, and had been sent to the post, and he had eaten his solitary and rather early dinner, he found that his mind would not settle upon the problems presented by the author of *The Yellow Hand*. He read on in a cursory mechanical way, making little effort to solve the enigma of who had committed the three murders, and was only mildly interested when he discovered that the two last had been perpetrated by the apparent victim of the first, who came to life again in the last chapter. His mind wandered continually, by some trick of association, from the news in his son's letter to the romance of his own youth, and to the wife that he had buried seven years ago in a grave that he had no will to visit again till he should be laid in it himself.

He thought of the first year of his marriage, when he had been earning not much more than two pounds a week. He had had no happier time. Of course, two pounds was more then than it was now. But there was no lack of money today, for the things that people will have. No lack of petrol and tobacco. People grudged it only for their children's lives. That was not entirely fair. Not entirely true. But all his thoughts were tinged, all his recollections fouled, by the words that he had overheard three days ago. Of course, there was no radical difference in the nature or the ways of men.

Even in those early unsullied days of his own marriage he had vaguely known that such vices existed. But they had had little objective reality. It had been three years, or nearly that, before Nina was born. It had seemed to Frida and him in their inexperienced youth a very wonderful, rather sacred thing. Nina had been a child of loving and very lovable ways. Suppose at that time her mother could have foreheard the words that had come to him last Sunday afternoon? In those first days, in her passionate pride and love for her first-born child. He remembered that when Nina was born, they had advertised the fact in the Hunnerton papers, a custom more general then than it now is. And subsequently there had been circulars from illicit manufacturers of contraceptives, and he had shown them to Frida, and they had looked at them as something curious and unclean, and thrown them on the fire together. It had never crossed his mind that they should touch such things with their own hands—with their own thoughts. Nor, he was very sure, had it occurred to her, or it would have been said at once. They had been too intimate, too frank, for the thought to have been left unsaid. It would have been impossible for such a thing to have intruded into the atmosphere of their own lives. Of course, there had been times when the full joy of marriage had been frustrated by illness or weakness. Once for a long time. But they had never thought of such resorts as those. Yet he would not be unfair. There must be many thousands today whose lives were lived simply and honourably; who met the high cost of the necessities of life, and the pressure of merciless taxation, with industry and self-sacrifice. Who gave battle to the cruelty of circumstance, rather than buy its clemency with the *danegeld* of the childless home. And there must have been many in the earlier days, perhaps with less excuse, who bought their pleasure at the modern price, or what had those circulars meant? Only there was the difference that the vice that had slunk past, as though aware of its own foulness, was now shameless and unafraid, bold even in the assertion of its own baseness. Assemblies of Anglican bishops had done it homage in cowardly equivocal words; abashed to bless, and yet afraid to curse it.

He wandered out into the garden, and to the orchard beyond, but the memory of the old days was upon him, and everything on which he looked had its own suggestion of word or incident, of things that were dead for ever, except as far as they remained in his own mind, where they must stir at times to a momentary resurrection, not knowing but that it might be their final consciousness. What is more desolately doomed than a memory which was dearly shared with one who no longer lives?

He went upstairs to his own room, conscious that he had stayed out somewhat too long. He could not endure the increasing chilliness of even a summer evening such as this, without risk of illness, since he had been wounded at Bethune. An undignified abdominal wound, of which he did not speak. There had been nothing romantic, nothing picturesque, in his short military experience.

He unlocked a drawer of old papers and letters, and of the diaries that Frida had kept intermittently from her schooldays. It was not as full as it once had been. He would go over it at times, and always end with the reluctant destruction of something that he did not wish to survive him—something that should not fall even into his children's hands.

But he had never felt the impulse of destruction as he did now. Those chance-heard heedless words had made real to him, as nothing had done before, the isolation of the past. Soon the empty grate was filled with papers that he no longer ought to keep, but only to cover away from unsympathetic, uncomprehending eyes. He left little but the children's letters that his wife had kept. They were written by yet-living hands. They could remain. But, for the rest, let the dead bury their dead. He might die at any time, and he would be the more content that he had left no records of what was private to himself and to one who was already dead. He cared nothing that he destroyed evidences which would have rejected the slander that he had overheard. Let them think as they would. As a million others must have done before him through the slow hours of night, he read on, letter by letter, and closed each memory from the sacrilege of alien eyes with the finality of the protecting fire.

## CHAPTER FOUR

FRIDA LAWSON came on Friday with her two children: Christine, whose fifth birthday had been a week ago, a brown-haired girl, with quiet happy eyes, keeping near her mother for the most part, and somewhat maternal in attitude to a sister fifteen months younger. If we look longer at this younger sister, we only do what is the common occupation of those around her. You might love Peter or not as you pleased—she would be unlikely to concern herself whether you did or not, unless you should get in her way—but she was not one who could be ignored. She was a child of innocent wide blue eyes, of fine-gold curls, of a delicately-dimpled chin, and with a delusive aspect of fragility which came from her small-featured face, and was not supported by an inappeasable appetite, and a tireless energy both of mind and body. The emotions she excited in those around her were somewhat varied, with the one monotonous circumstance that she was never overlooked for long.

Today her conduct had been of a perfection which a child of two or three years will very seldom attempt and will attain even less frequently. Quiet, polite, and smiling, she had seemed incapable of any evil thing. Since last night, when a nearly-tearful Christine had gone to her mother with small red tooth-marks on her arm, and Peter, being interrogated, had replied with a disarming smile: "I don't know whether I been naughty or not, but I did bite Christie's arm," she had had an immaculate record. And with this record still unflawed, her mother put her to bed at last in the night-nursery always kept ready for these frequent visits, and left her sitting up in her dressing-gown with her dolls around her—Christine, quietly tired from a day of travel, and quietly happy to have come to the house which she loved to visit, being already sleeping in a bed at the other side of the room. And Frida Lawson, feeling that the cares of the day were over, went down to dinner to meet her father, somewhat later than usual in coming home, and her husband, who had arrived on the evening train.

Chester Lawson, a long lean man, with a thin brown face, and brown humorous eyes, was in the midst of an anecdote which is best left at the start, for it was not destined to end, when his musically-inflected drawl was interrupted by his first-born's voice, and Christine stood white-robed in the doorway. "Mother, I wish you'd speak to Peter. She *won't* let me sleep. She says I'm to sing to her red baby-dolly, and I *am* so tired."

Her mother rose at once. Going to Peter was so frequent a part of the evening routine. She came back in a few moments, her manner having somewhat less than its usual placidity. "Chester," she said, "if you've finished, I wish you'd come to speak to Peter. She won't take any notice of me. I've got to change everything on the bed." She did not really expect that Peter's father would have more influence than herself, but she regarded it as a proper family procedure to call for a father's intervention in domestic emergencies.

Peter, clad in a light-blue dressing-gown which buttoned at the back in such a way as to make it as difficult as possible for her to get out of it, sat demurely on the edge of her sister's bed, watching her mother and Mrs. Case remaking her own from the resources of the airing-cupboard, her expression only changing to a sudden excited protest if a careless foot or a ricked sheet should threaten the safety of the seven members of her innumerable family who now lay in a row on the floor with only a shawl to cover them.

She greeted her father with a confident happy smile, and opened the conversation with the swift obliquity which was her usual first line of defence in such emergencies.

"My red baby-dolly had a bad pain."

"I didn't come up to talk to you about a doll. Mother told me that you'd been a *very* naughty girl. I can't think how at your age...."

"I very happy with my father and my mother," she suggested diplomatically.

"Then you shouldn't give your mother so much trouble. I'm afraid you'll have to have a really bad punishment this time."

Peter studied the unrelaxing severity of her father's face. "I don't like this con'ersation," she said definitely.

"Then you shouldn't do such things. I can't understand how you could when you were wide awake, and in grandfather's house, too. I'm afraid we shall have to give you a punishment that will make you remember."

She looked at her father with reproachful eyes. "We mustn't talk now. My red baby-dolly's had a bad pain, and she's just going to sleep."

"Then I shall put her into mother's room till I've finished talking to you."

For the first time a look of real alarm crossed the innocence of the baby face. Quick hands clutched at the invalid that had been lying on the bed beside her.

"Sorry," she said hurriedly. "I won't do it again. I won't do it again ever." She gave a side-glance at her mother, to judge the prospects of appeal in that direction, should her father persist in this dreadful threat of removing her offspring.

"I very happy with my mother and my father," she repeated desperately.

"But we're not happy with you, Peter. You make mother very miserable," Frida interposed. "It's no use saying you won't do such a thing again. Your father's talking about you having done it now. You must answer him properly if you don't want him to take Beryl away."

"It isn't Beryl, it's Mary Ann."

"Then if you don't want Mary Ann to be taken away."

"I couldn't get my feet cold on the bare floor, so I said 'Escoose me', and wet the bed."

"Nonsense, Peter," her father answered severely. "The floor isn't cold at all."

That was true. Even linoleum is not unpleasantly cold on a warm August evening, but both her parents recognized the full subtlety of this defence. It was only four mornings ago that she had been admonished severely as to the danger of cold bare feet, when she had been found in the garden at four A.M.; and there was a carpet on the floor of her bedroom.

"I think we'd better say that you'll have nothing but dry bread for breakfast."

She looked at her father with doubtful eyes. She thought the worst moment was past. There had been an occasion when she had met the same threat with a bland, "I like dry bread, I'll have dry bread two mornings," but the sequel had not been such as to tempt her to repeat that *riposte*. "I don't like grape-nuts," she ventured noncommittally.

"You know you don't like dry bread, Peter," her mother answered, "and you don't like to give mother this trouble, or Mrs. Case. You'd been such a good girl today."

"I sorry, Mother." There was a genuine and angelic penitence in tone and face, which passed into a brisker manner as she added: "If my red baby-dolly wets the bed, I smack her hard."

"But, Peter," her mother expostulated, "we don't smack you when you're naughty. You should talk to her, and try to make her a better girl." Peter saw the crisis was over. Laughter gurgled in her throat as she answered firmly: "I smack my red baby-dolly hard, if she wets the bed."

Christine, a silent absorbed spectator of her sister's skirmish with authority, lifted head from pillow to speak for the first time. "I never smack Jezebel. Peter's always smacking her dolls. Peter's dolls have always got pains. She doesn't feed them at all some days."

It was true that Peter's dolls had a lively and precarious existence, in contrast to the monotony with which Jezebel was washed and fed and put to rest. But the cherished Jezebel was an only child. Christine was not a believer in large families.

## CHAPTER FIVE

THE children were allowed to have breakfast with their grandfather and parents. It was not an early meal, John Oakley having adopted the post-War practice of staying at home on Saturdays. He came in from the garden at the sound of the breakfast gong as Peter was being lifted on to her chair, and gleefully informing the maid who did it: "Ada, I been a *dreadfully* naughty girl. I having dry bread."

Peter's table manners were incalculable. Liable to be of a kind which would shock a Zulu, they were about equally likely to be of a standard which made her family appear boorish around her. On this occasion she had given hostages to fortune, having promised six of her dollies that they could have breakfast with her because they hadn't got up before they were told to, and knowing that her mother's permission to lay them in a row beyond her plate at the end of the table was dependant upon her promise to set them such example as a parent should. (The others had been of such deplorable conduct that they were thrown into a heap in a corner of the nursery floor, with no prospect of any breakfast at all. Jezebel had been dressed and washed and fed, and was now back in her cradle, sleeping peacefully, as a baby should.)

"Gran'father," she informed him happily, "I been *dreadfully* naughty. I got to have dry bread for breakfus." She commenced to eat it with good appetite.

"Frida," Chester remarked, surveying the row of dolls, "we made a mistake when we named those children. It's Peter who ought to have been Christine. You know Owen Seaman's *To Christine.*

"Child of the silk-soft, golden hair,
The sweet, grave face, the serious eyes,
Mother..."

"Christine," her mother said, "why didn't you put on your other dress? I told you not to wear that again till I'd mended it under the sleeve."

"... of dolls, a constant care
That makes you prematurely wise."

"I won't trouble you with the rest."

"Sorry, Mother, I forgot," Christine said absently. Unlike her mother, she had a habit of listening when her father talked. Her mother listened only when they were by themselves—or, of course, when he talked about anything that mattered, which was less often than not.

"He's the editor of *Punch*, isn't he?" Mr. Oakley inquired. He was not deficient in humour, but he often found it difficult to tell whether Chester were serious. He wished Frida wouldn't be so unresponsive when her husband was talking. But Chester never seemed to mind. He knew that they understood each other in their own ways. But he had missed the joke on this occasion. He was not sure that he ought not to have laughed.

"Yes," Chester answered, "it's in an old *Punch Annual*. But it isn't comic. Of course there's 'my future lies behind my back.' That's rather neat. Seaman always is. But he's naturally quite a serious poet. Only, he once wrote some amazingly good parodies, and he was never able to change his clothes afterwards. The British public objects to any man doing that while it's looking on."

"Isn't it today that Elsie's coming back from the Westcotts?" Frida inquired of her father.

"Yes." That was so. Elsie, her younger sister, had been spending the first part of her vacation with a college friend. She was intending to enter the teaching profession through the avenue of a brilliantly-won scholarship and a training-college. She was a strenuous young woman, both in work and play. There would be incessant tennis on the lawn, and incessant talk at the table. Frida was glad she was coming home. She liked the tennis, and was indifferent to the talk. She said: "I wonder whether Miss Carfix plays?"

They were interrupted by the sound of the telephone-bell in the library, which adjoined the breakfast-room. "I expect it's something from the office," Mr. Oakley said, as he rose.

He came back in a few moments, looking somewhat worried, but with something of the more alert manner and decisive tone which had been habitual in earlier years, and were liable to be resumed before any need of action or confronting difficulty.

"Frida," he said, "I've got to go down to the office. I shan't be long away. Let Perkins know he's to bring the car round at once. Miss Carfix is due at 3:20. Of course, she must be met. But I shall be back long before that. You may expect me for lunch. Alwyn will be on the same train."

"He didn't say anything in his letter—" Frida began.

"No. But he will. Chester, I want just a word with you before I go."

The two men passed into the library together. "I just wanted to be sure that there's no more trouble than usual," the older man said, as the door closed.

"There's no trouble at all."

"Well, I'm glad to know. It might have been rather awkward at the moment, but you know if it were really needed——"

"Yes, I know that. But I shouldn't ever let your money go into their pockets. It's good of you to ask, all the same. Of course, if Frida'd been different, it might have been a hell of a mess, but, as it is, it always seems more or less of a joke."

"Well, I'm glad there's nothing special."

John Oakley was a businessman. He could not look at things with his son-in-law's eyes. He cared nothing for social prestige, but his financial reputation was a precious thing. Now he was on the way to his office in response to a message that there was a disquieting letter from the bank, and the cashier had hesitated to present the wages-cheque without first informing him of it. He could not have faced Chester's financial crisis in Chester's way, and yet his son-in-law's attitude, with its cool logical honesty, and contemptuous indifference to the conventions of commercial life, may have been of subconscious value in giving an added tone of confidence to the morning's negotiations, which were to be even more difficult than he anticipated.

# CHAPTER SIX

EXPLANATIONS are tedious, and a good tale should not look backward, but go ahead. Yet an explanation must be given, and it will be best to get it over at once, and as shortly as it can be made, while Chester is scribbling a leading article for the *Morning Chronicle* on the little lawn where Nina had talked so carelessly a week ago, and Christine's mother is mending that slit under the arm, and Peter had been persuaded to reluctant sleep with promise of excitements to come in the afternoon, and is lying in cherubic innocence among a litter of dolls, including three that have been restored to a precarious favour, and John Oakley is sitting in a bank-manager's private room.

Two years ago, Chester Lawson had found himself heir to the estate of a cousin younger than himself, who had been killed in the usual modern manner, and who had left him his entire possessions, with the exception of some legacies of (as it seemed) comparatively small amount.

Basil Lawson had been a merchant doing a moderate turnover, mainly on the Australian market. The lorry had run over him in the course of its routine progression. It had not been going at more than twenty-eight miles an hour, which its driver described as ten, according to the numerical conventions applicable to such incidents, and a coroner's jury were unanimous in exonerating him, five of them having driving licences, and knowing that they were under a constant liability to similar annoyances. It had distributed his brains on the smooth surface of the road without allowing him any interval for adjusting his affairs, or explaining them to those who would take control. He was believed to be a man of substantial means.

Chester was not too indifferent to money to receive the news of his inheritance with satisfaction. But on investigating the position, he found no evidences of the reputed wealth outside the business itself. He had to face the question of continuing or closing it down. The manager, a Mr. Henry Tibbetts, had been emphatic in recommending its continuance. He agreed that it would yield little if it were broken up. But as a going concern— Do you value a racehorse by the amount of meat on its bones? He pointed to the very considerable sums which Mr. Basil Lawson had drawn out of it during recent years. There appeared to be no doubt about that. How he had spent the money subsequently was less clear, and less relevant. Would Mr. Tibbetts be prepared to continue to manage it? Yes, for a reasonable increase of salary, Mr. Tibbetts would. In fact, Mr. Tibbetts did. He managed it for nine or ten months, at the end of which time he had managed to produce a position which was no longer manageable. Mr. Tibbetts went.

Chester Lawson lacked both the experience and inclination to take over the control of the business. He lacked the commercial knowledge which might have enabled an energetic man to steer it clear of the shoals to which it had drifted. He consulted the accountant who had dealt with its affairs in his cousin's time. He instructed him to take temporary charge, and to prepare a report. The report was promptly made, and was a decisive document. It blamed Mr. Tibbetts, who seemed to have lost his head when placed in control, and the continent of Australia, which appeared to have mislaid its prosperity. Mr. Tibbetts had bought too much, and sold too little. Worse than that, he had sold to those who were unlikely to pay. Without fresh capital, the business could not be continued. Capable management was equally necessary. If both these could be provided, the business might recover—or it might not. The depression on the Australian market might be prolonged. The accountant, a man destitute of imagination, but with the ability of a cool precision, on being interviewed, advised closing it down. Chester Lawson was inclined to like the idea. The last Balance Sheet had shown assets of £10,000, against liabilities that were £7,000 less. It was true that he had withdrawn about £2,000 (which was an additional reason for the present shortness of capital) to discharge the legacies, and to satisfy the claims of taxation. Still, £5,000 is a useful sum. How soon could the business be realized?

Mr. Birkett pondered. "I don't think," he said, choosing his words carefully, "that, if I were you, I should anticipate any considerable surplus on a forced realization. It might be the other way."

It had been the other way. Chester learnt that the late manager had shown a true perception of the position on at least one occasion—that on which he had used the metaphor of the meat on the horse's bones.

The incidents which followed are outside the direct course of this narrative, and can only be briefly indicated, though an analysis of them would illuminate much of the comedies of commerce and of humanity. There was some effort to sell the business of B. Lawson & Co. as a going concern, which failed owing to the depression in Australian trade, and the quantity and nature of the stock which Mr. Tibbetts had accumulated. This negotiation led to a rumour that it was in financial difficulties, which reached one of its largest creditors, who rang up the Foreign and General Trade Protection Society, who philanthropically collected his debts without any charge to himself, and asked them to get in this one immediately. Mr. Sinkwell, the manager of the F. & G.T.P.S., rang up the solicitors to the F. & G.T.P.S. and asked them to issue a writ. (The F. & G.T.P.S. did not expect to receive any of the resulting costs, because it would be illegal for it to do so. It lived on air.) Having scrupulously allowed his first client twenty-four hours' start, Mr. Sinkwell rang up a number of other firms which, from the curious records that his office contained, he knew to have dealings with Basil Lawson & Co., and said that he was "acting for other creditors in this matter," and might he do so for them also? Within a fortnight he was in a position to wreck the business. Basil Lawson & Co. was understood to be dying, and, as vultures drop from a clear sky, the medical and surgical specialists and undertakers gathered to receive their fees.

Mr. Birkett, C.A., recognized the position without expressing surprise or any other emotion. He advised a Deed of Assignment, with Mr. Sinkwell as Trustee. He explained frankly that he should have liked to have been Trustee himself, but that Mr. Sinkwell was too strong. If that gentleman were not Trustee himself, Mr. Chester Lawson might be confronted with the unpleasant ordeal of bankruptcy.

Chester Lawson became difficult. He said that he hoped that the business, at the worst, would realize sufficient to pay the creditors, and, in any event, he intended to do so; but he saw no occasion for filling Mr. Sinkwell's pocket.

Mr. Birkett was patient in explanation. He saw no occasion for paying the creditors in full. In view of the circumstances of the case, they were not likely to show any hostile feeling. He understood that his client had no other property, except his journalistic income? Very well. An assignment of the business assets should meet the case, Mr. Sinkwell assenting. If Mr. Sinkwell were Trustee, he would most certainly assent. Otherwise not.

Chester Lawson was not a businessman, but he was accustomed to the discovery of facts, and to their valuation. He saw the position clearly enough, with the obstacles of inexperience, but with the advantage of novelty.

He said that he would never sign anything which would be to Mr. Sinkwell's gain. He was determined that that individual should not profit by the crisis which he had engineered. Mr. Birkett told him that he had really no choice. If the business were forced into bankruptcy, Mr. Sinkwell would still be elected Trustee. The programme was inevitable. So many hundreds of pounds for Mr. Sinkwell; so many shillings in the pound for the creditors; so much discredit for Mr. Lawson; and in twelve months the whole matter would be forgotten, and Mr. Sinkwell's teeth would be scraping on other bones.

Chester Lawson had taken this reverse of expected fortune so equably, had shown so little excitement of voice and manner in Mr. Birkett's office, that that experienced professional gentleman did not feel serious doubt that his advice would be taken, however unwelcome it might have been on a first hearing; but he found that his client would not be moved from his decision. He would pay his debts (as far as he could) without Mr. Sinkwell's assistance. He gave battle in his own way.

He obtained the assistance of a friendly solicitor, to whom he had once done a service for which he had expected no return. He asked him to delay the various legal attacks which were being made upon him under Mr. Sinkwell's able direction. Mr. Percival Hatchett proved to be the right man for the emergency, though he had been somewhat discouraging at the first interview. He was of an habitual and even unscrupulous loyalty to his friends and clients. He took up every case that entered his office with an unhesitating belief that he represented integrity, and that the other side ought to get what was coming to it, and probably a bit more.

Yet he looked somewhat gloomily upon the first and largest of the writs that were laid before him.

"I can enter an appearance, of course," he said, "but I don't suppose I can hold it up more than about ten days if I do. Not unless you're prepared to pay the cash into court." He spoke mysteriously about the disastrous consequences of a Summons under Order XIV.

Then he brightened somewhat to ask if Mr. Lawson were quite sure that there wasn't any defence. Mr. Lawson admitted that he hadn't considered the point. He had assumed that Field & Fletcher wouldn't issue a writ unless the account were owing.

"You just go back," Mr. Hatchett replied more cheerfully, "and look up every scrap of paper about these transactions, and send them round here. You don't know that the account's due for payment. You don't know that you owe it at all."

After that there were consultations, and affidavits, and the expected "Summons under Order XIV", and an adjournment of it. There really did seem to be a doubt as to whether Mr. Fletcher had not been somewhat too impetuous in assumption that the whole account was due when the rumour of failure had first disturbed his mind. Finally, there was the afternoon when Mr. Hatchett returned in triumph from the court with the news that he had obtained "unconditional leave to defend," which meant, in plain words, that Mr.

Lawson could not be forced to pay £300 for some months to come, and would then have the pleasure of paying anything up to £600, if he should be able to do so.

And meanwhile, Chester Lawson had not been idle. A too-hurried auction sale had disposed of Mr. Tibbetts's deplorable stock for an even more deplorable price: Mr. Birkett had found a firm of Eastern merchants who wished to extend their operations to the Australian market, and who would purchase the book-debts for something more than they would be likely to realize, if the goodwill were included. At the end of three weeks, Chester was in the interesting position of having about £3,000 in the bank, and a list of creditors' accounts amounting to £4,368 3s. 9 ½d. very neatly written out by one of Mr. Birkett's clerks, on the table before him.

This was in Mr. Hatchett's office. Mr. Birkett was there also. They held council of war. The professional gentlemen concurred in the advice they gave.

Mr. Lawson demurred. He wished to make liberal provision for their own costs. (There were no objections to that.) Then he wanted them to divide the money *pro rata* between the creditors, sending the cheques to them rather than to their professional representatives, and without reference to any legal proceedings which might be commenced.

Mr. Hatchett was sorry he could not undertake that. It was futile to attempt to ignore costs which had been incurred. Also, there was professional etiquette to consider.

Mr. Birkett felt the same. He said further that if their client would hand the money over to them, there was little doubt that they could arrange the whole matter in such a way that he would have no further worry.

Mr. Lawson still demurred. He would clear the debts which Mr. Tibbetts had incurred in his name, as quickly as he was able, but he would pay not a penny more, except to those whose help he had sought. He would send out the cheques himself, with a letter stating that he would pay the balances of the accounts as early as possible.

Subsequently, he gave way on two points. He agreed to recognize the hoary legal inequity by which payments for rents and rates are preferential to other debts, and to leave the question of the conditions on which any payments should be made to Messrs. Field & Fletcher in Mr. Hatchett's very capable hands.

It is an idle but interesting speculation to consider how far his erratic method of dealing with this fortuitous financial crisis in his affairs might have been deflected by the influence of a different wife, or of a variety of circumstance. But Frida had accepted the approach of an apparent prosperity, and the fading of that illusion, with the unruffled cheerfulness and unswerving attention to the practical details of daily living which appeared to render her impervious to the majority of human ills, and which caused some to think her incapable of any strength of passion, and others, even more fatuously, to suppose her a fool.

In fact, she perceived very quickly that her husband was deriving sufficient satisfaction from the issues of his own obstinacy, and from the various expedients of delay, evasion, neglect, or defiance, with which, under Mr. Hatchett's half-amused advice, he met the subsequent assaults of the more aggressive of his adversaries, to give considerable compensation for the proportion of his uncertain income which he alienated to the reduction of their demands.

Seeing his lazy cheerfulness to remain unruffled, she left him to deal with his financial emergencies with the uninterfering confidence with which she would expect him to regard her preparations for the next day's dinner, while rendering any aid that was in her power as inevitably as she would have expected him to leave a message at the butcher's, had she asked him to do so.

Frida had that rarest of human qualities, the capacity to see things in their true proportions, and when the first bailiff sat awkwardly on a kitchen chair, she saw no more than a somewhat disreputable individual, who had hired himself contemptibly, and who was needing his tea. She was complaisantly aware that the furniture was her father's gift to herself, and beyond the reach of a grasping hand, and when, three days later, Messrs. Field & Fletcher had been converted to the same opinion, and withdrew, somewhat poorer men, she sorted out some of Christine's outworn clothes for an invalid child of her unsavoury visitor with no consciousness of generosity.

She had regarded with a similar equanimity the three tradesmen who had appeared at the back door with their books made up within a few hours of Messrs. Field & Fletcher's bailiff being deposited upon her, and the opposite attitude of Mr. Bulpit, the Birchett's Wood grocer, who had found himself too busy to render the usual weekly account on the following Saturday, till she had interviewed him with a disconcerting directness, and convinced him, with an open purse, that she would not be inconvenienced by discharging it with her usual regularity.

# CHAPTER SEVEN

THE institution of tea as the third meal of the day is an established ritual throughout the whole of England, but it is one that varies in its solemnity with the longitude of its observance. In the Northern Counties it is a portentous feast, delightful or dreadful, as you will, but not to be casually undertaken or lightly left. In the South it is more apt to be a matter of fancy cakes and fragility, even to the abomination of the knee-balanced cup, and the absence of a supporting platter. But the Midlands have been disposed to avoid these extremities, and there are countless well-ordered homes where it is a light and pleasant meal, served in comfort and eaten at leisure, not too slight to draw the household to the convenience of a common table, nor too heavy to leave the appetite undamaged for the dinner of the later evening.

It is at such a meal that acquaintance may be commenced most naturally, and with the minimum of discomfort for those who are uncertain of their reception, or self-conscious of an inevitable appraisement; and there was a kindly tactfulness in Frida's request to her father's housekeeper that it should be somewhat earlier than usual, so that those who would arrive on the 3:20 would find it ready by the time that the car had brought them home, and they had cleansed themselves of the dust of travel. Elsie also (coming from Worcester) would be arriving at the station about the same time, and Perkins could wait the few minutes that would be necessary to bring her up with her brother and his new friend. During his solitary weeks, John Oakley rarely invaded the dining-room, preferring that his meals should be served in the library, or in the little breakfast-room which adjoined it, but when his children came home, as they were always free to do, whether for weekends or for longer periods, meals were laid again on the long oak table, and the large mullion-windowed room which his wife had loved was reawakened to something of the liveliness of the older days.

Now his daughter Frida sat in her mother's place, and he on her right, in the seat which had been his since that table had been bought twenty-seven years ago, and his youngest daughter, Elsie, a self-possessed young lady with a very vigorous appetite, sat beside him. Chester Lawson sat opposite, with Miss Carfix on his left, and Alwyn on her farther side.

The children had been subjected to a short inspection, during which they had been examined and praised in the customary manner of English women, as though they were incapable of sense or feeling, a procedure to which Christine had opposed a mask of demure indifference, and Peter an impatience which she saw no reason to hide. "I don't *want* you," she had protested to the kissing Elsie, "I want my tea." Now they were having the desired tea with Mrs. Case, in the housekeeper's room, and even Peter's voice was unable to reach her parents' ears as she explained, with the smile of one who wishes to tell a happy anecdote in a way which will be pleasing to all; "I don't know whether I wasn't naughty or not, but I did bite Christie's eye."

So while Frida is asking Miss Carfix "Two lumps or one?" and remembering everyone else's preferences with the accuracy that Elsie applied to mathematics of less useful kinds, and other members of the assembled family are passing plates of bread-and-butter, and small dishes of jam, and making the tentative conversational openings which are indicative of a stranger's presence, we may take a leisurely view of the Oakley family and their guest, and commence to listen to the conversation when it becomes worthwhile to do so.

Looking at Frida first (for she is at the head of the table), should we say she was married, if her left hand were hidden, and we did not know it already? Yes, we think we should, though it is something less than a confident affirmation. At twenty-five she has the slim figure of healthful youth, as she may still have it when she is twice that age; slimmer, indeed, than the robust and athletic Elsie. Her children have come easily, as they most often do to those who marry in happy youth. And yet her eyes, greyer than Peter's, but with a curious likeness, have a restfulness that is rare in youth unless its experiences be complete, and its passions satisfied. Her face is clear of the cosmetics by which women have combined to challenge the meaning of emancipation, and to blazon the indigestions of soul and body which they aim to hide.

Her father, quieter than his children, more observant, more aware than they of the living scene as a whole, may be slower to speak, but expects by the custom of twenty years that there will be a silence when he does so, which will be less readily accorded to others. He is loved and respected by his children, with a trust that has been justified as often as it has been tried, but they would be surprised to learn that it is as a basic fact that they regard him, rather than as an individual. He is static, like the house itself in which they were born, and round which centre the memories of their own changing developments. We have seen him as an individual, but they are scarcely able to do so. It is natural that he should think of them but they are occupied with the fullness of their own lives. We must not call it the tragedy of age, for age is not tragic, except through disease or cowardice, but it is its condition that it is isolated, neither by its own difference or indifference, but by the blindness of youth, which cannot understand that the soul does not lesson nor change as the body weakens. A thing inevitable, because the body is the visible expression of the soul, and in age it is no more than a blurred sign, or a broken note.

But John Oakley did not count himself old (who does while any balance of health and vigour remains?) in spite of thinning hair in which there was little of colour left, and the wound of which he did not speak. In fact, he looked somewhat younger than usual this afternoon, and sat somewhat more upright, as his thoughts wandered continually to the morning's interview in the bank-manager's room, and to the increased realization which it had brought that he might have a harder fight even than had been the case already during the last five years, if he were to pull the business through. He had fought that fight for longer than his children's lives, fluctuating in its intensities, but never ceasing (except for that restful irresponsible time that ended at Bethune), with one to sympathize while his wife had lived, but accepted by his children as though the benefits which it gave were theirs by the operation of a natural law.

"Pleasure to have it none, to lose it pain," so will the child most often regard the social status, and the comforts, of its parents' home.

Elsie sits next to her father, light-haired and grey-eyed, solving the problem of eating and talking all the time without apparent breech of good manners, with the ease of one who has practised it for about nineteen years (she was twenty last April), and indifferent to the fact that her meal includes the paint with which she smeared her lips in the train half-an-hour ago (but it had not been much, for she was still young enough to be conscious of her father's disapproval, and believed that she had successfully gauged the maximum that he would pass unnoticed—a delusion that ended when he kissed her carefully three inches away).

Now she is sparring with Chester, and is reduced to five seconds' unexpected silence by a confusing retort, so that Frida uses the pause to turn the conversion toward Miss Carfix by asking if it has been warm this summer in Normandy? And Joy Carfix lifts long lashed lids in a quick shy glance at her hostess to say, in a lower tone than those that have been contending around her, that it has been rather cold and wet.

It was a pretty voice, was the general thought. Perhaps pretty was hardly the word. It was a voice that was low and clear, that would carry far without effort. And when she lifted her eyes—well, you could understand Alwyn being gone on her. Any boy would. But was there anything there? Anything worth pursuit and discovery within the small head of lustrous black-brown curls, made more emphatic by the scarlet of the simple one-piece dress, with its out-of-date old-silver brooch at the throat? It was the year in which fashion was beginning to shorten its close-fitting dresses. Calves were for the common gaze, but the knee was still one of woman's private parts, to show which was a gesture of indecency. It was the following summer that dresses were cut so that knees were covered when erect, but less easily when sitting, so that many thousands of women in train or tram were simultaneously occupied in a continual skirt-smoothing for the intermittent covering of those useful joints. Not that they were embarrassed by these preliminary revelations, as a boy would have been in a corresponding circumstance. There is probably no part of her person, back or front, high or low, that a woman would not exhibit with a demure unconsciousness if her sister were doing the same; a fact which it may be indiscreet to observe, and on which it would be more so to comment. It is enough to recall with gratitude that having inflicted their legs upon us, they set to work to improve them. Many of them needed it urgently. But we were to listen to the conversation, not to wander like this. Elsie is talking of tennis. She has learnt a smashing service from the college coach, which she is anxious to practice upon the family. She says that it will be too hot for Father to play this evening. (He had once said that himself, and she had always remembered it when a four could be made up without him.) She looked round the table. There were still five, unless—

"Do you play tennis, Miss Carfix?"

"Yes—a little." That might mean anything.

"You'd like a game after tea?" Alwyn asks her, quickly. He can count, as well as Elsie.

We look at Alwyn for the first time. A shy-mannered, rather handsome boy, darker than his sisters. We may look now as much as we will, but there is only one thing to see. His eyes are for Joy Carfix, anticipating her wants before anyone else can do so. There is no doubt where his thoughts are. As to her, you may guess as you will. She has looked at him once or twice in a friendly intimate way, but for the most part her eyes, and her occasional words, are for Chester on her other hand. Chester is reminded of a hen pigeon standing with a complacent affectation of unconsciousness while the cock coos round her. But who knows what the pigeon thinks? She may be engaged in an honest effort to make up her mind.

"I should like half-an-hour with you, Alwyn, in the library after tea," his father interposes, "if Miss Carfix would like to join the others at tennis. It will save time on Monday, if I have the week's report now."

That suits Elsie. Chester can play well enough, but she thinks herself his match, if not more. She will have Frida, and he can make the best of the foreign girl, who doesn't look as though she could use anything but her eyes, and Frida is a safe partner always. Elsie goes through life playing to win, and for twenty years she has made a good job of it too, picking up everything that was lying round— everything, that is, that seemed worth the effort of a stretched hand—and has done it with very little friction indeed. Popularity and good repute are two of the worthwhile things.

"I don't believe in husbands and wives playing together," she says, in a half-serious tone, "they always lose first, and then quarrel between themselves."

"Indeed—" Frida begins.

"Oh, yes, we do," Chester interrupts, "like hell."

Frida, smiling, lets it pass. It is too silly for further words. Elsie asks how long they are staying this time? Longer, she hopes, than the weekend. "Usual thing, I suppose? Left everything locked up, or is Margaret looking in?"

Frida admits, smiling again, that it is the usual thing. They have left the cottage closed, Margaret Potter, a woman who came in daily to help in the rougher work, having taken a fortnight's holiday, visiting friends at Reading. It wasn't bailiffs this time. It was a man with a judgement summons that had to be served personally upon Chester, and after a time it would expire, and Field & Fletcher would have to take out another for a later date. That was how she understood it, but Chester could explain better than she.

Chester said that would do. Anyway, it pleased them to think that the man would knock at an unresponsive door. Of course, he would have to go up to Town once or twice, but he could send in most of what he was on now by post.

Alwyn looked uncomfortable while this conversation proceeded. He was wondering what Joy Carfix thought. Her face gave no sign. Aiming at explanation, he began: "I wonder you're not ashamed to talk of bailiffs in the way you do. I don't know what people—"

"Why should we be ashamed?" Frida asked, "You're not ashamed of what other people do to you. It's what you do yourself…."

"We used to call you Victorian," Elsie said, looking at her sister with speculative eyes, "but you're not that. A Victorian woman would have about died. No, you're not Victorian. And you're certainly not modern. I wonder what you are."

Frida showed no inclination to attempt solution of this problem, and Chester took up the conversation.

"As a matter of fact," he said, "the bailiff era is over. It began with one who was with us, more or less, for three days. After that there were several others, but they lost heart more quickly. There was an occasion when we had two at once. Frida read Tennyson to them.

> "We were two bailiffs on one chair,
> There is no comfort placed *au pair*,
> The wind is—"

"You know I didn't."

"No. It was Wordsworth. 'A bailiff on the kitchen-chair, a simple bailiff was to her, and he was nothing more.' After that we had the era of Bankruptcy Notices. Hatchett told me not to take much notice of them. It appeared that they are an inferior article. Cheap but ineffectual. A Bankruptcy Petition is the real thing, and no one is very willing to invest in one of those, if they think it will be successful. The idea is that it's to be adjourned, till you've paid all you owed, and a lot more. When Hatchett let them know that there'd be no adjournments for me, they lost interest in those experiments, and concentrated on Judgement Summonses. The idea of them is that if you don't pay when you get them, you'll get into gaol more likely than not."

"I thought," Elsie said, "that imprisonment for debt was abolished after Dickens exposed it."

"Most people do; but you thought wrong, all the same. The idea is much what it was then, to blackmail the prisoner's friends, but the imprisonment, if the bluff fails, is a very different thing. At least, so I'm told. Dixon says he'll pay me a good price if I'll do three weeks, and find out what it's like."

"I'm afraid all this is rather puzzling to Miss Carfix," John Oakley remarked. "Perhaps a little explanation—"

Chester gave this very willingly to his attractive neighbour. She was a good listener. He was in doubt of how much she understood, and could guess her thoughts even less. "So you see," he concluded, "as I wasn't willing to pay those who were making the trouble, or to pay less than I owed, and as I'm not willing to pay twenty-five shillings in the pound now."

Joyce Carfix looked puzzled. "Twenty-five shillings in the pound?" she said. "I thought there were only twenty."

"So there are. I should have said twenty-five shillings *for* every pound that the business owed."

Elsie, listening, wondered again, was there anything there?

# CHAPTER EIGHT

ALWYN followed his father into the library. The request that he should do so, if not entirely welcome, had not been surprising, and did not necessarily imply that he was to give report of the guest who had been brought to the house at his asking. He had entered his father's business five years ago, and had been tried "on the road" at his own desire, as soon as he had felt sufficiently familiar with its details to talk to customers effectively. He had won success in that capacity which had surprised his father, and may have been beyond his own anticipations.

For two years past he had been established as a manufacturers' agent with an office in London, representing not only his father's, but several other Midland firms, and making a moderate but steadily increasing income. Looking somewhat younger than his age—he was twenty-two—and having a natural courtesy of manner, he had found himself generally liked, and his customers had found him not only capable and reliable in his dealings, but having a regard for their interests and requirements which was more than a professional pose. The fact was that he enjoyed his work. He had the quality of imagination that makes romance of any occupation. While he carried on business in a single, partitioned fourth-floor room in a side-street off Aldgate, badly furnished, littered and piled with samples, staffed with one semi-illiterate girl, who manipulated the ancient typewriter he had bought for £4 15s. before he had sufficient experience to know its real value, he saw himself in imagination handling a country's trade, and forming international combines. It was of his nature to have an instinctive loyalty to his family, and particularly to his father, to whom he was bound by a strong affection, and an unusual degree of mutual confidence. It was an untested bond, and none could tell the degree of strain which it would bear without snapping. That there might be an approaching strain they were both aware, but it was not the first subject on which his father spoke.

"What have you been able to do for us this week? Have you got Millward's contract? I thought you would have written yesterday, but there was nothing at the office this morning."

Alwyn was surprised, with some reason, at the implication, slight as it was, of these opening queries. His own mind was preoccupied in another way, and he was unconscious of any fault of omission.

"I didn't think you went in on Saturday mornings. I got Millward's contract renewed yesterday. I thought, as I was coming down—" He went into details of the business which he had done, and was interrupted by the query: "Did you get Herman's cheque?"

"Yes. I've brought it with me."

"If you'd only sent it on! Is it for the whole account?"

"No. It's for May. They want some allowances off the June account that I couldn't pass without asking you."

"Could you get it on Monday?"

Alwyn did not look pleased at this proposal. He knew that Joyce had come prepared to stay for a few days if she were sufficiently persuaded to do so, and he had intended to take a short holiday himself. He said: "Yes, I daresay I could. Tuesday, anyway. Edward Herman isn't always there on Monday. Is it important?"

"Yes. Money's very tight at the moment, and the bank's beginning to kick. August's always a bad month." He went into details.

Alwyn said he would catch an early train on Monday.

After that there was a moment's silence. Alwyn, half-inclined to obey an urgent impulse to get into the garden, but feeling that there was something that must be said first, broke it with: "Thanks for asking Miss Carfix."

His father hesitated in his answer. "She seems a very attractive girl. We'll have a talk in the morning. I expect you'll want to get out now." His mind was occupied again with the business problems that the conversation had brought up. He was not in the mood for talking of other things.

But as Alwyn was going out, he called him back: "Miss Carfix understands that we are informal here? She won't expect us to dress for dinner?"

# CHAPTER NINE

"WHAT do you think of her?" Elsie asked her sister as they made their way to the nursery together. Dinner-time was approaching, and Chester had wandered off with their father to look at livestock. Alwyn and Miss Carfix had disappeared down the orchard.

"I think she's lovely."

"Yes—of course. Anyone can see that. Chester did in particular."

"Yes. I should hope he could."

"Don't you ever—no, I suppose not. It must be a queer feeling to be so sure. What I meant was, do you like her as a prospective sister-in-law? She seems to be applying for that position."

"She's a good loser."

"Yes," Elsie conceded. Her new overhead service had proved as devastating as she had hoped, and the sisters had won three sets out of four from their opponents. Only the last had been lost, after a prolonged struggle. Joyce Carfix had played an agile game, but without subtlety or force, only really exerting herself to win in the last set, when Chester had urged her to do so. Not that she had seemed to lack interest in the game, but she had laughed equally whether she won or lost. Elsie conceded that, adding: "But she didn't care. She only cares how she looks, if you ask me. I doubt whether she's got the brains of a hen. I suppose," she added, somewhat inconsequently, "Alwyn's kissing her now."

They found the two children having the glass of milk and biscuits which were the routine allowance at bedtime. At least, Christine was having them. Peter had announced that she preferred some jelly which she had seen on the kitchen-table. She was arguing the point with her usual ability. If her hope of victory sank when she heard her mother's approach, she allowed no sign of disquiet to appear.

"I couldn't eat it, Mother," she explained, "I couldn't, re'ly. My teeth got too tired."

"Then you'd better leave the table."

"They're not too tired to eat jelly. It couldn't bite."

"If your teeth are so tired, you'd better stay in bed tomorrow."

A look of sudden consternation came on the small face at this unexpected development. Tempest threatened. Then it cleared as suddenly, with shrewd realization that the threat was only to induce her to clear her plate.

With a sigh and smile for a battle lost she picked up the biscuit.

"I'll hear your prayers when you've finished, before I go down," Frida said to the children.

"Yes, Mother," Christine answered. "Jezebel's said hers."

Peter looked up rebelliously. She loathed any alteration in established routines. Prayers were *always* said after you had got into bed, and might be used conversationally, and with the introduction of impromptu variations, as a means of keeping your mother with you for considerable periods. "I can't say prayers now," she said. "God hasn't come"

"I've told you, Peter, that God's everywhere."

"He's in the other room."

"I shall hear Christine's first, and then yours."

"No" (with a swift change of front), "hear mine first."

"I shall hear Christine's first."

Peter knew when her mother meant what she said. She abandoned the point, to ask: "May I say 'shan't ever sin any more'?" That was an original addition of her own, its source beyond discovery, its interpolation in incongruous places so frequent that her mother had felt obliged to discourage it, especially as it was always said with an audible chuckle, as though its author regarded it as containing a quality of exceptional humour.

"You can say it once, if you're good. Now, Christine."

"God," Peter explained, as Christine commenced obediently, "is hearing my dollies' prayers in the other room."

Meanwhile, John Oakley had forgotten his business anxieties in the pleasure of showing his pigeons to an intelligent and interested auditor. It was Chester's strength and weakness that he could be equally interested in a thousand things. Now he was absorbed in obtaining up-to-date information of his father-in-law's efforts to establish a new breed of pigeons.

He had worked for some years to establish the variation, but with only partial success. Last year a cat had broken into the loft where these birds were breeding, and killed the best three, among others. But for that....

Alwyn had taken Joy Carfix down through the orchard to show her the wooded hollow of the little stream-bed which lay beneath it, and rose again to the meadow of Cawsett's farm. She had shown no reluctance to go with him, but Elsie's guess of their occupation was widely inaccurate. Inaccurate it would have been in any event, because there was something different here from the casual lovemakings of her college friends, but particularly so because Alwyn had to explain that he had promised his father that he would go up to

London again on Monday, and it had been implicitly understood between them, though with economy of words, that he would be at home for the coming week—at least, if she were invited and consented to stay.

Joy said, smiling, that she wanted to get back early herself. They could go on the same train. Only one who was super-sensitive to her moods, as Alwyn was, could have been disturbed by the tone or substance of this reply. He said that there was no need for her to go back. Frida had said a few minutes ago that she hoped she would stay longer than the weekend. He might be able to come down again on Tuesday.

Joy was somewhat placated inwardly by the evident wretchedness of his reply, but she could not easily regard a business reason as sufficient for such a desertion. But stay? Not she. She would be *terrified*. Terrified? What of? Oh, it didn't matter, if he couldn't see. Not of his father. He was rather a dear. Well, of Elsie, of course. Elsie wasn't—? No, of course; men never saw anything. Wasn't it time to go in to get ready for dinner? No, she understood that they didn't dress. He'd told her that in the train. It was much the nicest way. She hated formality. (But what is the use of bringing down a dress that you can't wear? And one in which you know that you look your best, too.) Well, it must be time to go in, anyway.

No, they weren't kissing at the orchard-gate.

Alwyn, conscious of thin ice, turned the talk to indifferent things, as they went back through the apple-trees from which some of the earlier fruit was already falling. The ground beyond the hedge on their left belonged to Mr. Bartleet, who had been M.P. for the division till the last election, when he had lost his seat to the Conservative candidate. Pursley Park, it was called. He was a free-trader, a Liberal, the founder and head of Bartleet's, the cycle-saddle makers, now one of the largest leather works in Hunnerton. He was also, it appeared, a singularly mean man. He told a tale of how, last year, his Persian cat had broken into one of the pigeon-houses, and killed about a dozen birds, some prize-winners among them, and others that his father could not replace. There had been no doubt of the culprit's guilt. She had been caught in the loft. Mr. Bartlett had expressed his regret, and asked what the damage was. His father had suggested £5—£50 would have been poor compensation. When Mr. Bartleet heard this amount, he had sent his cook in to say that the cat was really hers, and might she pay two-and-six-pence a week? Of course, his father had told her he did not want her to pay.

Joyce did not seem responsive to the tone of this anecdote. She said that perhaps the cat really had belonged to the cook. She had known of a cook who had two cats.

Alwyn felt that he was accused of making an unjust reflection upon a neighbour's character, and was led to tell another anecdote to justify it. The tale was good enough if properly told, and to an appreciative listener.

Until two or three years ago, his father had kept some peafowl—a peacock and two hens, which had wandered loose over lawns and orchard and field, doing some occasional damage in the garden, perhaps, but not too much. The hens made nests in the orchard grass, and had reared a number of young birds, for which there had been a ready sale.

Mr. Bartleet had discussed the habits of peafowl with Mr. Oakley, and had learnt that they are birds of somewhat polygamous habits. He had observed that his neighbour's peacock sometimes wandered into his own gardens, especially in the lonely days when the peahens were sitting. Mr. Bartleet bought two peahens of his own. They made nests. They laid. They sat. Mr. Bartleet had reasonably good grounds for supposing that pea-chicks would follow, as, in fact, they did. But under the influence of Mr. Bartleet's hens, Mr. Oakley's peacock had developed a habit of spending half his time (if not more) on Mr. Bartleet's side of the hedge, and when the hens commenced to sit, he was no longer a welcome visitor. Mr. Bartleet addressed his neighbour in a polite note. He hated to complain, but Mr. Oakley's peafowl had contracted a habit of wandering, and were really doing a great deal of damage. Now that the strawberry-beds— If Mr. Oakley could kindly keep them up more strictly till the summer would be over?

Mr. Oakley considered the letter for a day or two, and decided not to reply. He knew the facts. He had no wish to develop a quarrel with his neighbour. You cannot confine a peacock in a rabbit hutch. It has too much tail. Even a loft or a stable may prove unsatisfactory. Mr. Oakley sold the birds.

As an illustration of the meanness of (some) human nature, the tale had points. But Alwyn told it too hurriedly, both because they were approaching the house, and because his auditor appeared uninterested. He indicated its vital detail too lightly. He was aware that it fell flat. Actually, Joyce did not understand it at all.

As they sat at the dinner-table a few minutes later, and Joy turned to Chester on her other side, to hold her own, adroitly enough, in some light conversational exchanges, both she and Alwyn were conscious of an inward wretchedness for which it would be difficult to state any adequate cause, but the existence of which (in the other) should have been satisfactory to both of them, had they had sufficient emotional experience to understand its significance. But there are new opportunities either to join in closer alliance or to drift apart in the shoals and eddies of the conversation which is before them, to which we may do well to listen, while Christine lies awake in the room above considering with gravity the encouraging fact communicated by her mother a quarter of an hour ago that the Commandments are no more than ten. If there are no more than ten sins in the world, it should not be difficult to avoid them with reasonable care and forethought. Anyway, it should be less trouble than the care of Peter's innumerable family. Her arm goes round the beloved Jezebel. She, at least, did not miss her meals, nor lie uncovered in the chilly morning hours.

But Peter lies on her back with a carefree mind. A smile dimples the innocence of her face as she recalls the good-night conversation with her mother, who had reproached her with the misdeeds of the earlier day. "But I'm not naughty now, Mummie," she had protested, with a natural indignation. "I've said 'God make me a good girl!'"

"Do you think He will?" her mother had replied, with an intended severity, and a consciousness of indiscretion that came a second too late to arrest the words. But Peter had not appeared to hear. She had remembered a necessary appendix to her prayers, "God bless my pretend children," and Frida had been content to leave the question unanswered.

Now Peter's mind went back to the problem which her mother had thrust upon her. "He didn't last time," she says at last, in a doubtful wonder, which breaks into sudden laughter at a thought into which it might be indiscreet to penetrate further.

She has promised her mother that she will not get uncovered again, but it is a warm night, and her only garment is already on the floor at the bedside. Short but vigorous legs are kicking rhythmically at the bedclothes. "I shan't ever sin any more," she chuckles, as she kicks off the last vestige of sheet. Her legs rise to the perpendicular.

## CHAPTER TEN

THE addition of one to five has made six so many times that we are reasonably justified in the supposition that it will continue to do so, but the addition of one chemical element to any other five will not produce the sum of six, but something incalculably different. It is so with the intercourse of individuals, verbal or otherwise. Even while she was a silent auditor of a conversation which was singularly impersonal, as conversations at the Oakleys' dinner-table had always tended to be, and especially so when Nina was absent, the presence of Joy Carfix had its impalpable influence; and when she spoke, she changed its current entirely with five words which seemed to her to state an obvious platitude, and which no one there would have been prepared to deny.

The talk began about the homing instinct in pigeons, continuing something which Mr. Oakley had been saying to Chester as they had entered the room together. It was a subject on which he had a very definite opinion. "I don't say," he went on, "that pigeons haven't got instincts, or that we haven't, for that matter. What I do say is that a pigeon finds its way home by sight alone, and there's no mystery about it, and never would have been if people hadn't been anxious to make one, because they don't like to allow that a bird can have any sense. There are the individual differences, to begin with. Some birds will take a lot of trouble to find their way home, and others won't. Then if you want a bird to fly home for a long distance, say two hundred miles, it's no good taking it straight there, however good homers its parents may have been. You've got to train it gradually, first five miles, and then ten, and then twenty-five, till it knows a wide stretch of country round its home.

"Then look what it does when it's loosed in a strange place. It rises high in the air, and flies in widening circles till it sees some familiar landmark, and then, if it's a good bird, it makes straight for home. If it were guided by instinct it could go on flying by night, which it never does. Even when it's over the sea, it can't keep its course during the night, which explains why so many hundreds of the best birds are lost in those ghastly races from France and Spain, which ought not to be allowed."

"Probably," Chester said, "an eagle or a falcon would act in much the same way, if it could be tamed equally to make its home at your door, and to be flown loose…I believe there is some evidence that the gyrfalcon does cross the Atlantic at times, though it seems hard to credit."

Alwyn suggested that he might mean the peregrine.

Chester said it didn't much matter which he had meant, because whichever he meant he was probably wrong. Elsie said to Chester: "You never really believe anything, do you?"

Chester protested, though without indignation: "Oh, I wouldn't say that."

"Even that," Elsie retorted, "you're not sure about. What I mean is that you have opinions, but no convictions. And even your opinions don't seem to be of any importance. Not to yourself, I mean. You'd always be about as willing to write an article on one side as the other. I shouldn't be surprised if you've done it on both before now."

"So he can," Frida concurred. "He wrote the leading articles for two papers last month, one on each side. It was to help someone who was suddenly ill."

"I don't know how you can."

"No one's fit to write at all who couldn't do that," Chester replied. "However much there is to be said on one side, every fair-minded man knows there's at least a column to be said on the other—and probably a lot more."

Mr. Oakley blocked this diversion, holding to the previous line of the conversation. He had seen sea-mews in the Atlantic, a thousand miles from the nearest land, after a night of storm in which it had seemed impossible that any bird could endure either on the surface of the water or in the air. They had been skimming the sea in easy tireless flight, adjusting their motion to the heaving of the water, and their own relative positions, in a way which was itself a wonder to watch. Where had they been the night before?

Chester said that if he had the choice of another incarnation he should certainly be a bird, though he was less sure which particular one he would choose. Probably a sea-bird. They still had some measure of freedom in a world where men had left none for themselves, and very little for any other creature that they were able to dominate. Men assumed their superiority, but if he were Creator or Controller of the world, and were reducing its varieties, he thought he should wipe out the human race much more willingly than many other species of birds or animals.

He spoke so seriously that Joy Carfix looked up at him with puzzled eyes. "But animals," she said, "have no souls." It requires some consideration, some analysis, to see why the conversation paused for a moment, as though someone had struck a note of deliberate discord. It was said with an obvious innocence, as a statement of elementary fact; something beyond dispute. It was not a proposition that anyone was disposed to challenge. Even had it been so, it was not a table at which divergent views were unwelcome. To John Oakley it was an integral part of his religion to believe it. But there was a consciousness that it was not spoken as a proposition to be asserted or defended. It was a thing she said because she had been taught, or rather, had been told to believe it. It was the voice of dogma, not reason. The voice of authority in religion.

John Oakley was a member of the nonconformist church in Hunnerton, though he had ceased to attend regularly since there had been a change of pastorate which he did not welcome. His religion was a fixed point, from which his mind wandered far in its speculations and interests, but to which it always returned. There were a number of articles of belief which he would not allow to be questioned in his own mind. They were settled things. Yet he believed (and it was partly true) that he had reached them by his own mental activities; that they were approved at the bar of reason, rather than accepted with the authority of tradition. Frida held without discussion to the same faith. What she thought herself, or how far she thought herself, would be shown (was being shown already) by the way in which she influenced and taught her children. What Chester believed (if anything) was difficult to discover. Elsie's phrase that he had opinions rather than convictions was shrewd enough. Elsie's own mind was the home of various confident beliefs and disbeliefs of the moment, with which she was well-content, but which might ultimately find it difficult to lie down together, being of mutually-destructive kinds. Alwyn had a mind like his father's, one to speculate and explore, but with a less firmly-rooted foundation of initial belief. It had its moorings, but in the storms of controversy the anchor would be more likely to drag. Yet they were all alike in that they might be quick to assert, but less so to assume.

But the voice of Joy Carfix was that of one who states what she has been told, and because it has been told her. Subtly, it was the voice of Rome. It gave to those who heard it the feeling that a man may have who argues points of faith or dogma with the priest of any church. It is difficult to treat him as a reasoning being. He fences with his feet fixed to one spot. You take such contest, if at all, with a buttoned foil. You do not strike too hard, feeling that there is an element of indecency in offering an argument which he cannot meet. You observe him to be unaware of his own weakness, and, indeed, he can hold his own well enough if he can keep his feet to the chosen spot. His weakness is in his rear. It is in that which he would have you assume without argument.

The talk paused for a long second of silence, and then broke out from all sides at once. Alwyn said jestingly that if Chester hadn't got a soul he didn't suppose that anyone would notice the difference. Chester answered Joy seriously: "I suppose it's a question of what you mean by a soul. I'd agree with you that animals haven't got souls like men. I think some of them may have a better kind." Frida said: "I hope you'll choose one that keeps clear of the Arctic regions. You know how I hate the cold."

Elsie was silent for once, observing Frida's assumption that she and Chester would wish to continue their companionship, even under such conditions. Her sister's marriage did not fit the common talk of her college friends, which was inclined to condemn marriage as an ancestral folly, a bondage hindering the free exploitation of individual "sex". Some of our parents might have accepted it willingly enough, being slow-going folk, or, at least, have concealed the misery they endured; but we were born to a freer age, and know the harm that such inhibitions cause. Frida's evident happiness was an affront to the emancipated generation to which she belonged. It was an enigma also, intriguing her sister's mind.

Mr. Oakley spoke a second later than the younger people. He was an opponent of vivisection, and there came to his mind a reflection that he had made more than once before, and with which most of his hearers were familiar already. "The modern scientist always asserts that the differences between men and the other animals are so small that they're hardly worth noticing, unless he wants to cut an animal to pieces while it's alive, and then he forgets what he's just said, and tells you that an animal's nothing more than an automaton, and even when it cries out, it doesn't mean that it's really hurt."

Elsie said: "But the Behaviourists really put men in the same category."

"Scarcely that," Chester objected. "They deny personality rather than physical consciousness."

"Anyway, no one takes them seriously except themselves."

"But even they," Chester suggested tolerantly, "have had their use. They have demonstrated a falsehood by reducing it to an absurdity."

Joy had listened in silence. She did not follow the conversation clearly, nor did she wish to show her deficiency. She recognized that it trod the forbidden borderland of religious belief which she had been withheld from exploring. She did not want to talk religion, in which she was not over-greatly interested. She had come here to wear a new dress (which was upstairs), and to be wooed by Alwyn Oakley (who was going to London on Monday). She felt disappointed, and she recognized a potential hostility in the mental atmosphere around her. With a perversely nervous inclination to stir trouble which often led her into needless difficulty, she said: "I suppose you don't really believe in God or His Mother?"

Chester answered that with a more definite affirmation than might have been expected from him. "On the contrary, God is about the only fact of which I am quite sure." He ignored the status of the Mother of Christ.

But Elsie was less scrupulous, or less diplomatic. There may be courtesies to be observed to a guest of another creed, but if she herself— Elsie had (as it happened) come little into contact with members of the Roman Church. Her college set, had they regarded the doctrines of the Virgin Birth or the Immaculate Conception, would have done so only for derision. But, in fact, they did not regard them at all. They were interested in other things. The two girls were soon in an animated discussion, to which John Oakley listened in unusual silence. Alwyn was silent also, desiring only an opportunity to divert the conversation. At Treswick Grange there had been no talk of religion, in which he did not think that Joy took more than the normal interest of a healthy girl. By what perverse fate must it break out now?

The argument itself was not on a high level, and may be left unrecorded. Miss Carfix held her own well enough, helped obliquely by Chester on more than one occasion, who, without taking her side, contrived to obstruct her opponent. The doctrine of the Virgin Birth is held (as far as any beliefs are definitely held at all) by the Protestant churches. He mentioned this. Elsie asked him if he believed it himself. He replied that if you accept the super-humanity of Christ, both the evidences and the inherent probabilities are about equally balanced. Elsie said, with some contempt, and some truth, that that was the attitude he took about everything. Her own argument assumed that no one really believed it. Miss Carfix fell into a natural and rather helpful error when she failed to distinguish between the various sections of English Protestantism. To the Roman Catholic mind the Established Church is its real opponent. The Nonconformist churches regard the Anglicans also as their most natural foes. When she mentioned the intellectual anarchy of the Anglican church, as she had been taught to regard it, she found that she was saying something on which all could agree. It is a point on which it has no defence. You may sympathize with the views of those, such as Bishop Barnes or Dean Inge, who have renounced Christianity, or with those who sit on the doorstep of Rome, but it is true of both that they are betraying that which they are vowed, and which they are paid, to teach. The leaders of the Nonconformist churches are in a similar uncertainty as to the ditch into which they would prefer to fall, but they are not (all) equally pledged to fixity of belief.

Alwyn diverted the conversation to these differences. Frida turned it into a practical channel by explaining the distances of the two nearest Catholic churches, to one of which she supposed that

Miss Carfix would want to go in the morning. One was on the farther side of Hunnerton; the other in the opposite direction—a long country walk. Neither was very easy for a stranger to find. Perhaps Alwyn would show her the way?

Alwyn said that he would. If he came with her in the morning, would she come with him to their chapel at Hunnerton in the evening?

More than one of those who listened recognized a new aspect of this introduction of an alien church. They might themselves have gone once tomorrow—or they might not. Excuses are easily found in fine August weather. They were not such devotees of church attendance that nothing was allowed to supervene. But here they must behave, as it were, in the enemy's sight.

They were diverted from this realization by Miss Carfix's reply. She would be very glad for Alwyn to come with her, but she was not allowed to attend other churches herself. They had new light at once upon the arrogance and the discipline of the Roman Church.

Chester smothered another query from Elsie which might have led into deeper quagmires by reverting to the previous discussion. If the Anglican churches were empty today, as they mostly were, he suggested that it was not so much a matter of vestments or dogmas as that they had ceased to teach or practice the high code of the faith they professed. He instanced the case of a London church which appealed widely for public support to enable it to keep open, in the absence of any sufficient congregation to finance its requirements. It let off its Vestry Hall to a secular society, and when it happened that this society was a little late with the quarter's rent, the rector had put the bailiffs in without even a preliminary warning of his intention.

"Well," Elsie objected, being in the mood to argue with someone, "why shouldn't he, like anyone else, if they didn't pay?"

"I don't say he should or shouldn't. I only say that he should have resigned first. How could he teach a faith in which he had ceased to believe?"

The conversation became animated in this discussion. Should a priest be expected to observe a higher code of conduct than that of other professing Christians? Was the forcible recovery of debt consistent with Christian principles under any circumstance? If so, what were they? If not, what would be the social consequences?

Chester said, to this last, no one could tell, for it had never been tried. England was officially a Christian country, but English law had always firmly rejected the principles of Christianity. The common interpretation of Christianity was that barbarities were inevitable, but they must be committed in a decorous way. In the instance he had mentioned, he had no doubt that the Rector had acted through a Church Council, who had acted through a respectable firm of solicitors, who had instructed a respectable firm of auctioneers, one of whose members held a bailiff's certificate, whose assistant had been employed to seize and, if legally possible, sell the Society's chairs; and when the money had been obtained, in whatever manner, it had found its way unobtrusively to the treasurer's hands, who had found it very convenient for the payment of the organist's salary. *Let not your left hand know what your right hand doeth* had always been a very popular Christian text.

"Do you know," Frida inquired, "that we've been sitting here for more than an hour?"

## CHAPTER ELEVEN

JOYCE CARFIX looked out from her bedroom window over the trees and lawns of the falling gardens, dimly seen in the starless heat-haze of the August night, and was uncertain of what she felt.

It was so few weeks—scarcely more than days—since she had escaped from the firm though gentle discipline of a convent school; had exchanged the cold clean austerity of her dormitory cubicle, with its narrow white-quilted bed, for the luxuries of her uncle's home. With feminine quickness she had adapted herself to the changed conditions, with avid hands she had caught at the quick romance which life had offered—and it had brought her here. Her mood was doubtfully happy, timidly adventurous, only certain that it felt unsure. There was a strangeness about these people with their keen impersonal interests, and readiness to question the most fundamental things, from which she shrank. But Alwyn's hand had touched hers—was it chance?—as they had risen from the dinner-table, and from that moment something of shadow had left her mind. He would not go back on Monday unless he really must. He knew that *les affaires* must be taken seriously.

She had never worried much about religion. It was an accepted thing. It seemed here to be, somehow, more vital, though it was so loosely held. Vital—and, perhaps, menacing. She had been taught that England was a heretic country—worse, in that way, than France, which was merely infidel. And she must remember not to depart from the principles of her faith, or (they should perhaps have been stated first) the observances of her church. Not that she was likely to do so. She was of a natural loyalty. Her family had been Catholics when the power of Rome was at its highest in England,

and through the bitter years that had followed; and in these indifferent days they were good Catholics still. Actually, she was repelled by Protestantism, as she understood it. A cold faith for one who has been taught to feel the nearness of many saints, and of the dear Mother of God.

What had Mr. Lawson said? She remembered a phrase with which he had turned the point of something which Elsie had directed at herself: "The difference between the Protestant and Catholic churches is that the one does not know what it believes, and the other does not know why it believes it." Carelessly and rather crudely worded, and of a grammatical construction which might be capable of defence, but seemed to need it, it yet contained a truth which was evident even to her limited knowledge. And like most of Chester Lawson's truths, she saw that it was double-edged. It was not the part of every private in an army to take control. She believed what she was told by the Leaders of the Faith she held. Were they not the more competent to decide? This was not less easy to accept when it was contrasted with an alternative anarchy.

Well, anyway, it was time for bed. Yawning, she closed the curtains, and switched on the light upon the restful comfort and quiet harmonious colours of a guest-room in which the spirit of the woman who had made that home still lived, though she had died ten years before.

Having no standard of comparison, Joy could not realize how kind Fortune had been in guiding her so straightly to an English home of the older kind, in a flat-and-bungalow period of ill-made, hire-purchased furniture, without aspect of permanence or stability, without reverence for its own past or faith in its own future, where the talk is most often of sparking-plugs and carburettors, and the laughter of children is seldom heard—a time which is yet only half-alarmed at the substance of the stones which science gives its followers when they ask for bread.

Yet the room had its influence upon her. There was a quiet stable peace in this large-gardened house. She recognized the atmosphere of a home, which is a woman's deepest need, though she saw also that it might be something less than a home to her. This was of what she felt. What she thought was of the dress that she had not been able to wear, and not long of that, for sleep comes quickly to the young.

John Oakley, in the next room, was occupied with thoughts which gave way less easily to the need for rest. His mind fluctuated between his business anxieties and this sudden infatuation of Alwyn's. He wished to do what was right. To consider Alwyn's interest first—of course. Even if it were a thing which he could not approve, it was a matter for advice rather than opposition. He tried to decide what his wife's attitude would have been, had she lived, as he would always do when such questions rose. He knew that she would feel very much as he did himself, and yet, relatively, be realized that her concern would have been just a little more for the character of the girl herself, just a little less on this question of religion that disturbed his mind. Both by ancestral prejudice and personal conviction, he disliked the Roman church. He disliked its priestcraft, its monasteries, its confessions, its superstitions of transubstantiation, and of the worship of saints. He disliked its prayers for the dead. He held strongly to certain tenets of belief which he thought to be essential to personal salvation. At least, he thought that he thought so, which is a not-very-different thing.

He had not quite the same kind of hostility for the Roman that he had for the Anglican church, for it was by the latter that his own church had been persecuted in its earlier days, neither had he quite the same degree of contempt. The Roman church was more remote. But it was also the more formidable opponent. Everyone, friend or foe, recognizes the sagacity with which it is directed. It has a rigid discipline. It speaks with authority. Its enemies may call it Jesuitical, meaning no praise, but they do not accuse it of any foolish simplicities. Beside, it, the English church, holding to its "establishment" for the revenue it brings, and grumbling inconsistently that its prayer-book should be controlled by a parliament of Nonconformists and Jews, without internal self-discipline or self-respect, is an object for derision rather than any stronger emotion. Hatred weakens as contempt grows.

Gradually, the relative positions had changed since the memory of which his father had told him. It was a village school, to which his father and his brothers had entered for the first time, their own father having bought a farm in that district. A village where the vicar held unquestioned authority, where dissent was a despised and persecuted, almost an unknown, thing. The school-master, a small-minded, mean-souled man, had received these boys, who were not allowed to be present at the school-prayers, with jeers in the open classroom. He had questioned them as to why they should be absent. "Don't you call yourself a Christian?" he had said to John's father, and the boy, to whom the word implied adult baptism, and being "aware of salvation" and of many strange and difficult things, had answered, "No, sir," with a shamefaced courage, to be met with a loud-voiced sneer from the master: "Boys, here's a boy who says he isn't a Christian!"

After that, there had been ostracism and playground persecutions, till the boy in desperation had caught up a line-prop, and laid out one of his tormentors with a badly-broken head, and that trouble had ended.

It was an episode such as could hardly have happened in John Oakley's own experience. A tale of the middle of last century, impossible in any school of today. Much of the bitterness was gone, but the old antagonisms, which were not only of creed, but political and social also, though they might seem dead today, would stir at times, as though they had been buried alive. And might they only be dormant thus because it was an age in which all faith had weakened, in which whatever religion men might profess was a lighter weight in the scale than it once had been? What were the words of the Founder of their common faith? *I came not to bring peace but a sword.* She was a charming girl. He would find opportunity to talk to her tomorrow, if it could be done naturally. It was not a thing to be forced. There were ways in which he would have been glad for his own daughters to be more like her. He thought plurally, but it was Nina who was in his mind. Not Frida, at least. There were things that Elsie had said that he had not been pleased to hear. He must talk to her, making occasion if it did not come of itself. But he did not delude himself into thinking that he could have great influence now. Those days were past. If their mother had lived. But all he could do now was to keep the home so that they would feel that they could always come when they would, and be ready to give help or counsel if he were asked.

"I can't go to bed just yet," Frida said, as Chester closed the bedroom-door. "I've got some sewing to do. It won't take long. I hope you're not tired."

"No, I should like a pipe. I can lean out of the window."

"There's no reason you shouldn't smoke downstairs."

"I know that, but I never feel quite comfortable, knowing your father doesn't like it."

"Nina smokes when she's here. He never says anything."

"No, but that's how I feel. Like you would if you did that mending downstairs tomorrow."

"Mother never had sewing about on Sunday. I think it was a good rule, though I sometimes do it myself at home,"

"I don't say it wasn't. What's the verdict?"

"I think she's charming. So I told Elsie. Elsie doesn't like her very much yet. I expect she will. I hope they'll be very happy."

"You talk as though it were all settled, and they'd been married yesterday."

"So it is, or at least it soon will be. Even a man might see that."

"People sometimes change their minds."

"Alwyn wouldn't. You ought to know him better than that."

"Well, he is rather like you. There wasn't much chance for me when you'd made your mind up. I'm glad I've not got to marry her, anyway."

"Why?"

"Because she's as soft as a padded room, and would give way about equally."

"Yes. I know what you mean. But she wouldn't have been silly enough to marry you. She'd know that you'd murder her in about a week, just because she couldn't be sensible. But Alwyn's different from you."

"You feel sure that she'll have him?"

"You can trust Alwyn to see to that. How long has he taken to get her here?" Frida, having disposed of the only subject of importance on her horizon, became silent, but Chester was in a talkative mood. He had probably never had an anxious moment concerning the destiny of his own soul (nor would he have used the word, which he considered obsolete, except for those who are drowned at sea), but he was as keenly interested in religion as in the problems of Indian Government, the effects of tariff-barriers, or the composition of the next test-match team. He went on: "They'll come a cropper over the religion question more likely than anything else." He talked for ten minutes about the possibility of it ending in Miss Carfix leaving her Church (which he thought unlikely), and upon the significance of the fact that those who do forsake the Roman communion rarely find any alternative anchorage.

Frida may have listened. When he stopped, she said: "Peter wasn't asleep when I went in just now. She said she was too hot, but I put the sheet over her, and one blanket. Mrs. Case thought it was hardly necessary, but the nights often get colder before morning at this time of year."

It was just then that Elsie knocked at the door and asked if she had gone to bed yet, and, if not, would she come to her room for a few minutes, as she wanted a talk? The voice was unlike Elsie's usual confident tones, seeming to be controlled with difficulty to an effect of casualness at which it only partly succeeded.

# CHAPTER TWELVE

"FRIDA," Elsie said, "I suppose I'm a fool to show this to any-one, but I know I can trust you not to talk, and I've just got to tell someone. It's such cursed bad luck—and all about nothing, too."

She held a letter in her hand as she spoke, and then passed it over, adding: "You'd better read what Con says."

Frida read the letter in silence, and then looked a second time at the date. "You must have had this since last Tuesday."

"Yes, I daresay I have, but I've only read it just now. Con's al-ways scrawling something."

"It isn't easy to tell what it's all about."

"I should have thought it was plain enough. Mr. Perrott's being sent down, and Gladys Cooke's in a ghastly mess, and there's no knowing how much more trouble's to come."

"But I don't see why you should mind. They can't be a very nice set."

"It wouldn't matter if they hadn't found out about Welwood."

"But, Elsie, you don't mean—"

"Well, why not? It's what everyone does now. Everyone up to date. Besides—"

But we are regarding a conversation which can have little mean-ing without fuller knowledge of the circumstances from which it rose—a knowledge which cannot be adequately gained from Miss Constance Monkswell's incoherencies.

Mr. Edward Perrott was one of those young men who might possibly have developed into a decent citizen had he been trained in industry, self-discipline, and self-respect. Possibility is a sufficient word.

But there was none whatever when his parents filled his pockets with money, and sent him to the potentially idle life of a University. The responsibility was largely theirs. They did not expect him to excel in any direction of scholarship. They wished to be able to say that their son had had a University education.

He had been vicious at school. He would have lived viciously at college under any circumstances. But it was his misfortune (and that of others) that he entered college at a time when certain of the basest of human degradations were openly advocated, and defended by those who held positions of authority, and who found that they could do so in specious ways, and still retain the respect of a proportion of their fellow-citizens. A year ago a man prominent in scientific circles, and of international reputation, had delivered a public lecture on social morality, in the course of which he had made the statement that *"in view of this modern knowledge of contraceptives, it is difficult to discover any valid objection to the experimental intercourses of young men and women who may not be in a position to marry, or who may not desire it."* It would be wrong to regard this utterance with severity. A man who can make such a statement seriously may not be *non compos mentis*, but he is sufficiently near to that condition to render him comparatively irresponsible. It is more difficult to exonerate the newsvendors who give it publicity. It was discussed (with other more or less familiar absurdities uttered by those who were commercially interested in the propagation of vice) among the young people whom it advised, and particularly in the high schools, colleges, and places of business where they congregated. It was warmly approved by Mr. Edward Perrott, and others of his kind.

Mr. Perrott had obtained some control over, if he had not actually bought, a cottage in a lonely district about fifteen miles from the University, where he was prepared to introduce any girl-undergraduate who would go for a ride in his car to the doubtful pleasures of experimental fornication. He called it the equality of the sexes, emancipation, having a good time, free love, being up to date, and a number of other things which it very certainly wasn't, while avoiding its more appropriate adjectives. Gladys Cooke, a young woman in whom the more elementary human emotions were rather strongly developed, and with the self-control of the average imbecile, was one of those who had been "taken a ride" in this somewhat worse-than-the-American use of that expression. Something had gone wrong with her first experiment in contraceptives (if the first it were), and after an interval of three months she had pleaded illness, and gone home shortly before the end of the term. She had confessed her condition to her parents, who had not taken it with scientific complacency. They had called in physicians, imploring them to do "something". In response to this urgency, the medical gentlemen had vainly administered a drug which is well known in certain circles for its value in procuring abortion.

Her parents were religious people, who would not do anything wrong. One of their medical attendants hinted discreetly at the possibility of an operation for a sufficient fee. But to this they would not agree. Not openly, and with the knowledge of each other. It is a sort of thing that should be *done* without the indecencies of decision. The child must be allowed its life. Gladys went on a long visit to an aunt of whom no one had heard previously.

But her father "took the matter up" with the vigour which had made him a power in the Covent Garden markets, and which had provided the funds which had taken his daughter to the college life which had so abruptly terminated. He took it up with the University authorities, and with the parents of Edward Perrott. Edward denied strenuously that he could be the father of any child of Gladys Cooke. He may have believed it. For all we know, he may have been right. But there were things that energetic inquiry disclosed which were beyond denial. Not only was he being sent down, but three girls (so Con had heard) who had been seen with him at Welwood had been politely requested not to return—which appears to show that it is a dangerous thing for girl undergraduates to take their scientific advisers too literally. They would do better to realize that a man who spends a sedentary celibate existence investigating the composition of atoms may know less of the realities of life than the average charwoman. They might consider the dreadful example of a leading physicist who has become the public dupe of the charlatans who exploit the lying cult of Endor; and who finds no difficulty in believing that Julius Cæsar, after nearly two thousand years of conscious existence since he was assassinated in the Roman senate, has still nothing better to do than to obey the voice of an illiterate medium, nor more interesting to report than that it is roses, roses all the way.

"You mean—" said Frida, looking at her sister without excitement, but with a well-founded incredulity.

"No, I don't. Not what I suppose you think, anyway. I did go with him, but I got funky at last. If I'd felt like I did the Wednesday before when we fixed it up.... But I got cold when the time came, and I wished I could back out, but I knew they'd all think me a fool. Everyone envied those that he asked.... I mean everyone in our set; of course, there are a lot of the slow sort that don't count, the sort that aren't really alive, though I suppose they think they are. But I didn't like something he said in the car, or the way he behaved, and we had a few words then, and when I found there was only one room, and he began to undress. Well, it seemed horrid."

"Yes, I should think it would."

"I don't see why you should say it in that tone. People don't expect men to keep away from women. They never did. And I don't see why girls shouldn't have just as good a time."

"But you didn't have a good time?"

"No, it was just a mess. But that doesn't alter the argument. If I'd been feeling differently, or if I'd liked Ted Perrott a bit more than I did."

"I don't think you would," Frida answered equably. "I shouldn't be too sure of that. It's easy for you to talk. You've got Chester. We all want the same thing, really. I don't see why I shouldn't have a boy if I want, as much as Nina or you."

"Nina?"

"Yes, of course. You don't think she doesn't know what's what with her boy friends. What do you think she gets all those presents for, if it isn't that? She gets money as well. Besides, when I was up with her in London, she told me a good deal."

"Nina isn't always quite accurate."

"I know that. I know she can blow it big. But I saw enough for myself. Things she took care Alwyn shouldn't see when he came."

"You wouldn't like to think that Alwyn went on like this Mr. Perrott?"

"No, of course. Alwyn's different. He wouldn't touch a girl's hand without saying: 'Are you sure you don't mind?'"

"Don't you think it makes Miss Carfix rather a lucky girl?"

"Oh, Frida, don't preach! And, besides, most women wouldn't agree. Most women like a man that's had some experience. And women have just as much right to experience as they have. We're like the first women that took to bicycles. When once people get used to the idea of free love—"

"Isn't it rather a funny word to use? I shouldn't think there was much love of any kind in Mr. Perrott's cottage. I should think hate would be a much likelier thing."

"You needn't rub it in. You've got Chester... I know I've been a fool, however you look at it. It was when I noticed the oil on his hair. The question is: what am I to do if they find out? Would they write to Father, or me?"

If Frida had a passing curiosity to know whether her sister meant that she had been attracted or repelled by Mr. Perrott's oleaginous ornamentations, it was not strong enough to become articulate. She addressed herself to the final question: "I don't know to whom they'd write, but I shouldn't think you'll hear anything now. If Con's letter's right about these other girls, they must have heard a week before this, if not more. They might think that they've made examples enough."

"I shall have to see the letters before Father gets down."

"I don't think I should try that. Besides, you couldn't. He's down too soon. Anyway, there can't be any tomorrow."

Frida spoke without any warmth of reprobation. It might not have been her way, but if such a letter were intercepted it might not be the worst thing that could happen. She thought that her father had troubles enough without that. She added: "I don't think I should worry, if I were you. If we hear anything more about it, we shall probably find a way of dealing with it."

"Thanks, Frida. You're a good sort when anyone's in a hole. I'm sorry if I've said anything unkind. But I've been in such a funk since I read the letter. You know how old-fashioned Father is. He wouldn't understand in a blue moon."

Frida thought that her father might understand very well. Might even understand Elsie better than she did herself, but she did not say it, any more than she had said that she probably knew how much truth (or how little) there was in Elsie's surmises about Nina, having had her elder sister's confidences only three weeks before. She thought that the whole incident had some not unsatisfactory features, and that a good fright might do Elsie no harm.

Elsie felt much less frightened than she had done an hour ago. Telling Frida things usually had that effect, their proportions appearing reduced by the quiet reception that met them. She said, as Frida showed signs of going: "You won't tell Chester?"

"No. There's no need."

"Nor Alwyn?"

"No, of course. I'd much rather he shouldn't know. Good night, and sleep well."

"So I shall. Good night, Frida."

Chester had gone to bed when Frida got back to her own room. He asked sleepily: "What's the row now?"

"Nothing really. Elsie's got a letter about one of her college friends who's in trouble."

"Got a baby she doesn't want? That's the usual trouble these days."

"Right first guess. You're almost brilliant when you're asleep."

"Boy or girl?"

"It's too early to tell."

"Well, you needn't say any more, if you don't want to."

"So I supposed."

"I hope you'll have a boy next time. Three girls would be bit off, wouldn't it?"

"Oh, I don't know. I think I'm rather good at girls. Of course, if you make a point...."

"I'd rather leave it to you. If I had to bet, I should put my money on twins."

"Then I just hope you'd lose it. Though they would be rather fun in some ways. I think I should like twins once; but not just yet. When I've more time. Funny you mentioning them now. Peter's going to have twins next week. I've promised her those two little blue dolls at Mercer's if she's good till we go home."

"There's not much chance of that."

"Oh, yes, there is, if she wants the dolls. She'll be so good she'll make us all feel uncomfortable. I promised you'd tell her, 'Asolved to Mally' in the morning. I never can get the boys' names right, and she always spots it if I go wrong."

"I don't know why you let me corrupt her innocence with those horrible tales."

"There's no innocence about Peter. Make more room, please. I'm not going to lie close on a night like this." Mrs. Chester Lawson switched off the light, and got into bed.

## CHAPTER THIRTEEN

JOYCE CARFIX waked early, dressed with the celerity of youth, though not without a thought of the effect she was producing (about which she had an unanxious certainty), and found her way downstairs and through a yet-bolted door to the cool green peace of the August morning. The gardens fell away to the south. The low sun to leftward was yet hidden by intervening trees. The sky was a hazy blue, threatening heat to be.

Sunday morning has a difference to the English Midlander of which he must be conscious, though he may not perceive its cause. It is not only that it is a day of worship, of leisure, or of recreation, as his habit may be. That is the common experience. But the hundred thousand chimneys which pollute the atmosphere of three counties have ceased issuing their filth since the previous noon, and the air is changed (to the native's eyes) to an unnatural clarity. There is a similar though slighter change on the same day in the long ditch which is London.

Hunnerton is on the edge of the Midland inferno, and sufficiently distant to be out of sight or suggestion in this green garden, but it was only when the wind blew from the west for many continuous days that its influence was driven from the sombre skies.

Joyce thought nothing of this. In fact, it would be scarcely true to say that she thought at all. She was of too keen a physical consciousness at that moment; thought was lost in sensation, as her blood responded to the peace and beauty of dawn.

Following the gravel paths, for the lawns were still wet with the dew of the summer night, she went down to the orchard, where a trodden track made dry passage possible through grass that grew unmown around the fruited trees. A brood of half-grown chickens, slim, glossy-black, scattered before her feet, and delayed her eyes for a moment with an unfamiliar beauty. She went on to the wooded hollow below. Surely Alwyn was not asleep on such a morning as this? And when he might.... When she.... She heard the click of the orchard-gate, and knew who was coming down the path at a quicker pace than her own. There was no need to look. But she turned, even with the thought, to call a light "good morning", and to ask as he approached: "What do you call those black fowl? I never saw any like them before."

"They're Black Hamburgs. Father hates what he calls the modern mongrels. He says poultry-keeping hasn't changed in the last fifty years. Everyone still reads about the hen that lays three hundred eggs, and keeps the one that lays eighty-three. It's only changed in all the beautiful old breeds having been wiped out. That's what he says. I wasn't born then. Oh, and it's changed in the price of eggs. The more the hens are said to lay, the dearer they get."

"Yes," she said. "I believe they're dearer here than in France." What did it matter what they said? They were aware of each other rather than of their own words.

"There's a pair of kingfishers that have a nest in the stream-bank just below here. You can often see them if you come down early and keep quiet. You'd better let me go first. I can show you the driest way." He looked down at her feet. Small, beautifully-shaped feet, too thinly shod for the deeper grass. He did not think he was wasting his time. Nor did she.

We need not follow or listen more. They will not be likely to say any profound or brilliant things. In fact, we are best away. There will be a moment—but it is an hour from now, which may be ages in the game which is so old to the world, and was so new to them—when he will have a sudden, irresistible impulse to kiss her hair. "Oh, Alwyn, don't I.... You know you mustn't...." But what protest can be made through lips which are being kissed, and with this heartbeat that chokes the throat? "Oh, Alwyn, don't! Don't, *really*." She is loosed at last. They must adjust themselves to an altered world. We are best away.

* * * * * * *

The breakfast is set now, but the room is still empty. We have time to think. We observed before that the bread that science offers to men is very frequently stones. It has not found the elixir of life. It has not abolished age, nor greatly delayed death. Yet it has gone a short way on that path, and would do more if it might. Could it offer the gift of a life of continuing vigour, it would not pause, and we should be likely to take it with snatching hands. Yet there might be a bitter price to be paid, and it is of the nature of the gifts that science brings that we must take them first, and the price will be known at a later day. It gave us the rapid movement of the road-car, but it did not tell us that the price would be not only in many thousands of our own deaths, but in the tragic mystery of a million of unborn lives. Yet we might have thought that rubber and petrol would be useless to feed a child, and that the result must be somewhat different from what would have followed had we all been busy in growing wheat.

If it should conquer death, we might make a boast that would be silenced with the knowledge that it was not age but youth that had left the world. For we may see that it is by the device of the multitude of quickly-ending lives that the marvels of childhood, and the glamours of love, and the joys of the making of homes, and the miracles of parent-hood, may be repeated continually. They are old things that are always new. If we be reincarnated, as many think, is it not better than could be the experience of one continued life? Is it not for the freshness of each adventure that we should forget what is behind, and be ignorant of what is before? This may be so, or the truth may be of another sort. Yet we may conclude that the Creator may have more imagination that we, as He has more power. He may have designed life and death in a good way, though He did it without our help.

\* \* \* \* \* \* \*

Breakfast is late on Sunday mornings. It is to be at nine o'clock. It is five minutes earlier when Chester enters the room, with Christine and Peter following, laden with dolls. Christine is holding Jezebel in both arms in the orthodox peace. Now (if they are good) they may have their dolls on the hearthrug while their elders feed. Peter addresses her father with her usual directness, "Mother says you're to tell me 'Mallied all six.'"

"Married all six" are the concluding words of one of a series of tales which Chester had composed for the amusement rather than the instruction of these young women for whose existence he was responsible. They had no uplift. They were called "Mothers and Daughters"; were constructed with a degree of skill which is unusual in nursery rhymes; and were alike in disclosing the evil-doings of a gallery of unholy mothers, and the reactions of, and (sometimes) the retributions they experienced at the hands of, their afflicted children.

Christine knew them by heart, being fascinated by the pits of wickedness which they disclosed to her inexperienced eyes, but Peter would not allow her to say them, they being her father's property. Her mother might; but only on condition that she should make no error in recitation. Ada, bringing in the bacon, lingered for the doubtful benefit of the one that was now demanded. Its proper title was

*Cora Clare.*

"Now Cora Clare was resolved to marry.

But her mother said: 'That poor thing, Cora!
I'm sure that a husband would only bore her.
I must keep her from Ikey, and George, and Harry.
And the Jones's twins, and young Jack Parry.'

"So her mother wrote to the boys, and said
That Cora was getting too old to wed.
But when Cora discovered her mother's tricks,
She escaped up the chimney, and *married all six.*"

"And now," Peter ordered, "we'll have 'doll named Werna.'"
    "Very well, if there's time."

"Now Gertie James had a doll named Werna.

But her mother said, 'You naughty Gertie!
I never have seen a doll so dirty.
You mustn't go out with that filthy Werna.
I shall take her down to the stove and burn her,'

"And though Gertie cried, next day she broke her,
And pushed her down in the flames with a poker.
But she did not know, as with glee she eyed her,
That *her own best brooch had been stuffed inside her.*"

"And now Sissie White."
The room was still vacant and her father began obediently.

"Now Sissie White was too good to live.

And her mother said, 'That sweet young Sis!

She'll never grow up if she lives like this.
It's only when—'"

"Peter," said her mother, "I don't call this being good. I shan't get you the blue baby-dollies if you let people fall over the ones you've got."

Peter was off her father's knees in an instant, to the rescue of a trail of dolls in various stages of dilapidation, which had been scattered between the door and the hearthrug. "It's all right, Mummie," she cried, in hurried propitiation, "they've just been crawling."

"You ought to publish those tales," Elsie said, having entered behind her sister.

"So I ought, but the publishers differ."

"They're better than Milne."

"No, they're not. They're not nearly as good. They're not in the same class. But that's not why there's no competition to get them. They say, for one thing, there aren't enough to make a book of the orthodox size. But the real point is that the parents wouldn't like them, and it's no use writing for children unless the parents approve. You can't get through. But my theory is that just as we like to read a murder story without immediately poisoning all our acquaintances, so a child enjoys tales of what would be equal crimes on the nursery scale, and they don't do it any more harm. Anyway, you couldn't teach Peter anything wrong that she doesn't know."

Peter's head rose from the floor from which she was retrieving her dolls, with a quick side glance at her father as her name was mentioned. "I won't ever sin any more," she remarked, the blue eyes in the small-featured face having a look of almost angelic innocence through its tumbled curls, "I'm Frida's good girl." She bent down chuckling.

"You shouldn't call mother Frida," Elsie told her.

Peter went on picking up dolls.

## CHAPTER FOURTEEN

BREAKFAST had been commenced for some minutes when Alwyn came in. Did he know what had become of Miss Carfix? Yes. He had been showing her round. She had gone upstairs to change her shoes.

Frida asked: "Do you think she would care to stay after tomorrow, as you're going back?"

Yes. He thought she would, if she were asked. He might be able to be back by Tuesday afternoon.

Frida had learnt all that she wished to know. She said that she was sure that Father would like her to stay as long as possible.

Joyce came in as she said it. Elsie, looking at her with appreciation that touched the borders of envy, admitted that she was a lovely girl. Even more so than yesterday. There was a soft radiance in her eyes, and she had colour which she rarely showed. Her voice, too, with its scarcely-perceptible foreign accent, was low and clear in a self-possessed smiling apology for her lateness. Joyce did not feel self-possessed, but she had the ability belonging to many people of nervous temperament to conceal her feelings successfully.

Elsie asked which way they had been.

Alwyn answered, along the stream.

"Down or up?" Elsie asked, not without guile, her eyes on Joyce for an answer.

"Down."

"You couldn't go far that way."

That was true. You couldn't go thirty yards down the stream unless you should wade in. It was fenced in that direction beyond easy climbing. Upstream you could go for a mile or two, or get out on to the road if you would.

Alwyn looked somewhat disconcerted, but Joyce said calmly: "We've been watching the kingfishers." She turned her eyes to Mr. Oakley to ask about those lovely black chickens—"Homburgs, wasn't it?"

John Oakley rose to the bait. He talked poultry. They heard about the introduction of the heavy, feather-legged fowl, and of the mongrel breeds that have resulted. All the beautiful old European breeds were threatened with extinction. Some of them had heard it before. When he said that they (it was not clear who) deserved hanging, Chester adroitly led the conversation to the ethics and incidence of capital punishment. That was a fruitful subject enough, branching into that of the change of manners which led us to hang our criminals in a quiet shed instead of a public square.

Were we generally more reticent than our fathers? There was citing of contradictory evidences. It is a new thing that a woman will paint her face in a public vehicle.

Elsie said: "But everyone does that," with less than her force.

"Not quite everyone," her father answered. "There are still some decent women."

Chester said that there was no longer any novelty in seeing a woman paint her lips in a bus, but he was still watching for the first one who would begin painting her knees. That would be news.

But Elsie, confident in the support of a million of her fellow-women (how many women are there who will not go with the crowd?), and conscious of certain articles on her own dressing-table, would not pass her father's remark in silence.

She said: "What about Nina? Isn't she decent?"

It was an awkward question. No man likes either to say that his daughter isn't a decent woman, or to withdraw a remark that he has just made. And it was indisputable that Nina's face had been seen by no one except herself for several years.

He replied, rather weakly, that it was always best to keep personal references out of an argument, but Nina knew what he thought about that.

Still unsatisfied, Elsie pressed the discussion, confusing different facts with some adroitness. Were not the women of today more vigorous, more healthy, and more sanely clad than their grandmothers? Did her father want them to resign themselves to a frumpish old age before they were forty? Besides, she expected they painted their faces much the same in the old days, but they hadn't the honesty to admit it.

There was matter enough here for several voices to contend in its confutation.

Chester, regarding the argument with his usual detachment, quoted a seventeenth-century poet, and went on to suggest that if a Victorian lady could be reincarnated today it would not be the absence of old women that would impress her, but the fact that there are no young ones. Paint, to her, would be a sign that the complexion of youth had gone into a chronological rear. He admitted that she might observe other differences, but could only speculate as to what she would think of them. She might wonder at the height of this generation of women. Sports had certainly lengthened their legs.

Her father answered the other horn of her attack. No doubt there had been face-painters in every stage of our own, and probably all other civilizations. There were certain classes of nineteenth-century women who painted habitually. It was like an inn-sign or a barber's pole. Probably the lines of demarcation were less sharply drawn today. He hesitated to be more specific, with a reticence which was certainly more characteristic of his generation than that which has followed. Elsie was on the point of saying something which she checked on recalling a conversation of the previous night. It is so easy to generalize—and so different.

Her father went on to the contention that we are unfair to the Victorians when we accuse them of hypocrisy. If you have vermin in the stables which you cannot—which you may not even be much concerned to—exterminate, is it any reason that they should be allowed to run over the dinner-table?

Alwyn spoke, almost for the first time. He was not usually so silent, but at the moment his mind had little room for more than the single thought—how soon could he marry Joy? He did riot think in terms of years, scarcely of months. Days were too long. His mind faced the financial difficulties (sufficiently formidable), not asking "if" but "how". Prudence has its place in the conduct of life. It has also its time, and that time should not be when love enters to those who have kept its temple clean. There are those of strong prudences or weak desires who may wait for half a lifetime in mutual faith, and find a goal worth reaching. There is the case of the poet Crabbe. There is the case of Alfred Tennyson. There is the case of his sister.

> "Oh, true and tried so well and long,
> Demand not thou a marriage-lay,
> In that it is thy marriage-day
> Is music more than any song."

Perhaps it was; but it was music that might have been better heard a few years earlier. We may observe that the evil of deferred marriage is not new. It must arise in any social order as it moves upward (if that be the direction) from the elemental things. When, in a word, children become less an asset than a liability. It is the fatal sign that the pillars of a civilization are rotting at the base.

After that, there may be delay. For a time, we may hide the fact that we no longer breed vigorously, moving our British levies to Scythia, and our Scythians into Gaul; but the time must come when the rafters of a burning Rome will fall on our children's heads, stilling their bewildered protests that they have all been sent to the best schools.

Alwyn did not think of waiting half a lifetime, or half a year. He would not wait an hour more than he must. That there would be obstacles, the contentions of indifferent or colder things, he could vaguely feel. But they were for him to overcome. That Joy would be complacent to such impetuosity was a question to be answered also. That was another victory (if she should offer such battle) for him to win. He had a dim premonition also (he would not have allowed it to be a fear) that there might be difficulties with her Church. Well, they must be broken down. It was for him to think of a way. Had he not held her close, feeling her heart beat fast (as a girl's will) through the thin rampart of the summer dress? Had he not kissed her lips? Even looked down on the slight smooth curve of cream-hued breast that had been offered by a movement of the traitorous dress, as she had turned in his arms? Would he rest for a needless hour till he had gained that more—that maddening more—which was yet to come? There is something different here from the casual carnality of Elsie's college acquaintances. Different not in kind, but in degree only? Not at all. They are the deadliest foes.

But we were saying that Alwyn spoke, and it might be supposed that we should listen to what he said. But it did not matter over-much. It was no more than a suggestion thrown into the eddies of conversation to the effect that the differences between the two centuries may be less of character than of circumstance. It sounded likely enough. It may be true. But two or three people were talking at once, and no one listened particularly. Why should we?

## CHAPTER FIFTEEN

WE had to come away from the Oakley's dining-table. We were getting nowhere. They talked too much at their meals. And there was Peter as well. Peter would fill a book before breakfast any day in the week. It would be as easy as swallowing her morning milk (and Christine's, too, on one occasion, though there was a reason for that). What I am trying to tell is an adventure of marriage (with a few other things), and we were getting nowhere at all.

The Victorian novelist has been accused of certain arbitrary limitations in the exercise of his leisured and spacious art. The accusation goes beyond truth, but it may be allowed that he would most often leave the hero with a sleeping bride in his arms. We must recognize that he might easily have selected an inferior curtain. It may be the greatest moment of life, if we except death, of which we know less, having neither personal nor inherited knowledge of that experience. From that habit of technique, and some reticences, it has been said, with exceptional folly, that the Victorian novelist only dealt with a half of life, which would be a truer word if it were said of those of our own day. Even to the convention which I have mentioned, there were many exceptions, Meredith, Thackeray, Dickens, and a score of others. They looked at life with a broader vision than we, and balanced it in a juster scale. They did not need to be taught that if you kiss filth on the lips, beauty will be slow to offer her own for an equal intimacy. We cannot blame her for that. She is of a fastidious kind.

But I am modern in this, if in little else, that it is a tale of marriage that I am trying to tell, which is some months away; and when I find that I am moving at a pace which will not advance forty-eight hours in a hundred pages—well, it is time to ring down to the engine-room.

Let us go ahead for three months, with no more than a backward glance at the intervening days, and then one at the new position which our pieces have taken on the board of life.

It is the trouble of all who would tell a tale, and would hold it in a straight path, that we do not live separate lives. There is none but is entangled with a score of others, so that it may be hard to draw a single thread clear. That was half the trouble at Birstall House, though I have said nothing of Mrs. Case's size, nor of Ada's unfortunate affair with the postman who came in the afternoon, nor of a dozen other matters that might have delayed us upon the way. For the moment, we will keep clear of Birstall, which is quiet enough, for its tennis-court is dismantled in these November days, and the dining-table is unused, and John Oakley is having his meals in his own room, as he does when the house is empty of those who grew up within its walls.

Elsie is back at college, having found no occasion to intercept her father's letters. She had met no penalty for her folly beyond some anxious hours, and a veiled warning from her principal which she could not resent, because to do so was to admit that she understood. She was left in doubt of what had occurred, observing that others had not returned, so that the set to which she had belonged was of an altered quality, so far as it still cohered, but she never knew that she owed her immunity to a remark of Edward Perrott (he being questioned concerning those who were disclosed to have been his companions in the Welwood excursions) from which it was rightly judged that the issue of the episode had been more to her credit than to his satisfaction. There was a general realization among her friends that, whatever might be the talk of the common-room, it would be wise to delay the practice of promiscuity (even with the expert advice of Dr. Marie Stopes to enable them to avoid the more unconcealable if not the worst of its natural consequences) until their college course should be completed.

The Lawsons are back in their Buckinghamshire cottage, and it is there we must look first for news of the time we have overlooked, and on this occasion we must not allow Peter to divert our minds. In fact, she is being good, which makes it easier, for we all know that goodness, however admirable, is rather a dull thing. She is being good on condition that she takes her orders from Christine, having considered that some of her father's remarks, when his intervention was called for, approached the intolerable. "I love Father," she told Christine, "when I'm good, but when I'm naughty, I *simply hate him*." And Christine has accepted the position with a cheerful seriousness, and gives her sister all the attention that can be spared from Jezebel's nearer and more natural claims. It is a game, Frida hopes, of which they may not quickly tire, for Christine has always been an advocate of the righteous life, and Peter's resolution to sin no more was unfortunately forgotten nearly three months ago—to be exact, about twenty minutes after she became the mother of the blue twins.

Frida's cottage is not of the size or quality of her father's home. When bricklayers obtained the benefit of shorter hours (if benefit be the right word in relation to an occupation which is difficult to follow in wet weather or winter days), and when they succeeded in convincing a post-War government that they had too many votes for it to allow anyone to build houses except themselves, they met the difficulty they had created very reasonably by building them with lower ceilings and smaller rooms. A nation which had won the War and followed America's suggestion that it should lose the peace with equal good temper, accepted its straightened quarters contentedly enough, even observing an advantage in the fact that they could be more easily swept and dusted, at a time when most of its women were too busy drawing doles to be greatly interested in domestic labour. That these new houses were very badly built was a quite separate circumstance. They were the natural product of a generation which had no use for Elizabethan oak, having lost confidence in its own capacity to endure. Give us our labour-saving contrivances, and the thickness of the walls is a more trivial thing, nor are we worried overmuch when we count the rooms and the nursery may be hard to find. Have we not sold our birthright for a tin of petrol? A generation of science has brought us here.

But Chester and Frida had looked for a home, and it had been the best they could find. Frida was one who accepted facts, looking at them straightly with steady eyes, and moulding them as she might. The cottage was in the country which they both loved. It was sufficiently near to London for Chester's needs. Looking round she had said: "Where is the garden?" Chester had been less concerned about that. There seemed a good deal to him. Those who have a large garden and few hands to labour may have five years' penal at Dartmoor and think it a home of rest. But Frida had been born in a Midland county. All English people love gardens. The subjugation of land satisfies at once their sense of beauty, and that deep-rooted Saxon passion for order which our politicians exploit so successfully; but nowhere are the gardens so numerous and so large as in the Midland counties; few great cities have been as stubborn as Birmingham in resisting the abomination of the ungardened flat. Frida had her way, and a piece of land, half-meadow, half-coppice, was acquired at the foot of the square plot that surrounded the cottage.

And for six years, in this gradually-furnished cottage, they had lived and loved, and joyed, and (of course) suffered also, and quarrelled at times, but with little of dramatic incident beyond the births of the two children, until the delusive wealth of Chester's lorry-obstructing cousin had been thrust upon them. "Blessed is the country that has no history." It is a half-truth, if not more. May not one of the reasons why the Victorian novelist was apt to end his tale with a bedded bride have been that there was a normal expectation of resulting happiness, and happiness (for three hundred pages) may be a dull matter of which to read?

Yet such homes as these may be worth regarding, for they are the hope of England today. We see the divorce statistics, with their dim appalling background of vice and cruelty, and say (with some truth) that it is the lesser evil that such people should be broken apart, but we may think also of the larger number to whom the thought of divorce would never come. We read of our birth-reduction, with its implication of women dishonoured to an unnatural barrenness. We read a best-seller which has for its admired heroine a wife who would have no more children because she lost some blood with her first (was there no one to send her a white feather, such as women would send to men in the early days of the War?). But we hear little of the valiant, patient, tax-ridden struggle in ten thousand happier homes that have not placated the modern Moloch with their children's lives.

England has had its earlier periods of apparent decadence, in Carolan and in an earlier Georgian time, but in the end the tree stood, and the rotten branches fell. "I, only I, am left," Elijah lamented, and the tempest and the whirlwind mocked him for the back-number which he had proved to be. But the voice of God was a quieter thing: *"There are yet seven thousand in Israel, those who have not bowed the knee to Baal...."*

They had been married six years ago, last May, ignoring the ancient superstition that it is a dangerous month, and Christine had been born in the July of the following year, and Peter about fifteen months afterwards. After that, there had been an interval of three or four years, and now there was good hope of a third.

The fox that had lost his tail sat down with his back to the wall, and told his friends that the brush is a very inconvenient and even dangerous thing to have. When three years passed without another child coming, three women out of four who spoke to Frida would affect assumption of a deliberate barrenness. "Of course, you won't have any more." "I think two's such a nice number." "I don't know why you had them so quickly. It seemed such a pity." When she said that she shouldn't mind if another came, they affected incredulity, or professed wonder among themselves that Mrs. Lawson wouldn't be frank like other women. It would be a mistake to say that their talk was like water on a duck's back, because a duck with a wet back is extremely uncomfortable Frida went her own way, and cared for none of these things, in which she was exceptionally fortunate. The herd instinct is very strong in the majority of women—so strong that they are not content merely to feel assured that they run with the crowd themselves, but they are restless with the desire to bait those who may decline to do so. And whether it be true or not that women talk more than men, there is little doubt that the woman has the more poisonous tongue.

But we have not come to the Lawsons' cottage to consider these circumstances, but because Joyce Carfix will be here tomorrow, and it is the best spot to choose from which we can learn what has been happening in the autumn months, and survey the position which is before us.

It is a moment of victory. Joy's letter that came by the morning post (too long for full reproduction) contained these passages:

> "So he told me that I might as well wear it as not, as he could see how it would end, and he should be late for the meat as it was. At least, I think that was it, I can't imagine Uncle missing a meal. After that, he was out hunting foxes all day. When he came back, he said he didn't know what he had said, or he hadn't said it, or something, and we had it all over again, but he had to give in in the end, and I've been wearing it ever since. I told Alwyn to leave Uncle to me. I'm going to see Father Fawcett tonight. That's the next trouble. I've got to get a dispensation from Rome. Father Fawcett told me he'd have to give me one of about six reasons, and it seemed to be rather difficult to find one of them that fits the case. He

asked me whether I should obey the authority of the Church if the dispensation were refused, and I think he wouldn't have minded if I'd said I wasn't sure, but I didn't like to say that. The most hopeful reason seems to be that if Alwyn doesn't marry me, no one else would, and I asked Father Fawcett why that wouldn't do, but he didn't seem quite satisfied, and when I told Uncle, he said he wouldn't put his money on that. I told Father Fawcett that if I said if I didn't marry Alwyn, I wouldn't marry anyone else, it came to just the same thing, but he told me he'd think it over, and I'd better see him again when I'd got Uncle's consent. But Uncle says the dispensation's certain to come. He's been a Catholic longer than I have, and he wouldn't lose any sleep about that. Anyway, it seems they'll let you marry almost anyone if they think it's your last chance, and quite right too. So I shall have to say I'm going bald at the worst, or something equally dreadful.

"Father Fawcett wants to see Alwyn too. He's got to make sure that I shan't be unequally yoked with unbelievers. I hope Alwyn won't say anything silly. I tell him he spends so much time selling things he doesn't know how to buy them. But he says he talked his father over all right, and that was the hardest job of the lot. I don't know about that. I'd had a few words with him before, and they may have helped.

"There's some trouble also about children. Father Fawcett wants us to agree that they'll all be Catholics, as of course they will, so I said to him why make a fuss about that? But you know what men are, and priests are just like the rest, as far as I've been able to see. I talked about it to Alwyn, and he said: 'Why not make it fifty-fifty?' And I asked him however many he thought we were going to have, but he said he didn't mean that. You don't understand English as well as you think you do when you've been away. So he explained what he really meant, and I told him it wouldn't do. Anybody could see that. And then he got quiet, and you can't do anything with him when he gets quiet, so I led from another suit, and...."

"Is that all?" Chester asked, as Frida's voice became inaudible in the midst of this sentence.

"No. It's not nearly all, but it's all I'm going to read to you."

There were actually about three further pages, but as Frida considered them unsuitable for publication, and as her judgement is probably as good as ours, if not better, we must let it go at that.

Chester realized that he must do the same, and contented himself with the remark that "the young woman does rather let out when she writes to you. I've always said you'd pull it off in the end, but I reckoned it'd take rather longer than this."

"I?" said Frida, "I haven't done anything."

"No. You never do."

It might be difficult to say exactly what Frida had done, and her exclamation of surprise may have been as genuine as such exclamations usually are. But, in fact, her steady, matter-of-course assumption from the first that it was a certain thing had been of a value which Joyce Carfix assessed with a clear-sighted accuracy, and she had written to her all along with a detailed confidence which she had not given to other members of the Oakley family. With Elsie she had established no more than a surface cordiality. Nina she had not yet met. She thought John Oakley "a dear", and considered that her victory over him had been almost absurdly easy. (Let Alwyn think what he would). She had learnt that the merest hint of tears— But it would not have occurred to her to give any real confidence to her prospective father-in-law. He was to be subdued and managed to the required end, and regarded with a watchful discretion, even though he were a surrendered foe.

"May I," Chester asked, "enquire the meaning of 'it'?"

"Yes, if you're as dense as you look. It's a ring, of course."

"I suppose they know what strain it'll stand," Chester remarked thoughtfully. He was not considering the ring, but, with an unhostile detachment, the amazing arrogance and discipline of the Catholic Church—a discipline which, though it is still exercised with more discretion in England than in the Latin countries, is probably firmer among its own adherents today than before the Reformation, when, century after century, the popes would write to the Archbishops of York or Canterbury, instructing them to insist that the priesthood should remain unmarried, and the harassed archbishops would write back to ask (in politer language) how the devil it was to be done?

The admonition of Paul against being married to unbelievers had occurred to the mind of John Oakley also, as he has considered his attitude to this sudden attachment. Circumstances yet to be explained had placed in his hands the power of delaying the marriage, and, as a general proposition, his observations told him that delay is halfway to prevention. Or perhaps more. But in Alwyn's case he was not hopeful that it would make any final difference, except to alienate him from the confidence and affection of his only son.

In any case, he had to admit that that particular text did not apply. The Catholic certainly believes. He appears to have an appetite for belief, insatiable and indiscriminate, which the Protestant can only observe with a half-admiring wonder, having always found belief to be a rather difficult thing.

For the measure of assent which he had finally given, he had convinced himself that an interpretation of the spirit of Christian charity, as suggested to his mind by the parable of the wheat and tares, and by Luke IX 50, were finally responsible. Joyce would have held this conclusion to be unjust to her eyelashes. We must take our choice.

## CHAPTER SIXTEEN

JOYCE came in the morning. "I wish," Frida said (without looking directly at the size of the cabin trunk she had brought), "we could have given you a better room."

"If you'd been in a convent for more years than you knew how to count— It will be just lovely being here with you. I'm so tired of Aunt Agatha being a Buddhist, or a Mahatma, or whatever it is. I always say she's the wrong thing, and she gets so cross."

This statement required no elucidation to Frida, thanks to the length of the letters she had received, but, having had fewer advantages, we must pause a moment to understand. Joy's uncle had an unmarried sister who failed to illustrate either the rule that children should follow their parents' faith, or the fact that most of those who abandon that of Rome appear unable to accept any substitute. Agatha Corchester had attached herself to one of the obscurer Indian cults, and was as unreasonably (or reasonably) annoyed when she was incorrectly classified, as a Particular Baptist would be should his friends insist on describing him as an Unitarian of the looser kind.

"I'm afraid you'll find it rather dull, at this time of year," Frida went on. "If you had come in the summer—"

But Joy said that it would be lovely now. In fact, November was kind. Pale sunshine; and the woods still held something of the autumn gold.

Having heard their voices, the children stood at the door.

"You've got our room," Peter announced. Not resentfully, but as one stating a fact.

"You shouldn't say that," Christine reproached; "we don't mind."

She offered ready lips. The dark-brown head leaned against Joyce affectionately.

Peter stood her ground in the doorway. She considered the visitor with grave and thoughtful eyes.

Not that she failed to recognize her. Peter never forgot. Her face broke suddenly into the smile which (as she well know) most people found irresistible. She said: "You can say *Judy Wynn*, if you like."

Not having heard it before, Joyce could only profess her inability.

"I can say it, I think," Christine volunteered. "No, you mustn't," Peter interrupted swiftly. "That's Father's tale."

"Is it something," Joyce inquired, "that I ought to know?"

"I expect it's one of the tales that Chester makes up for them. I hadn't heard that one before. They're all meant to corrupt the young. I daresay Peter could tell us, if she tried."

But Peter had disappeared.

Chester came in the evening. He had been persuaded to join in the production of a new literary monthly, in addition to his usual journalistic work, and was in London continually. He congratulated Joyce on her success with her uncle, which he knew to have been an essential victory, and was required to admire the ring—a stoneless platinum knot, which had been made to her own design. She had valuable rings enough that her mother had left her, though they were still in her uncle's charge, and she had told Alwyn that he had better save his money for other things.

Chester said, when alone with Frida afterwards, that this showed that she had a business head, to which he received a rather doubtful assent. Joyce, like most of us, showed some contradictions of character. She could be shrewd enough at times, but she had no thought of economy where her own desires were concerned. Not that she would pay a higher price than she need, but could any price be too high? The trunk she had brought for a ten-days' visit had its meaning also, though its fullness was partly due to a cradle for Jezebel, and a negro doll to be added to the countless family which Peter mothered so casually. She had impulsive generosities also, the amount of which might be to the limit that her purse contained.

Chester said: "Well, Alwyn's got a good business head, anyway. He ought to keep the ship off the rocks. He's working very hard now. He's coming down for a few hours tomorrow, but he said we mustn't expect him again during the week."

Frida allowed that he was working hard. As to the good business head, she knew him better than Chester. She made no reply. She knew that Alwyn took his occupation in the spirit in which (as the tale goes) Sir Richard Grenville had steered his ship into the heart of a Spanish fleet. The spirit of adventurous, rather chivalrous, war. He had less even than his father of the cold-blooded, calculating, commercial spirit. His weapons were energy and imagination, and some fine qualities both of brain and character. But a good business head? It is a question of what you mean. There is a margin of chance in all human enterprises. If we try to eliminate it, we cut at the root and meaning and the worth of life. We are on the verge of the Russian horror. But this margin varies. It might be too large for safety in Alwyn's enterprises. As to whether his resources were equal to that of marriage, he would be less likely to calculate than to resolve. They had got to be so. If they were not, he had got to make them. If Frida said no discouraging word, seeing this so clearly, it was because she also had married without counting the cost. In fact, there had been nothing to pay. The scale sank on the other side. But it would have been all the same if there had. When Alwyn met Joyce, she expected him to act in the same way. She knew that there were different standards for others. Nina's was different. Perhaps Elsie's also. But that was Alwyn's, and hers. But this conversation took place when they were alone at a later hour.

Now Chester, having approved the ring, asked what was the news from the seat of war? Joy said there was really nothing to tell. Nothing that she hadn't written already. Chester said he didn't know all that she had written. Anything read to him was severely expurgated. He understood that most of it was unfit—"Like the tales you make up for Peter," Joy interrupted.

"Oh, those— They're mostly about wicked mothers. I suppose they ought to be marked 'for adults only', but then the adults would feel had, as they often do."

"What's this one about Judy something?"

"Oh, that I That's not wicked at all. It's only silly. It's this:

"Now Judy Wynn was as fat as batter.

But her mother said, 'My Judy Wynn!
She's nothing but bones in a coat of skin.
If Judy Wynn were a fair bit fatter,

She'd be more like the Dormouse, and less like the Hatter.'
So her mother gave her a piece of pork
To eat when…"

"Joy," Frida said, entering the room at the moment, "the children want you to say good night to them before they go to sleep. Oh, yes, Chester'll always say verses for you, if you've time to listen. He makes them up when he's gardening, so when Peter wants another it's rather good for the lawn. He made up one of the worst while he finished forking up the potatoes last Sunday."

"May I hear it?"

"Yes. If Frida will let me finish this time."

"I don't mind, but you know the children won't go to sleep while you're keeping Joyce here."

"It won't take half-an-hour. I suppose it's *Mima Briggs* that you mean?

"Now Mima Briggs had a Persian kitten.

But her mother said, 'Jemima Briggs,
I've told you that kittens are worse than pigs.
Do you think you can keep that mangy kitten,
With a crawling baby that might get bitten?'

So her mother went to the garden lake,
And drowned that kitten, and no mistake.
But Mima muttered, 'I wish that you
Were in it instead.' *And she meant it too.*"

"You don't think it does them any harm to hear so much about mothers of that peculiar pattern?"

"No. Of course not."

"Frida," Chester explained, "is sceptical as to the power of environment."

"I only say they're quite different when they're born."

"You prefer heredity?"

"No. I don't say that. I say there's something different in each that you can't change. Something new."

Frida became expansive on this subject, forgetting the importance of sleep to the young. She said: "Chester came home last week and told me he'd got to write a column for the Sunday edition about a Conference that had been discussing the child-mind, or something equally silly. Half of them said that a child's character was entirely fixed by the something-or-others of the first six years, and the others said that the years of adolescence were equally serious. He asked me which side he should take, and I said he'd better tell them all to go home till they'd got more sense."

"Did you?" Joyce asked.

"No. I told Dixon what Frida said, and he said he'd no doubt she was right. It seemed to him that they all talked bally rot, but we couldn't afford to say that. People would think we were out of touch with modernity, and buy the *Sunday Echo* instead."

"What did you do?"

"He wrote," Frida was first to explain, "the kind of article by which you could only tell he was joking if you knew it beforehand. The children are in the book-room, on the right at the top of the stairs. I've left the light…. I'll have supper ready when you come down."

Joyce took the hint, and went, and Chester rose to help in the preparation of the evening meal.

When they were seated at the supper-table half-an-hour later, Joyce re-commenced the explanation for which Chester had asked her.

"The trouble was," she said, "that Mother left me £200 a year till I'm twenty-five, and some more after that."

"That doesn't sound troublesome," Chester observed, and then became silent at the memory of his cousin's will.

"Well, but it was. It wasn't Uncle having the money; we could have done without that. It's because it made me a Ward in Chancery, and whoever marries me has to go to prison the next day."

"And Alwyn thought it wasn't worthwhile?"

"No, of course not. I mean of course he didn't—anyway, I shouldn't have done."

That, at least, was true. Joyce had no love for publicity; no desire for martyrdom in any form. Few women have. The Five Bishops might burn. In fact they did. But their widows remained to draw the incomes of their estates. We may assume that without looking it up.

Gaol for Alwyn must be avoided at any cost. Her uncle's consent became an essential thing. It had not been easy to get. He had thought that she should wait a while, and look round. "Marry in haste", he had quoted looking profound, which he could do quite easily after the third glass. He thought that she might do better for herself than Alwyn Oakley, though he liked the boy well enough. Besides, he'd read somewhere that women should not marry till they are twenty-five. He rather thought it had been in a sporting paper, in which case it was not to be disregarded lightly. He forgot that he sent his own heifers—but we'd better not say that. Novelists who investigate the sewerage of humanity, with the aid of some second-rate carnal experience and a few cocktails, would agree with their women readers that we are being coarse.

Anyhow (weakening, as Joyce's eyelashes came into action), what did Alwyn's father say? Let him know that first. That was where John Oakley had found that the full responsibility was in his hands, and, in the end, he had temporized—if Alwyn could assure him that he was in a position to marry?— As to that, we may get some clearer light when we hear the proposal which Alwyn will bring with him tomorrow. It was one which he had in his mind about sixteen hours a day since he had seen his father a week ago, but it was one (he had decided) which would be better said than written, and with a commendable self-control, he had kept anything more than a series of indirect references to it out of the seven letters (or more) which he had written to Joyce in the meantime.

The lovers may have been fortunate that there was no woman in a position to obstruct their purpose. They had only to deal with the weaker sex.

Miss Corchester's belief in polygamy removed her from any active interest. She did not object to the marriage. She recognized that even polygamists must make a beginning. There must be a first wife. But it is an incident without religious significance. She turned her mind to the contemplation of more plural things.

## CHAPTER SEVENTEEN

"I hope," Frida said, when it came to the time of saying good night at the stair-foot, "that you won't mind breakfast being rather late in the morning. Mrs. Potter'll be here soon after seven on Monday, and we manage easily enough. She comes in all the week, except Sunday, but we've got to do without tomorrow."

"Can't I help?"

"Yes, of course, if you like; but I shouldn't get up early. Chester'll get up first, and see to the fires. You can get a bath about half an hour after you hear him moving about. The children will lie on, or come in to me."

"Can't I help with them?"

"No. There's no need. They dress themselves, or each other. Peter's really as good as Christine at that. I never let anyone else do anything for them that they can do for themselves. I say you can't watch children too much, or interfere too little, unless you see something going wrong. If all the adults went into a trance tomorrow, the children of the rich would die like flies, unless the slum children took charge."

"Well, I'd like to do anything I can," Joyce said. It would, in fact, be rather a game. This simple cultured *ménage* was something new at close quarters, and contrasted with the rather wasteful luxury of her uncle's home.

Frida would not have talked of a late breakfast or lying in bed herself a month ago, nor would she normally have considered the fact that her next child was an event of six months ahead, a reason for reduced activities. But the fact was that she was having some sickness and disability which she had not experienced with Christine or Peter. A child grows with no space to spare. It pushes the surrounding organs to right and left to make room for itself with the insolence of its youth, and it does not always do it quite in the same way. Other organs may resent this pressure, and assert their protest after a night's rest. It is an uncertain discomfort, to which any woman may be liable at such a time, and not only those who are under-exercised and over-fed, as most pregnant women are, though they naturally suffer most. Frida said cheerfully that she expected that it would soon pass, and Chester, teasing her that it was a portent of twins, kept her from getting up early, and gave ready help with the household tasks on the Sunday mornings when Mrs. Potter's assistance was not available.

Joyce might see here the possibilities of marriage at its best, resolving itself into a happy unselfish comradeship. Something which may be found, even today, in many thousands of English homes. Something which has no need for publicity, but which is as real as the disastrous wreckage that is exposed by the daily press. Those who marry for self-indulgence, or greed, or pride, with one eye on the possibility of the divorce court, can never know what marriage is, and may deny the existence of an Eden which they have failed to find. It is unjust to compare such marriages with the matings of animals. They are of a lower kind. The vital principle of successful marriage

> "To hold together, to lose or win,
> Till the very sides of the grave fall in,"

has been learnt by countless of our fellow-creatures, both birds and animals. But it is useless to go through life trying to buy its best with cheques that you fail to meet.

# CHAPTER EIGHTEEN

ALWYN came in time for the midday dinner, which (Joyce told him) she had helped cook. She had peeled potatoes. She had learnt something of the making of sauce. She was in sufficiently good spirits to be indifferent to some stains upon a dress which had been put to uses for which it was not meant. But she always had spoiled her clothes. It is a carelessness with a cheerful side. You feel annoyed just at first, but it is a good excuse for the pleasure of getting more. Joyce would have recognized her consciousness of this compensation with an unruffled frankness, had she been self analytic, which she never was.

The children shared the meal at a table which was large enough, though with no space to spare. Eating is a solemn function in the first decade of life. They would have been quiet enough if their father would have left them alone, which was not his way. He asked Christine why they each had two spoons. She knew the answer to that, having heard it before. But she did not know whether it were a fact or a joke. She knew her father to be an utterer of lawless words, so that his speech was full of pits for the young, but of the nature of this question (or rather of its answer) she could never be quite sure. She said: "It's so that we can lift one up while the other's coming down. So that we don't lose any time."

Peter looked sideways at her sister with blue inscrutable eyes. She understood her father's peculiar brand of humour better than Christine, better even than her mother. She knew that this was a joke. She knew equally well that Christine was not sure. She continued her meal in silence, her two spoons demonstrating the proposition with an industrious regularity. It was not a method of raising food which her mother approved, but Frida recognized that the time was not suitable for admonition. Peter may have realized that too. It is hard to tell. Anyway, she had cleared her plate. She said concisely: "I want some more." The words were not as unmannered as they may look. Her lips smiled. Her voice was a coo. Besides, she addressed no one. She announced fact, as we all may.

Christine said quickly: "You must say, 'Please, Mother'."

Peter turned to Alwyn to say happily: "Christine always makes me say please."

Alwyn seemed in good spirits, but was visibly tired. He admitted that work might have curtailed sleep, but not, he said, enough to matter. "I sleep in the trains." He had something to discuss with

Joyce that must wait till they were alone, but there were business matters on which he could speak without reticence.

He had made many efforts to increase his agencies during the past three months, with differing success, but the most important development had been outside his own initiation, and he had done no more than take advantage of opportunity. Among his previous agencies there had been one for a small but enterprising firm of aluminium saucepan manufacturers in Hunnerton. His first efforts for them had been indecisive. A mere acceptance of samples to be sent out by shippers to foreign markets. But last summer orders—substantial orders—had begun to arrive. Seeing that he represented a firm who could establish their market, he had been giving more time to their goods, pushing them hard in many directions, and content to wait results if he could get their samples into markets abroad. He had begun to reap the fruits of this policy, when they had written to say that their present output was limited. They hoped to extend their works, but he must go slower in the meantime. This had been disappointing. If they were slow to execute orders, his commission suffered. Worse even than that, customers might be offended, and lost.

A few weeks later there was news of even more disconcerting character. They had sold their business to Collett, Hayward & Co., one of the largest firms in the trade, and he must book no further orders in their name. Alwyn looked up his agreement. He had probably lost a very promising agency, but he was secure in his claim for commission on the business he had done already. Probably more than that. The position was not one which had been contemplated on either side when the terms of the agency had been fixed up. He might be entitled to compensation. It was a matter to think over before he replied.

That day he called on a firm of Eastern merchants, inquiring for any orders which might have come through. He was on good terms with the buyer, who asked him into his office. "I've got a good line for you this morning. Tell your people it will be worth their while to do this right, and they'll get something similar every month." It was an order for about £200 worth of aluminium goods.

Alwyn hesitated a moment. His first impulse was to put it in his pocket in silence, till he had had time to consider the position. His second was to be frank with a man he liked. He told him how matters stood. Frankness was paid in its own coin, as it often is.

"That's a queer thing," said the buyer. "It's Collett, Hayward's you've knocked out. They've had these orders for years. They've got so used to them they haven't troubled to call, and we've just posted them on. You got in by offering us a better finish, and about two per cent cheaper. Of course, bulk might not have been equal to sample, and then you'd have been out for good. Barker's their man. I suppose he'll be coming round to see us about this. But it's your order; if it's any advantage to you, pick it up."

Alwyn said he would take it, giving a promise that he would give prompt information if it could not be executed at the price under the altered circumstances. "We can't have any delay," said the buyer.

Alwyn was led to explain the doubt he felt as to his own position, and was met with the consoling reply: "Well, let us know if they treat you shabbily. It's your order right enough. We might have something to say, and Barker'd have to listen to us. We do a lot of business through him."

He went out feeling that he had done well to speak freely. In fact, he had been wasting his time, as we all do. The next morning he had a letter from Collett, Hayward & Co. They understood that he had been representing the firm that they had taken over, on the London ground. Would he make it convenient to call upon them at 11:30 A.M. on Thursday morning next?

Alwyn's first impulse was to resent the letter. It assumed that their time would be his. It said nothing about travelling expenses. His second thought (on which, very fortunately for himself, he most frequently acted) was that they would not have written in that way if they had merely intended to cancel the agency. He replied that he would keep the appointment.

When the day came he was interviewed by Mr. Richard Hayward, who offered him a cigarette, and talked of nothing in particular for about five minutes, and then came to his point with a direct brevity.

"Mr. Oakley, we bought out your firm because we'd got to come to it first or last, and the longer we put it off the more it would cost. That's nothing to do with you. It was because they'd got the best works-manager in the trade. But we found they'd got a good man on the London ground. You were getting your samples in where it isn't easy to do. And now you've got Hobson & Finch. Yes, I heard about that yesterday. That would have been another two or three thousand a year off our books. These firms that are hard to get in with are devilish hard to get back if they do change. That is, if they're treated right by the newcomer. Well, Barker's been under notice since January. I want you to take on our agency from the start of the new year. You can have Barker's terms. He hasn't done badly for himself. But he's got too much on. He thought he could leave our orders to take care of themselves, and just draw the commiss.

But there's one snag that you've got to face. If you take this on, you've got to start straightaway, but we're not going to pay commission twice. Barker gets it till the end of the year on every order from his ground, and we can't pay it to you as well. And there's another thing. You've got to take the ground between here and London, at the same commission. It won't pay in itself, but we're not going to separate it again from the London ground. On the whole, you ought to find it worth having. Barker's done nothing, and been drawing about £400 a year. If you work, you can make it £800. If you can't reach that figure, you're not the man that we want to find.

Alwyn thought quickly. He was good at an interview, or he wouldn't have been in that office then. He knew the offer was too good to miss. In the end, he'd have to take it on their terms. If they'd offered him a lower commission, he would have had to take it—after a struggle. But he saw also that they wanted him. He saw also that they were removing any difficulty for themselves in relation to his existing agreement. He saw that he was being asked to work for nearly three months without payment, and to take on an extra ground for which, standing alone, a higher scale of commission would have to be paid. He considered everything now in relation to his projected marriage, and he had an idea.

He said: "How do you settle commission, monthly or quarterly?"

"You have your cheque every quarter, as soon as the figures can be got out. There'll be no delay on our side. You could have a cheque on account any time, if you keep the right side of the line."

"You want to cancel the present agreement?"

"Yes. There's no need to ask that. We'll settle all commission due to you to date."

"Including Hobson & Finch's order?"

There was a second's hesitation. "Yes. That's only fair. Though your people couldn't have executed. They'd taken all they could have handled to the end of the year, as it was."

"It means working without any return for the rest of the year—and then till I draw commission on the new year's trade. If I take it on on those terms, do you mind advancing £100 on the next year's commission? I don't mean now. I mean on January 1st. I have my own office expenses running on."

"I don't know about that. We don't pay out money before it's earned."

Alwyn said nothing to that. He knew when to be silent. He waited for more to come. In the pause that followed Mr. Hayward also had an idea. There was nothing unusual in that. He was a very capable man. He had surmounted the three-fold disadvantages of a successful father, a public school, and a University course. He said: "It's getting about time for a bite. You'd better come out and have some lunch with me, and we'll talk it over.' An hour later the matter had been fixed up to their mutual satisfaction. Alwyn was to draw a sum in January on account of future commissions, which was not to be £100, but might be more or less, according to the amount of trade which had been done in the meantime. The agreement was to be drawn up that afternoon. He was to stay the night, and sign it in the morning. There had been only one thing to disquiet him. Mr. Hayward had mentioned his father, whom he knew slightly, with respect and liking. He had asked how business was going, in a casual way that might mean nothing, and had received a conventionally vague reply. But Alwyn had an intangible impression that there had been a real, though not unsympathetic, doubt or knowledge behind the question, and this impression was not removed when he saw his father that night (for he naturally went home, having to stay in the district till the next day), though there seemed to be hope that the worst of the strain was over, and that the crisis which had been produced by economic causes individually uncontrollable would be surmounted. But an old and valuable picture which Alwyn had known from childhood was no longer on the dining-room wall. A neighbour who had always admired it had been allowed to buy it for £50. The deeds of the house itself, which had been in his father's safe for over a quarter of a century, were in the hands of the bank. They had other charges also

John Oakley himself looked well. A constitution fundamentally sound had risen to the emergency. He worked longer hours, and with an increased concentration. He had lost some weight, which had annoyed him in recent years. He was of the temperament that is roused by difficulty, and though he had had some anxious moments to live through, he might be none the worse for them—if the worst were really over, as he was inclined to think. Business had certainly shown some improvement. Turnover had increased, and that after he had reduced his overhead charges considerably. Winterton's had been ordering largely, and had met their payments more promptly than had been usual in recent years. Providing they met the acceptances that were now under discount, about which John Winterton had assured him that there would be no difficulty…yes, he thought things would improve. But he wished to cut down his own expenses. He had reduced the salaries of his staff, including that of his manager, who was a married man with a rather large family. It was only right that he should curtail his own expenditure. He listened to Alwyn's account of his morning's interview, and then put the proposal to him which was to be communicated to Joyce this afternoon.

## CHAPTER NINETEEN

ALWYN had excuse if he told the tale with some satisfaction, though we may observe that chance had played its part in the course that events had taken. Still, it would have been no chance to him had he not shown energy and ability in his handling of the original agency. He had some right to boast if he would. He was careful to explain that the money would not be all profit. He would have to make some increase in his office expenses—had already advertised for an assistant who would call on the less important of his London customers. Joyce was not very attentive to that part of the narrative. She was not good at figures. He had been successful, as she had been sure he would. Most women look at results. Not that she might have been lacking in loyalty had the tale been of different kind. That might be happy pride, as they left the cottage together, and took the way that had been recommended to them—the way that led to the wood through Rickett's Lane, where the measles which had worried Frida three months ago were forgotten, and the children of the district went again to the Council School which would be distributing some other infection before the year would be over. If we must defy natural law by crowding our young together, it may defy our ingenuity to avoid paying the bill. What we have done in the last fifty years is to establish about half a dozen infectious diseases so firmly that they are now regarded as almost inevitable and natural episodes in a child's life; and if Nature has really enlarged its tonsils in a rather clumsy and abortive effort to resist infections—well, it has done its best to meet an emergency which it did not originate. The tonsils may have been sufficient for their purpose in clean air, and under natural conditions. Feeding a generation largely on coal-smoke was, in any case, nothing more than an interesting experiment; and some of its consequences might reasonably have been expected to be worse than they are.

Alwyn had much in his mind to say, now that he had got Joyce to himself for a precious hour—so much that he was in some danger of the fatal error of forgetting her to whom he spoke, but Joyce had something to say to him, too, and whenever that position arose, what she had to say must come first, and the sooner that he realized that— well, the better it would be for both.

She came to her point at once, as they left the gate.

"Dear," she said, "it was sweet of your father to offer it, but I shouldn't like it at all."

Alwyn exclaimed in surprise: "But how did you know?" He felt sure that the conversation had been private between his father and himself. He had not said a word to anyone.

"It's been in every letter you've written. Yes, of course, it was plain enough. What else could you have been hinting?"

There was discussion over this. Alwyn was incredulous that he had written anything that would have disclosed what he had meant to propose today. In fact, it had been intuition on Joyce's part rather than knowledge. Call it a good guess.

The conversation diverted to other things that the letters held, which Joyce said, and may have meant, were more than she deserved. They were very dear letters (she said) to her.

As a fact, they would seem rather commonplace, even dull, if they were reproduced, which there is no occasion to do. Feeling broke out awkwardly in an occasional phrase, but love had not had time to gain fluency of expression. Love is shy in its youth. It may become more articulate later. The kind of love-letter which is exposed in a breach of promise action, or the divorce court, is not typical. Such letters have probably arrived at their natural destination.

The diversion gave Alwyn time to consider a position which he was not prepared to abandon without a battle. Joyce had said of him that he could sell better than he could buy. He had something to sell here, so to speak, the value of which she might not be willing to see. He said adroitly that, of course, it should be her decision. It had been a suggestion only. Placated with the knowledge that she would have her own way (or rather that it could be obtained without difficulty; she had never doubted that it would be hers), he won her attention, as narrative only, to the details of his father's offer, and the reasons that underlay it.

It was, in short, that a part of Birstall House should be theirs, and that they should commence their married life under his father's roof.

It was an offer which contained mutual and substantial advantages, but it was one which many, perhaps most, girls would be unwilling to accept.

Small or large, a woman likes to make her own home, and to furnish it in her own way. She likes to be its undisputed mistress. Emphatically, she likes to feel that its servants are hers; that she can order it as she will. She may like to feel that she has privacy with the man of her choice. To many, a shared home is something less than a home at all.

"I thought," Alwyn began, throwing his main proposition into the front line, and avoiding the contentious issue, "that we could be married at Christmas. I know it's a long time to wait, but I can get off then better than at any other time."

"I don't think we could possibly—"

"I know it seems an endless time, but—"

"I wasn't going to say that. I was going to say that I couldn't possibly be ready by then."

There was a moment's silence. "What's the difficulty? I thought we'd got over everything."

"Well, there's the clothes."

"Let me have a list, and I'll get them for you."

"Don't be silly."

"Well, it's such an excuse! They couldn't take more than a week, or ten days at the most. I should have thought two would be more than enough."

"That shows how little you know about it."

"I don't see that clothes matter that much."

But Joyce did.

Alwyn saw that he was on a wrong tack. He said: "Anyway, you'd have more than six weeks. You can't say that isn't enough."

That should have been said at first. Joyce changed her ground at once. "We couldn't get a house in the time."

"Oh, yes, we could I wanted to settle that this afternoon."

"Not to furnish it."

"Yes, we could, or it might be rather fun to get it when we come back."

"Back from where?"

"From Paris, of course. I thought you'd like that."

Joyce did. She had a swift thought of a school friend, rather older than herself, who had paraded a Paris husband before her old school-fellows just before she had left the convent. He had been a small, rather bird-like man, going bald. Joyce would like to exhibit Alwyn to that self-satisfied young woman. It might be wrong to say that this thought turned the scale. Joyce would have honestly thought the idea absurd. Yet it is a fact that from that moment she listened to Alwyn's plan with a mind in which the central proposal (Alwyn might have said the only one that mattered relatively at all) was an accepted thing. She meant to be in Paris when Christmas came.

Alwyn accepted the measure of assent which her silence gave, and steered the conversation diplomatically to the circumstances of his own home which had led to his father's offer. The house, which had once been filled with a growing family, and the service which it entailed, had stood comparatively empty during the last three years. Nina had drifted away—he touched lightly on the way in which the eldest daughter, who should naturally have taken her mother's place, had spent visits to friends in London of increasing length, until she had announced that she had the offer of a secretaryship which would require and provide for her permanent residence there. Frida was married. Elsie at college. His own business had obliged him to live in London.

His father had said that the home would always be there for any or all of them as they might require it, and that was still his wish, but business conditions had been increasingly difficult, and when he had been there a week ago he had found that his father was seriously thinking of selling the house.

Now the conditions of his agreement with Collett, Hayward & Co. would necessitate frequent travelling between Hunnerton and London, and it would be comparatively unimportant at which end he should live. He knew how reluctant his father would be to sell what had been a life-long home. It would be a grief to himself to see it go. Seeing the opportunity of the new conditions, his father had made an offer which had been for Joyce to decide. They should have their own private rooms. They could have the existing furniture, or they could furnish freshly, as they preferred. They could share the household expenses on such a scale as would not be burdensome, but would make them feel independent. Joyce should take charge of the house as its accepted mistress. Alwyn told this as a thing now put aside. Viewing it in that light, Joyce saw that it had some attractive features, and her mind wavered. Alwyn began to talk of possible localities where they might look for a house, and found her a poor listener. "Will it really be sold?" she inquired And then: "Your father'll feel moving from there. It seems a pity to give it up."

The talk came back to the date of the marriage, on which Alwyn wished to be definite. The Saturday before Christmas? The Monday before? Christmas Day was a Wednesday. Yes, he was sure. Perhaps Monday would do. Where could it be? It must be (had he realized?) in a Catholic church. He had not realized or cared. To most men, young or old, a marriage service is an unavoidable nuisance. They want the woman. The woman, presumably, wants the man. But she appears to want the marriage service about equally. Alwyn would have married Joyce in a sewer. Joyce would only marry Alwyn in her best clothes. Alwyn discovered that, whether or not Joyce had had her thought on such an early date, she had given the event a much more detailed consideration than he would ever be likely to do. She knew her own mind very clearly.

There was a stile halfway through the wood. It was very quiet, and not cold. They stayed there till the short afternoon darkened, making love to each other with foolish words. They went back well agreed that December 23$^{rd}$ would be the right day. Joyce said, as they were near to the cottage gate: "Dear, does your father really want us to do that? I want to think about it a bit more. I'll tell you when I write tomorrow."

She wanted to talk it over with Frida when they were alone.

## CHAPTER TWENTY

ALWYN had his way as to the date. He married Joyce Carfix in the little Catholic chapel that is in the grounds of Treswick Grange, on the Monday morning before Christmas, and her uncle's car ran them swiftly to Folkestone by the Ashdown road, so that they were in Paris that evening as they had planned to be.

The ceremony of marriage is an unescapable vulgarity. It makes a parade of the intimate. That which should be supremely spontaneous has a spurious punctuality. Its assembled background jests uneasily, knowing that it should not be there.

This would not have been Joyce's view. She was a fact too central to herself for such an event as her marriage to be a curtained thing. Let the world turn to look. It was a very proper and satisfactory attitude. But in its actual intimacies Alwyn might find her to be of a less confident exposure. There she would be uncertain of what was done. She would seek propriety in its feminine meaning. She would do as (she supposed) others did.

During the period of the degradation of European women which followed the collapse of feudalism, and which is not yet entirely ended (a woman is still disqualified from sitting in the House of Lords, or commanding an army in the field, either of which she might have done—and did—in England a thousand years earlier), they owed much of the consideration they received to the influence of Mariolatry, and they had cause for gratitude, especially in the Latin countries, for that curious outgrowth of Christian faith. But the official Catholic exaltation of asceticism has always had a contrary influence. Many thousands of married Catholic women must go through life in the belief that they have classified themselves, by the act of marriage, as of a lower order than the celibate, and that their husbands are degraded alike by that which should be the most sacred intimacy. Others have more sense. Yet from two ideas which have little substance of sustaining reason there is bred a third of a better kind, that in motherhood lies the sanctification of marriage.

Joyce had no inclination to the ascetic. She would go through life alert in the acquisition of the things that pleased her. She would not be quick to forbid whatever impulse might urge her, were it love, or hate, or sympathy, or any higher or meaner mood. Now she was in the asserted youth of love, which was well for her. But she was convent-bred, and even at this consummation there were doubts and inhibitions that vaguely vexed her mind.

Paris, most feline of cities, now hard and bright in winter sunshine, wooed them in its own way.

Joyce spent. Alwyn, standing by, and solicited always for advice which may have been seldom taken, could observe her attitudes to those with whom she dealt. But he was not of a critical mood during those days. Surely not so to her. The mutual adjustments of thought and habit which are at the root of a successful life-partnership may be unconsciously taken. And in the smaller details of routine, and reactions to surrounding circumstances, he was more pliant than she.

He saw her meet the voluble politeness of the hard-featured Paris saleswomen with a jest which he could not always follow, or a timid-seeming propitiation, which was yet tenacious of its own will, and by no means indifferent to the price it paid, nor too timid to insist that the last thing that the shop held of the kind she sought should be brought out. Nor would any persuasion move her to take that with which she was less than pleased.

Yet, though she might not be indifferent to price, she would not be deterred by any cost from that to which her fancy led. What she would, she had.

The last of the bank-notes which her uncle had given with a liberal hand was in a money-changer's safe before the day came when an extra trunk must be bought to contain her purchases, and then, when the custom dues came to be paid—well, Alwyn must stop in London on their return journey long enough to call at his city bank, or their combined resources would not have enabled them to finish the journey to Hunnerton.

They had been a fortnight away—a time which Alwyn could spare with little loss, for the first week in January is a time of stock-takings, and of the balancing of books, when few orders are given out except for the satisfaction of immediate needs, and these can be sent by post, a traveller finding little disposition to welcome his solicitations at that period.

They came back with the memory of a happiness only once interrupted by any serious discord. That was when Alwyn had used the introduction of a business friend to a firm in the Boulevard Sebastopol, whose London agency he hoped to obtain. It was the only time they had parted. Alwyn's French was of the usual English kind. He could read a newspaper well enough. He could understand a separately spoken word. He could listen to one rapid sentence, comprehend it, and render it into English, but by that time three further sentences would have been spoken which he had scarcely heard. It was a difficulty which did not trouble him when in Joyce's company. She could talk for both, and translate for him, and was quite willing to do so. But on this occasion he went alone, it being a business call, and the partner whom he sought to see having shown that he could correspond in English. He agreed to meet Joyce in about an hour's time at a corner in the Rue Lafayette, when they were to end the day at a picture-house in that neighbourhood. The time came, and Joyce was commendably punctual, but Alwyn was not. He arrived nearly an hour later, and she was no longer there. He waited anxiously for half and hour, and then went to their hotel. But she was not there either. He went out again to a foolish searching of streets. What could have happened? Should he tell the police? He went back to the hotel, and met her coming in at the same time. She was cool, and of a tone he had not known her to use to him before. What did he expect? She had waited for him a long time. "Nearly two hours," she said, with no more than the degree of inaccuracy usual in such episodes. He denied that possibility. He had been there within half an hour or little more of the time agreed. He explained a delay for which his limited knowledge of the language had been partly responsible. He had been asked to go with Monsieur Lacoste to visit a warehouse which he had understood to be across the street, but which had been nearly a mile away. Those who speak a foreign language for a visitor's benefit may lapse easily to their own tongue. When they had parted, Alwyn had been in a part of the business quarter of Paris with which he had no previous familiarity. He may not have found his way by the quickest route.

Well, he should not have left her. Surely business might have been forgotten for a single week. Where had she been? To the picture-house, of course. Could she stand there forever? As it was, if he knew how the people had stared! There was a *gendarme* who had been watching her— They were nearer a quarrel than they had ever been. Both had had two preceding hours of a nervous wretchedness. Joyce had made her solitary way to the picture-house in an impulse of anger which had regretted its decision before she had reached the door, but had been too obstinate to give way.

Then there had been the inevitable reconciliation. It was a wound that healed too quickly for any scar to remain.

They came back to take up the new life together at Birstall House on a day of heavy skies, and rain upon still-frozen roads, but their own hearts were light and happy, with the joy of youth, and a love of untested strength.

## CHAPTER TWENTY-ONE

HAS it been a mistake? Is it this which was feared by the novelist of an older day? We might have watched the ways in which the desire for marriage was thwarted and vexed, and of all that was said and done in the autumn days that are now passed, and it might have been a better tale than it is. We should know several people more intimately than we do now. And we should have ended at last on the Folkestone boat, at the length of a modern tale.

Now we must steer into further seas, and they have a placid look. Even though the horizon be a year away, there is little flurry of wind or lift of wave; there is no blackness of rock, or whiteness of shoal ahead.

What is to be done? We may enter Birstall House, and it is a likely chance that we shall be at the end of a book's length, and in January at the best. It would be rash to swear that we should reach the year's end. There would be so much to be seen on a close view.

Or we may stand back, taking a remoter view of the events of the coming year. We may see how the pieces move, but we must be careful lest we listen to what is said and linger more than we should at a caught word.

We may agree that a book should cease at a tale's end, but a true tale has no end. If it seem otherwise, it is no more than a false thing. Yet if we go on at a quick pace we may come to where there is more both to hear and see.

Joyce Oakley is mistress at Birstall House. There is no doubt about that, though, after a few rather confused weeks, the details of housekeeping finance were returned to Mrs. Case's long-experienced hands. The last word was Joy's, if she would, but she had no mind for a comparison by which she would be judged to fail. It is one thing to start a new home, with a hundred things to be learnt by the simple process of going wrong, and to make jest of them when you are together at the day's end. It is another to take control of an established house, and to continue its ways, or to seek to alter them with results which are never quite what you think they will be. There were smiles, of some courage, and some private tears, but Joyce was too vain to fail. There was only once that there was any serious trouble, and then Frida came for the weekend with an opportuneness that was not as fortuitous as it appeared, and that trouble was over, without (Joyce was glad to think) either Alwyn or her father-in-law knowing anything about it. Being no more than men, was it likely they would, or that they would have competence to judge, or even understand, if they did?

As to Alwyn she was right. He was absorbed in his own affairs, and knew little more than that he had a smiling and obviously-happy wife. As to John Oakley, she was more nearly wrong, but if he lacked the blessed gift of masculine blindness, he had that of a watchful silence, which is a rarer thing.

Joyce was mistress at Birstall, and John Oakley was a much happier man. They saw much of each other, for Alwyn was away very frequently. The plan of living away from London had not worked quite as well as he had hoped—letting his judgement be swayed by the desire to fall in with his father's plan, which he had liked. That was the kind of error which he would always be inclined to make. It was true that he needed to be in Hunnerton once or twice every week, and that he had business to develop between there and London. True also that Collett, Hayward & Co. had provided him with a season-ticket between the two places. But his main occupation was still in the larger city. If he were at home, he left early and came late. Sometimes he would say that he must stay in London, even for two of three days together.

So John Oakley and his new daughter would breakfast alone, and she would be his sole companion at the evening meal, and a confidence and understanding grew between them. When he greeted her appearance with the quotation "Joy cometh in the morning", it was not entirely jest.

Even the borderline of religion was crossed at times, with cautious hesitant steps. He came to understand something of a kind of faith which seemed in some respects to be no more than a traditional superstition, rather loosely held, and in others to have actual power to control her life. In the smaller things, it had none. To say that it gave her a licence to sin would be inaccurate and unfair. But the habit of confession, the distinction between major and minor sins, has the effect on some minds of causing them to regard their own defects of habit or character almost with complacency, as admitted and unavoidable things, of an expected kind. But on the vital issues of life he saw that there was an influence here of an untested but threatening strength.

Something, to a less extent, she may have learnt also of a faith of a different, and, perhaps, of a deeper kind. A faith which, like her own, was not unencumbered with dogmatic assertion, though somewhat more discriminate and economical in the burdens which it selected for itself to bear.

Are we going to have a tale of the real kind, after all? John Oakley was not an old man. He was still in good health. His constitution was sound. He grew very fond in these days of a very attractive girl, whose husband was frequently absent. Did he not use the opportunity to seduce his daughter-in-law? Irresistible passion, and all that? No, he did not.

The fact was, that had he fallen in love with her in the wildest way, no possible physical pleasure that he could have obtained from such a course would have compensated him, not to a thousandth part, for the distress of his own mind. It was not even an idea that could have crossed the threshold of thought. A most uninteresting man? Very well. We must look elsewhere. It was understood that this would be a lean year.

Even Joyce gives us no help. She should be tiring of her husband by now. She should be jealous of his London absences. She should be looking over the hedge at another man. In fact, she is looking at nothing better than the Hamburg hens. They have a slim symmetry and sheen at which she is pleased to gaze. She thanks God for her happiness every night, even though there are mornings when she is a little difficult of mood before Alwyn leaves. No, there is no hope here.

And, as the year advances, she has a new excitement. There is the approach of a central fact to which the world is a background only. There have been important things before, such as wars, and there has been an earthquake here and there. But these are details now. The ultimate purpose comes. Joyce Oakley will have a child. Those, at least, were the relative importances in her own mind. If we fail to agree, there is an additional reason why we should not enter Birstall House just now. It would be unhealthy for such as we.

But for Alwyn having brought his young wife to his father's home, the house would have been quiet in these days, for both Nina and Frida have ceased to come. Nina wrote to Frida that she did not like Father giving her room to Joyce without asking her first, and finding her things moved into the little end room, which last had actually been done by Mrs. Case before Joyce came home, though Nina did not learn this. This may have been the reason, or there may have been others. She still wrote letters to her father asking for cheques, casually worded, but with a note of half-articulated urgency which had its reward, even in one critical week when the wages of the office staff were left till Monday, though the workpeople were paid about an hour after the usual time. That was through Alwyn going to London on an early train, and wiring the money he could draw from his own bank, which he cleared to the last pound. Of this (perhaps foolishly) Joyce was not told. She only knew that Alwyn had gone early to London instead of taking her out on Saturday morning as he had promised to do; and she was of a cool petulance for an hour or two after he returned, till her mood changed in its lightning way, and she would be petted, and must have chocolates, which he was glad to fetch. That was in the early days of the coming of new life, which was still a wonder to both, a thing sacred and strange and great. Mrs. Case, a woman of traditional superstitions, and experience as ample as her own girth, had told Joyce that the time of pregnancy is one of overpowering fancies, which must be gratified at any cost, even though they may be of a fantastic kind. Joyce liked the idea. Her fancies had always appeared to her to be of a much greater urgency than were the competitions of others. Now they became numerous, and of a licensed right. Theatres and chocolates were indicated continually. So were peaches, of which she had always been very fond. It was an excellent idea.

Frida did not come during the summer months, with better reason that Nina's, and Elsie went to stay with her in the vacation, and gave her what help she could in a vigorous, off-hand way. For Frida had a third child, and, for some reason, had lost some of her strength, for the time at least, and the clear-eyed courage with which she faced the chances of life told her that she must have hours of rest during the day, if she were to regain the health which a wife and mother needs, even though, for the moment, there might be shiftless ways, and meals ill-laid, and the state of Peter's clothes be something of which she must not think.

Joyce came to see them also, and to gaze at the small but vigorous life in the redecorated cradle that had held Christine and Peter, and that nothing could make as clean and fresh as it had been in its first days. It was a boy this time, as Frida had hoped. She had named him John, after his grandfather. Joyce was not pleased at that. She had had a secret thought that she would have a use for that name herself. She said: "I think it's a beautiful name." She did not mean Frida to read her thought, which few would have done. She thought it looked very small beside Christine and Peter. How much did he weigh? He had been rather small at birth, Frida replied, with an unwillingness to be exact, which was rare in her, but he was over ten pounds now—nearly eleven. Christine had been the largest at birth. Nearly nine pounds.

After that Joyce prayed fatuously every night that her baby might be more than nine pounds when it should be born. She had been inclined to make a bold push for twelve at first. A matter of such importance as the birth of her first baby was one on which the Queen of Heaven might be asked to do something rather special. But experience had taught her that if she kept her demands to moderation she was much more likely to find that Heaven did its part.

We may smile, but there is no cause for derision. Joyce, like most girls, had been taught nothing of motherhood, though she had been prevented for many youthful years from doing any useful work, so that she might acquire the accumulated knowledge and wisdom of men. She was fortunate only in that she had avoided the knowledge of how to prevent life, which is pushed upon so many girls who are never taught the alphabet of how to produce it easily. Had she been told that fat is bad on a mother, and worse on an un-born child, making the process of birth painful, and even dangerous for both—that a woman being pregnant, should live leanly and hard, and begin to eat well when she has the feeding of a separate life, she would have thought she listened to foolish words. Besides, what do other women do? That would always be a first question for Joyce. As to its answer, there is no doubt. They boast lyingly of a baby's weight, as an angler boasts of his catch. They are lied to, for their own peace. "What does he weigh, nurse?" "Just on eight pounds." The scales are held from her eyes. Tomorrow she may see, but does not everyone know that a baby loses weight for the first few days?

If the restrictionists who would destroy all liberty, not of birth alone, but of every human activity, would make a law to punish women who produce heavy children, they would, at least, be dealing with a matter more important than the hours at which a man is per-mitted to sell his own goods. But that is to postulate that they are men of sense, and such would not be making more laws on any earthly matter; they would be working overtime to repeal some of the curses that we already bear.

Yet, on this point, it is open to all to observe that the creatures which produce their young in a season's space, in the hardship of the colder lands, do not bear them in summer days, but when food is scanty and poor, and the lamb struggles to fleshless legs, and begins to skip in the sun, even as its mother's hunger is fed with the first of the spring grass. You may see this on the Welsh hills, and you may learn it again from its other side where shepherds toil to save the lives of heavy, turnip-fed Leicester ewes, producing their fattened lambs with as much pain, and far greater peril, than a human mother has with her first child.

Looking at the undrained fertility of the immense Amazon basin, at the unirrigated Saharan wastes, at half-inhabited Canada, at the solitary Australian plains, and at the growing numbers of those whom we regard as Asiatic inferiors—at a half-world that is empty of men—it might be thought worthwhile to teach our slow-breeding women how to produce successfully and safely, rather than how to render cancerous their unfertile wombs. But it may be—it is a more probable thing—that we watch a civilization that drifts to wreck on rock of its own luxury, as a thousand others may have done before it, while it trusts for salvation to the motor and the picture-house, its quaint and impotent gods.

Joyce was not a modern woman in this—if such be indeed the degradation of modernity—that she had no doubt of the value of her coming child. Fierce primitive instincts stirred. She dreamed great futures for the son which it would be her choice to have. Being told that he might be influenced by that which she thought or did, she read and thought and worked in unaccustomed ways. In other moods she would turn her mind to noble, gracious or lovely things. She prayed childish prayers. She imagined it already within her arm. Seeing a picture of the child-head of Ascanius, she gave Alwyn no rest till she had a copy hanging at her bed's foot. That was how he should be.

She happened to hear a doctor remark that, though he was a heavy smoker himself, he believed it to be harmful. He said that, among other effects, he believed that it reduced fecundity. She was not over-clear as to what fecundity was, and she puzzled her mind as to whether he had meant that a heavy smoker had fewer children, or merely that they were all a size smaller than they would otherwise have been, but she saw that her cigarettes had got to go. This was hard, for she had got into a habit in these easy half-idle days which was not easy to break. It was never easy for her to deny herself any indulgence that she craved, nor to consider any price too high. Yet the smoking stopped. She stipulated that Alwyn should not smoke in the house. It was a temptation to her. Besides, if she could stop, so could he. Why should the mother get all the unpleasantness? It was most unfair. She mentioned this also in her prayers. It was a point worth making which she did not intend that God should overlook. It should be good to cancel a sin or two of the minor sort, such as having made Alwyn love her when she knew he was very tired. It might even help her to get that nine pounds.

She and Alwyn were very happy, very intimate, in these days. The basis of marriage did not shift or pause, as it sometimes will. There are women who draw away from their husbands at such times. Physical passion is in suspense. They may be petulant and exacting, asking comfort and care, while reluctant of any physical intimacies. They test the strength and quality of the bond, and are fortunate if it remain unfrayed—as, of course, it should. There are others who are impulsed at such times in a directly opposite way. Joyce was one of these. She wooed Alwyn at times with a sudden fierceness of passion that would have its way, and that would not wait, even though an engagement were broken or a train lost. Once she thought him slow to respond, and it was not quite forgiven for several days. After these moods she had repentant doubts. She had been vaguely taught that a pure wife should be passive to a man's will. Marriage is what they endure. It is the curse of Eve. Had she committed a mortal sin? She confessed with an embarrassing directness, unusual even to the ears of priests. Most confessions are dull, and of an amazing monotony. But Joyce would never be dull.

When she went to visit Frida, it was to be for a weekend, but it lengthened to ten days, and in the autumn she went again for a longer time. She gave help, being more active than in her own house. She gained much, not only in that, but in other ways. She was insatiable to learn of Frida's ways with children. Bathing the baby, she would admire it till she almost forgot to pray that her own would be just a little bit better still—as, of course, it would.

She had a whim that she would make her baby's clothes with her own hands. She had told Alwyn that all mothers should. But she was not fond of sewing. The weeks passed, and the work dragged. Worse than that, it was not more than fairly well done. She had guidance from Frida, whose needle was an obedient tool, the extent of which Joyce was scrupulous to tell to Alwyn on her return, as a child confesses a fault.

Frida had been glad of her help, but reticent as to her own condition. As to that, the specialist she had seen had been of a non-committal speech. He thought there was probably nothing serious. With rest and care all should be well. He looked keenly at Frida. "Of course, it would be best to avoid any risk. Probably safest to give up the thought of more. After all, three was a good family for these days." He looked at a patient who was not quick to reply. Wasn't that what she had wanted him to say? They mostly did. But in this case he wasn't sure.

She answered him with a direct frankness. "No, I know I'm not fit for anything like that. That's why my husband still has the other room. Do you mean that you think there's any permanent injury?"

No. He didn't think she need be afraid of that. He spoke with more confidence than he had done previously.

Frida said: "I don't think I shall have an anæsthetic next time. It isn't like a first child, when you've had three. Don't you think they may interfere too much?"

No, he was emphatic that he didn't think that. Dr. Waters was a very skilful man.

Frida agreed to that. Dr. Waters was a man she liked.

The specialist went, taking five guineas, which he considered a very moderate fee, having come to her, as perhaps it was. She wondered somewhat why Dr. Waters had advised her to have him at all. Evidently there had been no need.

There had been three good reasons for that. It was the usual thing to do; it took the responsibility off his hands; and it procured him a percentage of the specialist's fee.

But Frida was not one to talk long of herself, or to make complaint. She said she was better, and would soon be well. As Joyce had herself to face the ordeal of motherhood, she was the more careful of what she said. If you are invalided home from the front, you do not whine to a new recruit. Besides, she was of no mood to whine, or even to regret. We must think what the cradle held.

# CHAPTER TWENTY-TWO

IT was not till Christmas came that Birstall House was as full as it had been in the older days. Then the Lawsons came again, after an absence of nearly a year, bringing the children with them. John was nine months old by this time.

Elsie was home for Christmas, though she would go to stay with friends at the commencement of the new year. Only Nina was not there, having written to say that she would come, and then wired that she was detained in Town.

Joyce was expecting her baby in March, or in the early days of the following month. There was no reticence about that. If Joyce Oakley were going to have a baby, it was an event of such importance that everyone should know it for ten miles round, or if not, it was time they did. It had not occurred to Joyce that babies were not very natural and expected things for married women to have.

The Lawsons came a few hours earlier than they had been expected, and Joyce was out. She came back from the exhilaration of a frosty walk, after having been confined to house and garden by several days of rain, and the dull skies that the Midlands know. She had left the road where the little stream runs under it, and came up through the orchard, entering through the French-window of the lounge, as her habit was.

Peter stood at the open door. She showed her sturdiness through her clothes more evidently than a year ago, but the smiling innocence of the ethereal face was unchanged. The negro dolly which Joyce had given her hung by her side from its remaining arm. It was dressed in a blue overall a size too small—a pathetic relic of a deceased member of Peter's too-numerous offspring.

"Good morning, Auntie Joyce," she said politely. "Can you see boggits?"

Not knowing what they were, Joyce said cautiously that she was afraid not.

Peter sighed her relief. "Father can," she said, with no pleasure in her voice.

Boggits were a recent ghostly invention, of uncertain origin. They are very useful things.

You can be frightened of boggits so that someone has to sit at your bedside holding your hand (and telling tales) till you go to sleep. You can see boggits on the stairs of a kind so formidable that you are unable to go down when you are called at inopportune moments. The same obstacle can make it difficult for you to go to bed, when you are more attractively occupied. A boggit may also be of an occasional friendship, and protect your toys in the night, so that you can leave them all over the floor, and no one can really blame you, when the explanation is given. In Peter's capable hands they were of a hundred utilities.

But, unfortunately for her, her father had discovered that he could see boggits, too. Indeed, he was of opinion that everyone would be able to see them when the red came off, with which Peter gravely agreed.

His boggits nibbled at Peter's toes if she got uncovered at night. They climbed into her chair at meal-times, unless she were there before them. They were boggits of a very troublesome, insubordinate kind.

But she played the game very fairly. If Father admitted the existence of her boggits, must she not extend the same courtesy to his? Besides, his descriptions were so vivid that there were times when she wasn't quite as sure that they were only pretend boggits as she would have liked to be. She knew that boggits cannot do any harm on Tuesdays, but Tuesday is quite an occasional day. It is much less likely than not.

She respected her father's boggits, but she had a natural anxiety to know that her aunt was not endowed with an equal vision.

Joyce was glad to sit down for a time before going upstairs to change, for it had been a long walk, and she had hastened her return when she had become aware of the time, and Peter came to her knee. She looked down at the dusky, one-armed infant that swung precariously at her side.

"I can't let Sheba lie down *anywhere*," she explained. "The boggits would get her quick. She can't put her hands together to say her prayers."

Peter may have persuaded herself of the truth of this curious imagination, with its suggestion of atavistic superstition. It was hard to say. It was certain that she would run to Sheba's rescue in a shrill-voiced panic, if a momentary forgetfulness had left the black infant exposed to this sinister danger. It was also true that she had set up a valid reason why her favourite child should remain beside her under every circumstance, even lying by her plate at meals, which well-trained babies very seldom do.

Peter swung the enduring Sheba by her remaining arm. "She's a nice dolly. You gived her to me," she said politely, with one of her rare lapses from a perfect grammar. "Have you got any dollies?

"I'm going to have a baby of my own next year."

"A *real* baby? Not a pretend?"

"Yes."

Peter looked at her aunt with wide-opened critical eyes. "You're not as fat as mother was. Not nearly. It won't be very big, will it? Mother says it's like hens laying eggs. The black hen was killed crossing the road. You can't smack boggits when you want to," she added thoughtfully. "They might never come back." It is a difficult world.

It was at that moment that Mrs. Case's voice was audible from the hall. The next, Peter was gone. Sheba's head getting a hard whack from the half-open door as she swung her though. Peter liked Mrs. Case, who liked her. At times there were things to eat.

Joyce went upstairs. She supposed Frida must be there. She had seen Chester as she came up the orchard, though he had not seen her. He had been in the kitchen garden, smoking where he felt he could do it without offence, and talking to the new boy. Chester was always talking to someone. Or, rather, listening if it were a stranger, and he could get him to talk.

Joyce found Frida with a sobbing, unconsolable Christine, on whose life black tragedy fell. Jezebel had been badly packed, or the trunk had been handled too roughly between train and taxi. She had a broken hand—Jezebel, on whom Christine had lavished three years of daily, almost hourly love. Jezebel who, though she had not outgrown her cradle, was now old enough to sit up and have proper meals.

"I *told* you, Mother, to let me carry her. I *told* you not to pack her like that," she sobbed passionately. "I think you're a wicked mother." This from Christine!

"I don't want another doll, I tell you. I don't want another. Not if it's *anything*. Jezebel's *hurt*. If you did want a baby boy, you didn't want to stop wanting me."

At that moment the baby boy, who may have felt that he had been forgotten long enough, introduced a higher note of discord from the basket-chair in which his mother had laid him.

"Christine," Frida said, with a quiet gravity, "you shouldn't say things that you don't mean, and that you'll be sorry about afterwards. You must go to baby now, and make him laugh. You know how to do that. I'll put something on Jezebel's hand, and bind it up so that it won't hurt her at all. She shall go to the hospital tomorrow, and have it made quite well."

"I didn't mean it, Mother," Christine answered miserably. "But I do love Jezebel so. And she can't ever say when she gets hurt." She went obediently to the duty which her mother's wisdom gave. She could always make baby laugh. She had a way of tickling him in a gentle way which he thought good.

She turned round with a sudden new terror in her eyes. "Mother, if I were dead, should you throw Jezebel away?"

Frida promised that Jezebel should be carefully kept in that remote-seeming contingency. But the fear remained in Christine's mind. No one would care for Jezebel as she cared. No one even knew what was good for her to eat. She might be punished for things that she hadn't done. Christine decided that she must be very careful not to die.

## CHAPTER TWENTY-THREE

"PETER says I may say two of Father's tales, because Jezebel's hurt her hand."

This was from Christine at the breakfast-table on Christmas morning, which the children had been allowed to join. It will be seen that Peter still ruled, and the privilege of reciting one of "Father's tales" was not allowed to Christine under any ordinary circumstances. But Peter had a heart. She had offered Christine the unconditional transfer of six of the more dilapidated members of her own household. She had assured her that the boggits approved, and had even suggested this arrangement. But Christine had only said that Jezebel wouldn't like it at all. The recitation licence had been a last effort to ameliorate the tragedy.

"Everyone doesn't want to hear Father's tales," her mother interposed. "She'd better say them when you're alone."

"Oh, no, Mother," Christine expostulated. "I want to say them now."

"I should like to hear them, if they're new ones," Joyce said. "If I may."

"Chester's all right when he jokes," Elsie said bluntly. "It's when he's solemn it's such bosh."

"I wonder when that is," Chester countered unruffled.

"Chester," Frida explained, with a sister's candour, "can write better in his sleep than you could if you sat up trying all night."

"I don't call that saying much. Besides, I couldn't do it. I should begin yawning at twelve-fifteen."

"Now Dulcie Day was a dreadful talker—" Christine commenced.

"I don't think I'd choose that one," her mother interposed.

"I suppose it's two personal for most of us," Elsie suggested.

"It might be for you," Alwyn said. "Most of us can keep quiet when we try."

"Chester can't."

"Well, he made it himself."

"It isn't because of that," Frida explained. "It's quite innocent in itself. It's Peter's footnotes."

"Shall I say *Clara Bell*, Mother?"

"'Kicked her mother, and made her squeal'," Peter quoted, chuckling.

"It's a mistake to begin with the climax, Peter," her father admonished.

"Shall I say *Betsy Vaughan*?" Christine asked. "That's quite good."

No one raising any instant objection, she commenced to recite with a slow exactness:

"Now Betsy Vaughan was as strong as horses.

But her mother said, 'My Betsy Vaughan!
Nurse tells me she's always awake at dawn.
She sits there yawning at noughts and crosses,
And the loss of a child is the worst of losses.'

So her mother told her to go to bed,
When she wanted to write on the slate instead.
The voice of her mother was close and clear,
But the pencil squeaked, and *she did not hear*."

"And that's what you call a good tale, Christine," Alwyn commented. "I call it dreadful."

"I meant her mother was good," Christine explained. "Most. of the mothers do naughty things."

"'Kicked her mother, and made her squeal'," Peter could be heard to murmur again in a private ecstasy, in the brief interval while her spoons were bringing more scrambled egg to its destined goal. And then suddenly: "Say *Sissie White*, Chris."

"Shall I, Mother?"

"Yes, if you like. I don't mind."

Christine was never sure about Sissie White. Had she done right or wrong? Had her mother been wicked, or merely wise? She felt that there was a catch in it somewhere, but she could not see it, and it worried her dreadfully. She used to lie awake at night puzzling over it. She had asked her mother, and got no real help, even from her. Her mother told her not to take Father's nonsense seriously. But was it nonsense? She might have asked her father, as the author of the enigma, but she knew from experience that there would be no comfort in that. Father would say anything. "Now Sissie White," she began carefully:

"—was too good to live.
And her mother said, 'That sweet young Sis!
She'll never grow up if she lives like this.
It's only when she's in bed she lies,
And she calls rice-pudding a nice surprise.'

So her mother told her she'd best begin
To practice the simpler kinds of sin.
And to please her mother, as best she could,
She disobeyed her—*by keeping good*."

Alwyn said: "You mustn't believe that tale, Christine. It couldn't happen."

"Why not?" asked its author.

"It contradicts itself. She wasn't good, if she disobeyed her mother."

"You mean if a mother tells a child to be naughty she can't help obeying, whether she likes or not."

"There's no goodness in doing what you can't help," Elsie contributed. "There's no badness either."

"I think," Peter remarked deliberately, licking empty spoons, "I think it's a funny tale."

"Perhaps," her grandfather concurred, "we'd better leave it at that."

"Can I say the good tale now, that you haven't heard?" Christine asked.

"Can I get down if I say thank God for a good breakfast?" Peter interrupted. She showed no interest in a good tale.

"Yes, if it's really good," Frida replied with some excusable incredulity "No, Peter. You'll sit where you are, till we've all finished."

"I'll wipe my mouth hard," Peter began, trying a business deal, and then stopped to listen, as Christine began:

"Now, Rene Reeves was a girl like I am.

And her mother said, 'My Rene Reeves,
These tales are nothing but make-believes
Except the mother of Queenie Platt,
Really—mothers are not like that.'

So her mother gave her a good night kiss,
To show that mothers are more like this;
And Irene thought, as she tucked her in,
'It's nice to be good—and to hear of sin.'"

"I think that's a really nice tale," Christine concluded.

"I don't suppose he meant it at all," Alwyn commented. "He's only ended them like that to get a publisher to take the lot."

"And found it a useless sin," Elsie added. "No publisher'd be such an ass."

"You're not far wrong," Chester admitted; and then to Joyce: "Who was Queenie Platt? Oh, never mind now."

"I think," Mr. Oakley remarked, "it might be well for someone to ring for dinner."

"Is it that time?" Joyce exclaimed in consternation. "I mustn't be late for mass."

"Not yet, but it soon will be."

"You're not really going?"

"You're not going to walk all that way?"

"Yes, I am. Alwyn's coming with me, of course."

"And now, Mother," Peter asked again, "may down?"

# CHAPTER TWENTY-FOUR

ALWYN found Joyce a little difficult on the walk home. He tried to accommodate himself to her pace, and was reproached for loitering so that they would be late for dinner "and everyone waiting now," and for hurrying with a lack of consideration such as is characteristic of masculine brutality. She asked if he would mind if she lay down in the afternoon. And then "Will they think it rude?"

No, he said, of course, she must lie down if she were tired. Everyone would understand. In fact, she hated this invasion of the house by those to whom she must always be something of an intrusion upon their own possession. She hated Elsie. It was a fixed belief in her mind that Elsie hated her. She had overheard something that Elsie had said about the changes she had made in her own rooms. Surely she could do that. Hadn't Alwyn paid for the furniture? It was not like having a home at all.

She was mistaken in what Elsie had said. It had been a remark of no hostile significance, forgotten as soon as made. But had she known this, it would have made little difference. Thinking that she had heard it had brought these thoughts to the surface of her mind, where they were always present, and pushing upward till she would thrust them down—as she did now. The Christmas must not be spoiled by any discord from her. But she knew that these moods were not easy to thrust aside. She had promised God that morning, and again in church. But it wasn't only what Elsie had said. She had heard Frida talking to Mrs. Case. She was fond of Frida. She had no quarrel with Mrs. Case. She knew that they were both fond of her, for which she could forgive much. But she had recognized that Mrs. Case had been reporting or explaining to Frida, as to one who had an ultimate right to know. It was a vague vexation, but no less real for that. The talk had ceased as she had come in from the garden

As to the furniture of the two rooms, it was true enough that it was legally as well as actually hers to do with as she would. Alwyn's father had owed him rather a large sum for commission at the time of their marriage. Alwyn had been content not to draw it till he should need it for the home which he had to make. And as the time approached, John Oakley had known that it would not be easy to find. He wished then that Alwyn had drawn it month by month as it fell due. That had been one reason why the idea had arisen that they should live at Birstall House. It was not only the commission money which had been applied to that purchase. Part of the sum which Collett, Hayward & Co. had advanced had been used in the same way. It had all been fairly done. His father, perhaps with better foresight than he, had insisted on a strict legality. There had even been a valuation. In the final arrangement Alwyn had taken over something more than the furniture of the two rooms.

Joyce had not been troubled with, and would not have cared for these details. At that time she took little interest in money, except that which was in her purse, and which she could spend as she would.

As you come round the bend of the road, Birstall House lies about a quarter of a mile ahead on the right. You cannot see the house from there, but you can tell where it is by the sign of a large chestnut in the farther field, which projects over the hedge. Alwyn and Joyce, taking this turn, saw a yellow car of a racing pattern, which stood at the gate. Joyce, alert always to the human element, forgot fatigue and irritability as she exclaimed, "I wonder who that can be? I don't know anyone round here who has a car like that. Do you know who it is?"

Alwyn said no. He did know that Nina's friend, Pauline, had such a car, but she was in London. He did not think of her. As they spoke, a woman came from the gate and jumped into the car. It gained speed at once, and came down the gentle slope of the road with a long penetrating wail as it approached the bend.

"That's Pauline," Alwyn said, as it shot past. She did not appear to see them. Her eyes were for the road, as they had need to be. They were only two people who stood quickly aside as pedestrians should.

They looked round at the pace at which she took the turn of the road. It was not lack of nerve or skill that caused the counterfoils of Pauline's cheque-book to show how frequently she contributed to the funds which are collected at the magistrates' courts.

"I wonder what she was doing here," Joyce said, in a natural curiosity, "I expect Nina decided to come, after all." It seemed a probable explanation. She hoped it was not the true one. Nina was almost a stranger to her. And her room wouldn't be ready. People ought to be more considerate, knowing her state of health. They ought to know their own minds. She was quite sure now that she would need to lie down in the afternoon. Why, she was so tired that she could scarcely get to the gate!

John Oakley stood in the hall as they entered. He stood irresolutely, taking steps toward the room in which he knew he would find Chester alone, and then turning back. As he turned, he saw them enter.

"Has Nina come?" Joyce asked quickly.

The question seemed to surprise, even confuse him. He said, "No."

"We saw Pauline's car at the door," Alwyn explained, "and thought she might have run her down."

"No," his father replied again. "She came on—private business."

It was awkwardly said, giving an explanation that was not asked, which, he was conscious, was no explanation at all. He was sorry almost as the words were said. What was the use in concealment? He supposed that everyone would have to know. All the country would know tomorrow. And he did not know much himself as yet. Not for sure. He attempted a natural manner. "Mrs. Case says the dinner's ready to bring in, as soon as you can get down." It was a reminder to Joyce that she must not stay talking there, though it may not have been so meant. They went up to their room.

"I'm sure there's something the matter," Joyce said anxiously.

Alwyn agreed to that. Somehow his father had looked—had looked old. And he felt that it was not a business trouble. There had been enough of those in the last two years, but his father met them in a different way. It was some trouble about Nina. Something of which he had not wished to talk.

Joyce felt the same. A quick impulse of sympathy swept away the fretful trivialities that had vexed her mind. That was from the fundamental contradiction which made her actions of an apparent and sometimes baffling inconsistency. Vanity was resident in her mind, an accepted guest. Jealousy, basest and most poisonous of human passions, was a sleepless snake that was ever coiled to strike. But generosity was there also, an instant sympathy with any trouble that she could understand, and a loyalty to those by whom she felt herself to be loved which would not easily find its price. There were contradictions here which had warred at times, with easy victory to either side, but they had never met in vital and decisive battle.

Now the impulse of sympathy at the shadow of a trouble that she did not know was sufficient to overcome the pettishness of her earlier mood (helped somewhat, perhaps, by the relief of hearing that Nina had not come), and strong enough to dull the sharp annoyance she would otherwise have felt on opening her uncle's letter (quickly sifted from out the pile that was waiting beside her plate) when she saw that the expected cheque was for £5 only. He had always sent her more than that, even when she was a girl at school. She scarcely glanced over the brief apologetic lines in which he blamed the condition of farming which had reduced his rents, and the burden of a merciless taxation, for the smallness of the cheque he enclosed. Of course, uncle had always had plenty of money. Everyone knew that. She supposed he thought she didn't need it so much now she was married. If he only knew! And she had meant to go out on Monday and buy that squirrel coat with the money that she had felt sure would come. Well, Alwyn would have to find it. She knew the end of the quarter was a good time for him. He got his best commission-cheques then. It would only mean a few extra kisses. A few hours' sulking at the worst. She thought all this as she laid the letter down, folding the cheque over as she did so. She was willing for all to see that she had a cheque. She was not willing for Elsie to know that she had got less than she had said she expected. She opened the next letter mechanically, noticing with a subconscious satisfaction that her pile was the largest, and then forgetting everything as she observed again the preoccupying trouble of her father-in-law's face.

John Oakley spoke little, except once or twice to the children in an endeavour to maintain the spirit of the day. They were unusually silent. They ate. Space had been found on the crowded table for the one-armed Sheba. Prayer-hindered, boggit-pursued, her black face could still grin happily, as it lay with its white eyes turned to the ceiling, and its head between the salt-cellar and the spoons.

He regretted already the impulse that had led him to say that Pauline had come on a private matter. He saw that they must be told. He wanted to talk to Chester now. There was no time to lose. But he had wanted time to think. He had not wanted to spoil that meal with a common knowledge of this hateful ugly thing. Yet its shadow was there He saw it in Alwyn's silence: in Joyce's eyes. He could not tell whether Frida suspected anything. She gave no sign. She was one who would carry on, though the skies fell. But she knew that Pauline had come. That she made no allusion to it might have its own significance. Had she known or guessed something already? He knew that to be a scarcely possible thing. Only Chester and Elsie were disputing across the table in their usual way.

Frida said: "You look tired. Was the walk rather long?"

"It was, rather," Joyce answered. "I think I shall lie down till tea-time, if nobody'll mind. I expect you will, shan't you?"

"No, I don't think so. I've stopped that now. I may a bit, when I've got the children settled. They've promised to try to sleep this afternoon, and they're to stop up later tonight."

Elsie glanced at her sister. "I'll look after them," she said, with one of her offhand generosities. "You'd better lie down. Peter's going to give all her family a proper meal for once, so I don't think you'd get her to sleep much before four."

Peter looked up at that. "I'm going to sleep," she announced virtuously. "I promised Mother. You can wash up for me, Auntie Elsie, if you like."

Evidently the dolls' dinner and the sleep were both on the programme for the afternoon.

John Oakley observed that his household had allocated itself, excepting Chester and Alwyn. That would be the best way. He would tell them, and get such help as Chester could give. They could tell their wives, and, of course, Frida would tell Elsie. He asked them to join him in his own room when the meal was over.

## CHAPTER TWENTY-FIVE

"SHE got her bailed out, took her home, and came straight here."

"She didn't lose any time," Alwyn commented.

"No. She's a live wire," Chester agreed.

"She says that she didn't give Nina any idea that she would come, because she knew that she would object. She was still hoping that there might be some way by which it would not become public, so far as she was concerned, but Miss Lufton thought that I ought to know."

"Does she mean that Nina was kept at the station all night?"

"Yes. I understand that she could have had bail from the police, but she could not get anyone on the telephone that she knew. It was an awkward night, and several friends to whom she might have appealed had gone out of Town. Pauline was not at her own flat, but Nina got in touch with her early this morning."

"Did the others get bailed out last night?"

"No. Pauline understood that the police would not arrange it on their own responsibility. They are detaining them till they can be brought up at Bow Street."

"Then they didn't really think Nina—had anything to do with it?" Alwyn suggested.

"I'm afraid we can't go quite that far. They evidently thought there was an important distinction."

"Shouldn't one of us go up on the next train?" Alwyn asked. The thought of Nina in that position— Surely something could be done, if they were on the spot.

"I telephoned the railway," his father answered, "before lunch. There's no train now today till the 5:45. But Miss Lufton said that she was going straight back to her, and she thought that for any one of us to turn up there would only trouble her more. She said Nina said she'd done nothing wrong, and she seemed quite confident that she could clear herself, but she dreaded the publicity. If we can do anything to prevent her name coming out—" He looked questioningly at Chester. "That was really why Miss Lufton came."

"That's a good deal to ask," Chester answered doubtfully. "It's the kind of case that's reckoned to make good copy. It's the Sunday papers that would be the most difficult. If it collapses, and there's plenty of later news to fill up, we might get them to give it the go by."

"There won't be anything in the morning papers tomorrow, anyway. Not if you've got the tale right. And most of them aren't being published in the afternoon. But after that, it sounds front-page, I'm afraid. But we won't leave anything to chance. I'll find out now."

He went over to the telephone and gave five numbers to which he wished to be connected in London. How long would it take? About an hour? He was afraid that wouldn't do. It was a Press matter. A matter of urgency. Would they put him through to the Superintendent? Well, then, Mr. Barclay would do. He talked rapidly for a few moments, ending with: "No, of course. I quite understand that. You have to take them all as they come. But you'll do the best you can? Thanks very much. I shouldn't have asked you, if it hadn't been quite exceptional."

"And now," he added, "if you'll both go out and feed the pigeons."

"Why?" Alwyn asked.

"Because I want to talk to one or two who may ask me whether we're being overheard."

"But you said the calls wouldn't be through for about an hour."

"They'll begin in about ten minutes, probably less. I'll let you know at once when I've found out anything important. There'll be lots of time for the train."

Chester had his way, as he usually did when he was sufficiently serious.

"It's no use them sitting here," he thought, "worrying to no purpose. There's nothing more to be said till we've got the facts."

Then the telephone rang, and he was soon listening to some interesting information from the chief reporter of the *Daily Mail*.

Half an hour later they were back in the lounge together.

"I think I've found out about all there is to know," Chester began, "and I've done what I could till I get on the spot. Riley says there won't be much done this week. Just evidence of arrest, and the police will apply for an adjournment at once. He thinks that's certain. He says he doesn't think they intend to oppose bail, unless it's in the case of Dr. Slitman, and they mayn't even with him, if it's fixed heavy enough.

"He knew all about it at once. The police give us the tip when there's good copy about, and we give them a leg up in other ways. But we've got to face the fact that it isn't anything that'll blow over. Riley says the police have been watching Slitman for the last three years, but he's been too clever for them till now. They reckon he's about the most popular abortionist in London, and been charging the highest fees. There isn't anything on earth that could stop the case against him, and what we've got to do is to find how far Nina's involved, and to get her out. She's charged with complicity now—nothing worse than that, and it's the kind of thing that's not always easy to prove, even if it's true, which we mustn't assume. Riley'll pass the word round that she's a young lady who's only drawn in through being Miss Porter's friend, and knew absolutely nothing about it. He says we'd better have a good counsel there to put a word in to that effect."

"I should think," John Oakley remarked, "that anyone could do that."

"Yes. It does sound that way. But it wouldn't work. If you get a big name, and everyone knows you must have paid him a big fee, the Stipendiary won't snub him when he gets up. He'll let him say a few words, if not more, and they'll get reported, and people will think more of them than if they'd been said by a solicitor they'd never heard of before—and those mightn't even get into the Press. You see, Nina's only a minor part of the show.

"Besides that, if the police see that you're training some big guns on to them for her defence, they may think it's not worthwhile, and just drop it as far as she's concerned. I've seen that happen more than once before now, when they've got one or two in the net that they weren't particularly anxious to catch."

"Have you got any more calls coming through?"

"No, I cancelled the others when I'd got Riley. He'll pass the word round, and he's got about fifty times more influence than I. It's lucky that I've done him a good turn once or twice. I wouldn't come up, if I were you. Not till after. Let Alwyn come up with me, and he can go and see her, while I get to work. Alwyn can tell her that I'll see that she's in good hands, and he can bring her home afterwards, if she'd like to come. I expect it'll be all over in about ten minutes, and there'll only be fixing up the bail after that."

"It's very good of you," John Oakley replied, "but I think I d rather be on the spot myself."

"Of course you would. But I'm thinking of Nina. She won't feel any better if all the family's there. It's no use making too much fuss. You'd probably upset her more than anything else."

"Well, I'll think it over. It's half-past three now. I'll decide between now and tea-time."

"Very well. I'd better tell Frida I'm running up."

## CHAPTER TWENTY-SIX

JOHN OAKLEY went to the solitude of his own room. He was still without any certain knowledge of the seriousness of his daughter's position. He neither knew with exactness what she had done, nor what she was accused of doing, nor what the penalty might be if she were convicted of such an offence. There was the bald fact that certain persons had been arrested, charged with a conspiracy to procure abortion, and that Nina was one of these. Pauline had said that "of course" Nina had only happened to be with Miss Porter, as a friend might. It had been "rotten luck". He thought that Pauline's view would probably have been that if one of your friends wanted to visit a surgeon for such a purpose, you couldn't refuse to go along. Not if you were a real friend. But that might be unfair to Pauline—a young woman whom he recognized that he did not like. She had been a good friend to Nina today…

And so Nina was to stand in a criminal dock. Chester had called her "part of the show". He had said many things that jarred in the last hour. Of course, quite unaware. He had the taint of the journalist, for all the aloofness of his mental attitudes. Yet Chester, like Pauline, was acting the part of a good friend, and one who might help in ways that few could. Was the fault in himself? That he was getting old? That he was too much out of touch with Nina's life? Had known too little of her occupations or friends? Had he been secretly afraid to inquire too closely? Was the fault his rather than hers that she was in this position now? He allowed, in justice to himself, that there had been no reason for her to leave home as she did, that she would almost certainly have resented and evaded too close inquiries. He had always found money for her when it had been asked, and sometimes it had been hard to do.

Yet he had failed. As a father he had clearly failed. And now Chester made it plain that he thought he would be better out of the way. Perhaps he was right. Did he suppose that he would use such a time to reproach her? To increase the emotional stresses of the ordeal that she had to face? That would be unjust. Yet he recognized that others might face the position in a more buoyant, a more incidental, way. There would be many who would even sympathize with her. Who would feel, as Pauline felt, that it was just "rotten luck". But there was no consolation in that. They were not the kind of people whose good opinion he would wish to have.

He had a feeling that this would not have happened had her mother lived, which must have been, in itself, true. Had her mother lived, everything would have happened differently. That is true of every death which has taken place in the history of mankind. Things might not have been better. They might have been worse. But different they would very surely have been.

But he did not analyse the mystery of human experience in that way. He only thought, if her mother had lived, this would not have been. And then he remembered a conversation of eighteen months ago. Had he been right when he had thought bitterly that it was better that she was dead?

Nina, their first child. He remembered all the hope and love which had been round her in infant days. He remembered the childish sayings of her earlier years. And tomorrow morning she would be in the Bow Street dock! He had not Chester's mental detachment, which would have told him that there was no necessary disgrace in that. How many of the world's best men have known the insides of its gaols? It is a list to provoke thought. It might almost be argued that a man who has not been imprisoned by his fellows has not proved his claim to pre-eminence. He is like one of reputed learning, but who is the holder of no degree. The dock does not open its door only to the worst of men, but to all who will not walk the way that their kind prefer. The way of transgressors is hard. That is a physical, which is sometimes mistaken for a moral law. That was how it was now. The transgressor annoys the crowd, whose progress he obstructs. But where does modern progress go? The momentum of generations still impels it in the old way. It has the law on its side. If the "modernist" view be correct that a woman should think three times before she has a child once, that it is a potential error, to be done away with by the best available method, then these people who were arrested now might be held as martyrs in a succeeding century. "In these barbarous times," people may say, "a man or woman could be imprisoned simply because they had destroyed a child that was not even born."

But John Oakley was not comforted by thoughts which he did not have—which could have been of no consolation had they come into his mind. The idea that an embryo child may be no more than a few ounces of offal to be cut loose by the surgeon's knife, and thrown to the ash-heap, was not one that would have appeared capable of debate. Chester would have regarded it differently. He would have considered it from a dozen aspects. An idea of any kind could be assured in his mind of a tolerant hospitality. But John Oakley's was of another kind. He believed did not merely profess, but actually believed, in the fundamental teachings of Christ; and whether birth restriction or abortion—between which there are little more than the differences of sentiment and expediency—be wise or foolish, right or wrong, whether they point the way to higher possibilities of life, or to the foundering of the social order which tolerates them, it is a fact which should be too evident to deserve discussion that Christianity is their final foe.

Perhaps it would be best to let Chester and Alwyn do what they could. If it were only a matter of an adjournment— And, of course, she must come home. He remembered that it would be very awkward for him to be away from business for any length of time. Indeed, awkward was an inadequate word. There were financial exigencies which might urgently require his presence at the office. Remembering those, he was the more disposed, for one illogical moment, to go at any cost, lest his remaining should misinterpret itself to his own mind as a putting of business considerations before his daughter's need. But the thought of the financial stringency which had become almost constant during the last year (though he would persuade himself that it had been somewhat less difficult since last midsummer) led by a natural process of thought to the suggestion Chester had made that expensive counsel should be engaged. Here was another burden to face, he knew not how, but he supposed that it must be done.

As he thought of this, the tea-gong sounded. He went down to meet those who looked at him and each other without the expected words. There were reasons for this, collective and individual. For one thing, Elsie had not been told. Chester had been talking to Frida till the gong had roused them to awareness of the passage of time. They could not begin to talk about it as something known to all.

Alwyn had told Joyce what he knew, vaguely as he understood it, and with a natural desire to represent his sister as casually involved in something for which she had no responsibility. Joyce might not like Nina, but in such a position there was no doubt of what her feeling would be. She was for the family to which she belonged. She would not be one to care greatly, or to inquire closely into questions of right and wrong. Nina's foes would be hers. But it was not a matter on which she would be likely to speak first.

The silence did not suit Peter at all. She could be angelically quiet while there was conversation around her, listening intently, with eyes that moved quickly from one speaker to another, and understanding—how much? But if there were silence, she was always willing to fill the gap. Now her mind was on the excitement of the night before, when she had been reluctantly persuaded to bed amid the confusion of the new toys that she had received complacently as the season's due.

"I might have been bit a lot," she said, in her clear, high note. A cryptic remark of this kind could usually draw a request for explanation, but now it was disregarded. She tried again more explicitly. "Mother oughtn't to have turned on the dark, when there were four boggits under the bed. I might have been bit a lot."

That drew Elsie to speech. "Now, Peter," she said, "tell the truth."

This was a new game that Auntie Elsie had taught her, that she had proved graciously willing to learn. She had seen little of Elsie till that time when she had come to her mother's help a few months ago, and she was still somewhat unsure, but, on the whole, inclined to approve. She knew that people differ; and that, if a child is to have a peaceful life and her own way, the study of these differences is a first necessity.

Her grandfather was wise in the ways of childhood, but absurdly easy to manage. Mrs. Case was as soft as the outer reaches of her own corpulence. Her mother was formidable, but without subtlety. Her father dangerously incalculable. Battle with him was to be avoided, if possible. Yet, if it became inevitable, it was to be undertaken cheerfully. It might turn out well enough. But Elsie was different from any of these. Peter did not analyse, but her consciousness was that Auntie Elsie was less concerned about conduct than some others around her, but, if so concerned, she approached it intellectually rather than morally, which is a much less uncomfortable way.

"Telling the truth" was a game that had been started at Birchett's Wood, and resumed this afternoon. She thought for a moment, and then said with a happy smile: "There weren't any boggits. I didn't want Mother to turn on the dark. I wanted to sit up in bed, and cut out elephants."

Mr. Oakley realized from Elsie's tone and manner that she was unconscious of the trouble which had invaded their household peace. The time had come for decisions to be made. He spoke at once.

"I'm sorry, Elsie, that we've had some bad news about Nina. I think all the others know, but you've been with the children, and may not have heard. There's no time to discuss it now, as some of us must catch the London train in an hour's time, but—"

"She's not ill?" Elsie interposed. The indirect method of approach which seemed natural to everyone in communicating the position was irritating to her normal impetuosity.

"No, she's not ill. It's a legal trouble. Some people have been arrested, and she was with them at the time. Pauline was here before dinner, and thought we ought to know."

"You mean she's got to give evidence? I don't think Nina'd like that. She'd be too nervous when it came to the point."

"I don't know that she'll have to give evidence. We don't know the exact position yet—"

Frida interrupted. "Father, we've been talking it over, and we're sure you'd better not go. Nina'd only get upset if she sees you. We don't want to have her crying all night.

"We think it will be the best way if Chester and I go up tonight, and Alwyn comes by an early train in the morning. I'll go and see Nina tonight, and let her know that Chester's getting a good lawyer to take it up. She'll find one of us quite enough."

It was a remark Chester had made when they had been talking upstairs that had decided Frida to go. She had asked: "Do you mean that she might be found guilty if she had merely known what was going on?" and received a hesitating reply. He had added: "I don't suppose that there's much risk. It's the sort of thing that's not always easy to prove, and they won't be really going for her. There won't be much risk if she tells her own lawyers the truth, so that they know how to steer her clear. I once heard a K.C. say that you could often get a guilty man off if he told you everything; and almost always get an innocent one off if he were equally frank, though it mightn't be easy, because when an innocent man's committed there's always a nasty tangle somewhere; but when a guilty man tells his own lawyers he's innocent, he doesn't give them a chance, and he always ends in the cells."

Frida knew that truth was not Nina's natural resort in any difficulty. She had better see her—and she didn't want anyone else there.

"I think I'll go with you," she had said at once, "and I'll get Elsie to look after the children while we're away."

Elsie looked round the table. She was very far from being a fool. It was clear to her that there was something more serious here than her father's explanation had implied.

She looked directly at Chester. "What is it, really?"

He gave a simple and explicit answer. "All we know yet is that there have been some arrests on a charge of conspiracy to perform an illegal operation, and it has been alleged that Nina knew of it, and had some complicity, which she denies. Probably it will collapse altogether as far as she is concerned, but we want to be on the spot, and make sure."

"Yes, of course. Poor Nina. She'd worry horribly over anything like that."

"You ought to start in about thirty minutes," John Oakley said, reluctantly accepting the position to which he had been allocated, and wasting no further words upon it. "What about money?"

"Can I help you to pack?" Elsie asked.

"No, I shall manage," Frida answered. "There isn't much to do. We shall be back as soon as we can, and Chester'll probably go to Birchall's for the night."

"Oh, I think we're all right for cash," Chester replied. "We've got two or three pounds between us, and we're not likely to need more." The words were more confident than the tone. The demands of Christmas had left his pocket rather bare, and he had been relying upon a cheque that was probably on the way now—that might have been delivered but for the congestion of the Christmas post. He knew enough of Nina to expect that it would be necessary to pay her fare if he brought her home, and probably highly desirable to settle various obligations at her flat before doing so.

"I don't only mean that," Mr. Oakley answered. "You said it might be important to get an expensive lawyer. Don't you have to give them cash down?" He was one who would always look a difficulty in the face, however insoluble it might appear. He did not see how he could safely draw a cheque of any large amount today, nor how he could fail to give needed help at such an emergency.

But Chester put that lightly aside. "Oh, no. Not if you know the solicitor. I'll fix that up easily enough, and they'll probably let me off a lot cheaper than they would you."

Joyce had followed the conversation with troubled eyes. Always sensitive to atmosphere, she realized that there was an unspoken difficulty about the money to which Chester had not really replied.

She said: "You'll want a lot, going up to London. I know I always do." (That was a fact, as Alwyn knew to his frequent cost.) She reached for the bag which was never far from her hand. "I've got three pounds. And here's Uncle's cheque. You'd better have that. He only sent me five, because he can't get his rents or something this year."

She passed the cheque and notes over to Chester, who hesitated to take them up.

"I think—" he began.

"Thanks, Joyce," Frida said. "We'll let you have it back in a few days.

"No, I didn't mean that. There's no reason you should spend it more than we. Besides, I don't want it at all."

"You'd better take it," Alwyn added. "You'll need it more likely than not."

Chester knew that to be true. He picked up the money.

"You'll find that cheque more useful," his father-in-law suggested, "if Joyce puts her name on the back."

Joyce was unconscious of generosity. She had done no more than the natural thing. Even the thought of the squirrel-coat had left her mind in the face of this sudden trouble...

Normally, she was vaguely puzzled by the financial atmosphere in which she lived. She could not fail to be aware of occasional tensions, of anxieties which were in the background, and sometimes took a more prominent position. She thought vaguely of her father-in-law, as of her uncle. They were normally wealthy men. That was an attribute of their positions. Such people would often grumble about the shortness of money. It was also normal. A way they had.

The house and garden had a gracious atmosphere of settled peace. It was a peace that had been uninterrupted for thirty years. Actual sordid trouble, the realities of penury, could not enter at such a gate.

Frida was about to rise. "You'll look after the children tomorrow?" she said to Elsie. It was a question, but it was an assumption also. It scarcely needed reply.

Christine looked up at her mother with tearful eyes. She knew that something was wrong. Something that threatened the stability of familiar things. "Don't go, Mother, I'm frightened," she said, holding to Frida's arm.

Peter's blue eyes had been wide open since she had heard the tone in her grandfather's voice as he had commenced his explanation to Elsie. Her ears had listened. Her lips had remained closed. She might understand much or little, but she would remember that tea-time talk to her life's end, even when she had forgotten many of the incidents of later years. Now she said: "You mustn't hold Mother like that, Chris. Mother's got to go." Christine loosed her hold.

"Of course I'll look after them," Elsie said. Friends were to have motored over from Faversham for her tomorrow. She wanted— no one would ever know how much she had wanted—to go. She had meant to have the day with Dick Taverton. She knew quite well why he was coming. And why he had refused the invitation to spend Christmas at Eastbourne. Why hadn't Frida asked Joyce? As to that, she knew well enough. Joyce did not know enough of Frida's ways. She had no control over Peter. She bribed with chocolates, and with coins. Peter took the chocolates politely, and went her own way.

Yet she had agreed, as she would not have thought it possible that she would do an hour ago.

There has been much written in recent years of the nature of war. Of its cruelty, diseases, and deaths, and of the debasements which it entails. It is largely and very terribly true. But it is not the whole truth. War calls out the highest as well as the lowest qualities of mankind, and not only in the areas of actual conflict. It rouses generosities and comradeship, it stills the meaner emulations and jealousies among non-combatants also. Or, at least, it does so in those of any natural nobility of mind, and it may demonstrate how large a majority of men are of such a pattern, when the ruthless economic strife which is at the basis of our civilization pauses at the noise of the louder conflict.

Every criminal prosecution is of the nature of civil war. It had threatened Nina, and both Joyce and Elsie had responded with generosities which they would have regarded as beyond any reasonable probability in the earlier day.

In the result, Joyce had the pleasure of giving, and life has little to offer us which is more than that. Elsie had some tears in the night, of which she felt contempt when the daylight came. Beyond that, she lost nothing at all.

On Friday morning, Dick Taverton turned over *The Times*, and read that Dr. Slitman and others had been charged at Bow Street, and that the police had asked for a fortnight's adjournment, after formal evidence of arrest.

"Nina Oakleigh!" he exclaimed to his host, "I say, Frobisher, isn't she Elsie Oakley's sister?"

"That's the name. Any address given?— Yes, that's it. I've heard Elsie mention it."

Dick Taverton took another mouthful of bacon. "Wasn't there some talk about Elsie and Ned Perrott before he was sent down? I don't think anyone got to the bottom of that."

Frobisher agreed so far as to say that she had been in that set.

Dick Taverton was in some doubt as to whether to continue the acquaintance. He was looking for a wife, and had thought of her seriously in that capacity. It showed how careful you had to be. But she might still be worth cultivating.

"Runs a bit loose?" he suggested hopefully.

"No. I wouldn't say that. I think she's as straight as most."

"I guess I'd better give her the go-by."

There was no loss to Elsie there.

## CHAPTER TWENTY-SEVEN

"I SUPPOSE things are kept out of the newspapers at times?" Mr. Oakley asked, in the awkward ten minutes of waiting when it was too soon to start, and Frida was talking to Mrs. Case about what the children would have for breakfast tomorrow.

"Yes," Chester agreed doubtfully. "I've known it done. In fact, it's almost easy if it's a matter of no great importance, and only one or two reporters have got it down. It's done through money sometimes, but influence is the usual—and the easier—way. But it wouldn't be easy to do in a case of this kind. And it's harder to get a name held back than to get a thing altogether ignore.

"The Home Office can do a great deal when it really tries. There was a book about the Savidge Commission. Most of the wholesale trade got the wind up and funked selling it, and the police went from shop to shop warning any bookseller who put it into his window. Of course, they couldn't alter the fact that it *had* been published, and no one had dared to challenge the things it said, and I think it did what it was written to do; but outside Feet Street and the

Law Courts there wasn't one man in fifty thousand who ever heard of it. The Home Office can do that when it pulls its weight. But, it's only the magistrates or the Press who can prevent the names coming out in a case like this. I don't say it's right or wrong, though I sometimes think it would be fairer if they weren't published before conviction. I don't see, anyway, how you can defend publishing the name of a man who's accused of blackmail, and withholding that of his accuser. It ought to be neither or both. It shows the way a man's guilt is assumed before trial. And, of course, it's a matter of making terms with the accuser to get him to prosecute. They know the defendant will be in the dock, whether his name's published or not."

Chester paused on observing that Mr. Oakley had ceased to listen. He did not resent this. It was a too-frequent experience. Frida did it. It was Chester's trouble that one thought always led to another which was equally interesting, or perhaps more.

However, on this occasion, Elsie filled the gap. She would have suited Chester well enough, or even better than that. But not equally well.

Now Elsie said: "So you're sticking up for blackmailers now? I think you'd defend anything."

"Of course I'm not. The only proper thing to do with a real systematic blackmailer is to break his neck. It's far worse than mere physical murder. But you shouldn't assume anything in advance. As a matter of fact, there aren't many things easier for a man who's under some obligation to a woman that he wants to shirk than to accuse her of blackmailing him, and the mere threat may be enough to choke her off, if he brings the police on to the scene. It's the Press blackmailer that's hard to catch, though there aren't many of those now. There aren't more than two now, outside the financial Press."

"Two what?"

"Two papers that make a system of personal attacks, which inevitably brings in the blackmailing element, even if the editor isn't actively in it. Every man on the staff is a potential blackmailer. He can write an article against someone and threaten to publish it unless he buys it himself for—"

"I've been standing here waiting," Frida remarked, with not more than pardonable exaggeration, "for about five minutes."

# CHAPTER TWENTY-EIGHT

"WELL, I've told you what I think," Pauline said with her usual uncompromising directness. "I think you're a fool. If you'd had any sense, you'd have wired him before now."

"My dear, you don't know him," Nina replied miserably. "He wouldn't understand in a hundred years. He's not our sort at all."

This was in the evening, in Nina's flat. If she had remembered little else that her mother had taught her, that influence, joined to a natural instinct for home-making, was in the harmonious colouring and quiet-toned comfort of the room, though there might be a thought of wonder as to how it was sustained on the salary of a doctor's part-time secretary.

Pauline said: "Nonsense. He'd understand well enough. Look where you met him first."

"I know I met him at the Yellow Cat. You're always rubbing that in. But I told him I'd never been there before. I'd been taken there by a friend, because I wanted to see what a night-club's like."

"Well, what about him?"

"I don't think he'd ever been in such a place in his life. Tommy Dukes brought him along."

"Yes, of course. That's always the tale."

"Well, it's true this time."

Pauline knew that it was likely enough. Half the night-clubs in London would have to close without the support of those who go out of curiosity for the first time. Folly envies vice, and vice fattens on folly.

"I don't know about that. But I do know one thing. If you don't let him know now, you'll be sorry afterwards."

"He won't know as long as he lives, if I can help it. It isn't bound to be in the papers. It mightn't be in one that he'd read anyway."

"Well," Pauline said dryly, "if you count on *that*."

As she said it, the door-bell rang.

"Oh, bother. I wonder who that is? I won't see anyone now. I can't talk any more, and I look a sight. I expect Mrs. Mutton's gone home. Just keep still, and they'll think I'm out, unless they've seen the light from the street."

The bell rang again. Pauline rose. "You shan't see anyone you don't want. I'd better send them away."

"You don't think it's the police again?" The terror of last night's arrest was in her voice.

"Of course not. They're all eating their Christmas pudding."

Pauline went to the door. Nina heard her say: "Yes, she's in. Oh, come in, of course," and the next moment Frida was in the room.

She kissed her sister warmly, but without any unusual display of emotion, and sank into the comfortable fireside chair, taking in the whole scene at a glance as a woman will: the air of quiet, rather affluent, comfort, the long shelves of Nina's books, the unobtrusive decanter, the high-piled ashtrays, the banknotes on the little table beside Pauline. She thought: "It costs eight pounds a week to run this," as she put her coat over the back of the chair.

"I thought I'd better just run in," she began, and Pauline wondered whether she intended to profess that it was no more than a casual visit; but that was not Frida's way. "I don't suppose I can do anything; but I thought you'd like to know that Chester's in town, and he says you're not to worry, as he'll have the best counsel that can be got hold of tonight.

"He only wants you to get to there half an hour before it comes on. He said, if you'd do that, you could just think about something else now, and go to bed."

"How on earth—?" Nina began.

"I let your folk know this morning," Pauline explained. "There had to be some common sense somewhere."

"Pauline came to Birstall this morning, and told us about it, so we thought we'd better come up, Chester and I, in case we could be any help."

Nina showed no anger at this. Now that it was done, she was conscious only of an enormous relief.

"Well, you're a good pal," she said to Pauline. There was no doubt of that. There was other evidence in the banknotes that were beside her arm.

Frida went on: "Chester said, the only thing that's really important is that you should tell the lawyer tomorrow everything fully. He says they can make it come out all right if they know all the facts, but if they don't they'll never know where they'll get ditched."

"There's really nothing to tell," Nina began, with an assumption of confidence, in the off-hand manner which was habitual with her in meeting difficulties. "I just went with Miss Portman because she asked me to go. How could I tell that there was going to be all this fuss? Anyone goes to a doctor when they're not well, and any friend goes with them, if they're worth having."

Pauline's long, slim, brown-tipped fingers pressed a cigarette-stump firmly down in the ashtray.

"I wouldn't waste time on that rot," she said bluntly. "The truth's always worth telling—among friends. How'll the lawyers know what lies to make up, if you don't? Mr. Lawson's right about that. The fact is, Frida, she's in it up to the neck, and you'll want a clever lawyer to get her out. That's why I've brought her this cash that she thinks I can't spare, which I can quite easily. It was going tomorrow in a worse way, being for the rent of my own rooms, and the old Jew can wait a month. It'll do him good. You know Nina never has any money today, however much she had yesterday. There's nothing really wrong, except that people will interfere, and the law's rot. But it's no use saying that. We've got to dance to the band. I'll put the facts short.

"Billy Portman's not married, and due to have a baby in May."

"Billy being a girl?"

"Being a girl. Wilhelmina for short. Billy's a civil servant. She get's three-ten a week, and she's got a mother to keep. If she has a baby, she has the sack. That won't help her to keep it. She asks Nina what she's to do. 'You're a doctor's secretary', she says, 'you ought to know'."

"Dr. Bolton's nothing to do with this?" Frida interrupted. She saw how much Nina would be prejudiced, in any event, by the nature of the position she held.

"No," Nina said quickly. "Nothing at all."

Pauline had a long moment of silence. "Very well," she said at last, "if that's the tale. Dr. Bolton had nothing to do with it, but Billy happens to know that she's a doctor's secretary. There's nothing wrong in that. She deals with his correspondence and keeps his books for three hours a day, and gets two-fifteen a week. But Billy asks her, and she tells her that she knows where she can get it done, if there'll be no talk, and if she can pay. The man that's in this has got one wife already that the law won't let him quit. He can't marry Billy if he would, but he's not a bad sort. He says he'll go up to one hundred pounds, and when Dr. Slitman knew that was the limit, he agreed, and Nina took her along, and they just walked into as neat a trap as the police ever set."

"But Nina had nothing to gain?"

"Nina was to have twenty percent. She's had it before."

"You needn't have said that. It's nothing really wrong," Nina interposed.

"I didn't say it was. You can't live here on two-fifteen a week. But I'm giving Frida the facts. I've told you I don't think it was wrong every time you've asked." She turned to Frida. "What was Billy to do? She couldn't afford to lose her job. She couldn't have a baby without anyone noticing, and she didn't know how to get rid of it without help. If she'd been married, without any excuse, there'd have been no fuss at all. She'd just have said to her doctor: 'Don't you think I'm too weak to have a baby just now?' and if that doctor didn't say yes, she'd soon find one that would. I know Slitman's a slimy sort, but I can't see that anyone's done anything wrong, and three people out of four would say the same, if they weren't afraid."

Frida thought differently. She thought everything was wrong, from end to end. There was, in the background, the wrong of, or to, the neglected or separated wife, who could not, or refused to, find legal release. That was too vague to judge. There was the wrong of a law which would not face facts honestly, and legitimatize the coming child. There was the cruel wrong of a system which could dismiss a woman from her employment for the crime of motherhood, when every hand should be stretched to help. There was the pitiable cowardice of the cornered woman, the greed of the murderer who would kill for hire. It was all wrong, sickeningly wrong, but she rarely occupied her mind with such analyses. She concerned herself only as to what should be done in the position which confronted her, and if you go on quietly from step to step—well, life's much simpler than if you insist on looking a mile ahead. Besides, you don't stumble quite as often, having your eyes more on the ground.

Frida did not lose time or words in discussing the ethics of abortion. (Suppose it had been Christine or Peter, or the nine-months baby she had left at this emergency in Elsie's capable but rather casual hands. But you don't think of such things. They are absurd.) She said: "Chester said it isn't likely that they'll go into anything at the first hearing. He thinks there'll be a remand for a week at least. Father thought you might like to come home when it's over."

"Yes," Nina said doubtfully. "You mean to Birstall?" She would rather have gone to Birchett's Wood. Just with Chester and Frida, and the children. They wouldn't preach. She didn't care to face her father. Nor to meet Joyce.

"We're all together there over Christmas. You could come back with us, if you'd like to." Frida knew just how Nina felt. She had not expected the offer to be received with enthusiasm.

"They mayn't let me come."

Pauline explained. "They let me go bail for Nina till it goes before the Stipendiary, but the Superintendent wouldn't promise anything beyond that. He said it rested with the magistrate, and he might fix it much higher, if he didn't refuse. They wouldn't give it to Dr. Slitman or Mr. Warner, and Billy said that she couldn't get any that they'd take, and anyway, she wouldn't try. She said she didn't care what happened. I don't suppose she wanted to face her mother. She hadn't let her have any idea, and, besides being an invalid, she's an old-fashioned sort."

"I don't think there'll be any trouble about that. Chester didn't, and there isn't much about those things that he doesn't know."

"Can he keep it out of the Press?" Nina asked eagerly.

"He didn't think it would be possible in a case of this kind. Do you mind that so much?"

Frida had contracted some of Chester's own indifference to that kind of publicity. She added, as Nina was not quick to explain: "Chester says it's all forgotten within a week."

Pauline gave the explanation: "You see, Nina was engaged only ten days ago, and she's afraid that when the man reads the report he'll get rather a shock."

"You ought to have let him know."

"So I told her, till I got too tired to say it again."

"You don't know Gifford," Nina put in.

"No, but I soon should, if you let me take him in hand."

"Hasn't he been here since?" Frida asked.

Nina answered that. "He's on leave till Monday. He's Chief Officer on the *Bostonia*. He's gone to St. Helens over Christmas where his people live, and he's to be back here on Friday."

"Couldn't we get a wire through?"

"I'd much rather you didn't try."

Frida had a moment's hesitation. She did not know the man, and was always reluctant to interfere. That Nina dreaded that he should know of this might be in his favour rather than otherwise. She did not minimize the importance of the decision. Nina married to a decent man would be Nina saved from herself. And he would get a good wife. She might bring him a rather damaged virginity, but she would very certainly be faithful to him, if he were so to her. Frida knew clearly enough that that had been Nina's need all the time. She was made for domesticity. Marriage was her natural destiny—and to have children about her knees. She was one of ten thousand women, made for better and cleaner things, who are caught in currents against which they have not the power or perhaps the will to struggle, and are carried where they would never have chosen to be.

But she did not think that there was any probable basis of happiness in concealment of such an episode, and, besides, it was plain folly. It couldn't be done.

She asked: "If he hears of it from others, or reads of it in the papers, won't it be worse than if you tell him first?"

"It couldn't be worse. Frida, you don't know him. I simply *daren't*. He thinks I'm a—a sort of saint." She gave a nervous laugh, and threw herself back upon the couch on which she sat. "It's no use saying any more. It's just a mess. I suppose I must take what comes."

Frida looked at her doubtfully. Was the man a fool? Anyone who couldn't see what Nina was—well, "sophisticated" is the modern slang substitute for a blunter word! She turned to Pauline.

"Have you met Mr.—Gifford?"

"Yes, once. I suppose, according to Nina, I'm another of his pet innocents. I don't say she's altogether wrong either, but I tell her he's got to know, and it's better done first than last."

"What sort is he?"

"Well," Pauline answered with her usual candour, "if you heard he'd won at a beauty show you'd know that they're giving prizes at both ends. He'd be a bit too simple for me, but he'd suit Nina down to the ground. Made in Heaven's the right word."

"Do you think he'll really take it so badly?"

"Ask me the next. He'll go in at the deep end, but there's no saying how he'll come up. He might wring her neck, or he might break into the Court, and carry her off over his shoulder. You just couldn't tell. But it might be just as well for Slitman that he hasn't got bail."

"Nina'd be a fair weight. Is he a giant?" Frida asked. She would like a somewhat clearer picture of this formidable seaman than she had yet been able to get.

"Oh, he's hefty enough."

Frida became conscious that her mind was made up. "We ought to get hold of him somehow. Couldn't we telephone to St. Helens?"

Nina admitted that she had had a letter that morning. She passed it over carelessly. "He can't write letters," she said frankly. "There's nothing private in that." Frida read it on this permission, though she had seen at the first glance that it gave them what they needed—a telephone number on the note-paper heading. But she wanted to learn all that she could. She found that he was not a very original correspondent. But he came to the point. He proposed that they should be married when the *Bostonia* "tied up" from her coming voyage. That would be in about three weeks' time. There would be three or four days during which he could get leave while the boat was "turned round".

She said: "The sooner we get through the better. The telephone's in the passage, isn't it?"

"Oh, have it your own way," Nina answered listlessly. You'll be sorry afterwards. There's a dreadful draught out there." She knew that Frida hated draughts.

"Then I'll put on my coat first. There's no knowing how long I may have to stand."

"You needn't stand. There's a chair."

Frida got through almost at once. Apparently telephoning was not a popular relaxation on Christmas night.

She found herself answering a voice that talked the English-American dialect usual among officers on the transatlantic boats, who hear both languages about equally.

But she found that she had to do most of the talking. When she paused, she was set going again with a curt and anxious question. Mr. Gifford—Gifford Smith was his full name—was more anxious to obtain information than to discuss it. He wanted facts, not comments. He gave no indication of what he thought till it was evident that they could no longer postpone the ceremony of cutting-off. Then he spoke decisively, and hung up.

Frida went back into the warmth of the lighted room.

"What does he say?" Nina asked anxiously.

"He says you're not to lose something—I think it was your shirt, but I couldn't hear very clearly. He's coming 'right along', whatever that means. He spoke as though it would make an important difference." After a pause, she added: "I think I should feel fairly safe with that man on the bridge."

Pauline threw her last cigarette stump into the fire, and an empty box after it. "I'd better be going," she said, "I've got to give a car a trial run before breakfast." She made a sufficient though precarious income through motor agencies and an occasional deal on her own, risking her life also at times for a fee, in the trade-promoted racing contests. "No, I shan't take them back. Mr. Lawson may do all you say, but you may find you need them, all the same. Let me have them, if you don't. Any old time will do." She reckoned in a business-like but generous mind that her friendship with Nina Oakley (or Oakleigh, as Nina preferred to write it) normally cost her fifty pounds a year in half-forgotten loans, after deducting those which were returned. But this was an unusual incident, and she knew that Nina had been depending upon the twenty percent commission which she could no longer anticipate.

As she stood up, the telephone rang again: "I'll see what it is, if you like, as I go out."

A moment later she announced: "They want you to hold the line. It's St. Helens coming through."

"I thought he would," Nina said. She looked excited, pleased, and yet desperately frightened. "I'd better go," she said, in a moment's effort of courage. "You folk stay here."

She closed the door upon them. Pauline sat down to wait. Frida said: "I hope she's telling him the truth now."

"Not she," Pauline answered with conviction. "I know that voice."

Frida recognized the point of the comment. Nina's voice had a different tone when she spoke truth frankly, as she often would.

They could hear the voice, but not the words. "It won't make any difference," Frida said easily. "He's not such a fool as you think."

Nina came back looking happier.

"He's to be at Bow Street to meet us there. I didn't want him to come here first. He's telephoning the *Morning Post* to know whether it's too late to get our engagement announced tomorrow. He wanted me to be ready if they ring up here for confirmation."

## CHAPTER TWENTY-NINE

JOHN OAKLEY, seated in his solitary office (for the works were closed for the Christmas holidays), and divided between the urgent anxieties of the letters he was opening, and the dread of what might be happening in London, received the expected telegram somewhat earlier than he expected. It was barely one, and he recognised a good omen in its time of arrival. It almost certainly meant remand—delay—time to plan, and to act. Then he saw its length, and had a new fear before he read it. Good news is soon told. There should have been no need for more than "All well. Coming this afternoon", with perhaps an ambiguous extra word which he would understand, but which would mean nothing to anyone through whose hands it might pass.

Not that he had delayed opening it, or at least not beyond the moment when the boy who brought it had closed the door, but thought and emotion are swifter than any physical movement.

Then he read this:

*All well fortnights remand returning tomorrow*
*nina engaged chief officer bostonia probably married*
*next week see morning post for announcement baby*

*will need another tin number three food tonight writ-
ing frida.*

That was good enough, and startling enough of its kind. It left
much to be explained. But he would know in the morning. He knew
that he would hear fully from Frida, even though she might be coming home by an early train. Some women spend their leisure in
smoke, others in gossip, Frida wrote.

There was no need to stay longer, now that the telegram had
come. He had told them to send it to the office. And it was unlikely
that there would be any more letters. That meant that there would be
no more remittances coming in. If that proved to be the case, he
would have to see the bank in the morning, as he so often did in
these days.

Well, he would go home now. He would have the afternoon free
to show Christine the pigeons as he had promised.

But he must get that tin of No. 3 Food first. He knew that Frida
liked it to be purchased in Hunnerton, having a (probably quite
groundless) doubt as to the freshness of the stock kept by the local
chemist. But would the Hunnerton stores be open this afternoon?
Not a chance. Frida knew that as well as he. Doubtless had it in her
mind when she sent the wire. Doubtless, also relied upon him quite
calmly to get over the difficulty. Frida had always made it clear,
without fussing, that her babies came first. And she had always relied upon him from her own babyhood to do anything that she asked
seriously. Well, there must be someone on the (or some) premises.
He would try what the telephone would do. It was a good thing that
he had risked sending the cheque last week, or it would be discon-
nected now. After all, a baby's need is a good plea to set up. We still
say "women and children first", though we want the children no
more, and the woman's right to preference was derived from the opposite presumption. (And there are women who are foolish enough
to think that they can have it both ways in the good times to come!)
Anyway, it was a good reason enough. The keys turned, and he got
the tin. In the morning he got Frida's letter also. Frida was not styl-
ish, but her letters had one constant quality. They were full of facts.
He read this:

"My dear father,

"I'm writing this from Nina's flat, as I'm staying
with her till tomorrow, when she's going to St. Hel-

ens, and we can all travel together as far as Hunnerton.

"We've had rather an exciting time, but it's over now till Jan. 10th. I don't think Nina meant to do anything wrong, but she's been in with a set who seem to value the wrong things. It's a kind of nightmare to hear them talk. 'Who cares for the next generation? It's done nothing for us'. I heard that almost word for word three times today. And the funny thing is that they seem to think that all English people think the same, or at least all the people that matter. I wonder who to. And you know how Nina always follows the crowd.

"You'll see what's in the papers, but it won't be much, though we did have rather an exciting time, but it was before we went into Court. We got there about a quarter to ten to be on the safe side, and Chester came and said there was some mystery about whether Nina's name was on the charge-sheet, I think that's what it was, and we had some hope that they were just dropping her out, and then Chester took us into a room where we could see the K.C. that he had dug up. He said he wasn't the one he wanted, but he was the best who was in Town. He seemed very good to me. He seemed to know more about the facts before he began than I do even now, and had the truth out of Nina in about three minutes. She tried fibbing once or twice, but each time he interrupted with 'What you mean to say is...and told us what it had taken us all last night and this morning to get her to say. Then a clerk came and said would he speak to someone else in another room, and he went out and left us there, Nina and me, and Chester and Alwyn who had just come in, and Pauline was there. I know you don't like her, but she's a good sort in her own way, if it isn't ours. And Gifford Smith, the ship's officer that Nina's going to marry. We about filled the room, it was a dingy little place, and sat there saying nothing, or whispering something as though we were in church, till the K.C. came back—I didn't get his name properly, he's something Blades, but you'll see that in the papers—and said that they didn't want to press the case against Nina if she'd be willing to help the prosecution by giving evidence of what she knew. And Gifford Smith spoke before anyone else could, and said there was nothing doing, and then Nina said she didn't think she should care to do that. And Alwyn said he should think not, and Mr. Blades, if that's his name, stroked his chin, and said perhaps we hadn't got much to worry about if we sat tight, and he went out again, and a detective or someone must have been waiting at the door for we heard their voices outside, and Mr. Blades said that Nina would have been pleased to have given the Court all the assistance she could if she'd been asked in the right way, though it wouldn't have been much, but they'd made it impossible by the way they'd acted, which wasn't quite what Nina had said, but it may have done quite as well, or a bit better than that.

"Anyway, we had to go into Court, and they'd said they'd arrange that Nina needn't go into the dock, but the magistrate wouldn't have it. He said he couldn't have any distinctions. And after that, it was over almost as soon as it began. But Mr. Blades got in the few words that he'd promised he would. He said that he didn't raise any objection to a remand, though his client was ready to meet any charge that could be made against her; but if there were a further application of the same kind he should ask the Court to dismiss the case as against her, and submit that there was no evidence against her, and she ought not to have been arrested at all. I mayn't have got it quite right, and Chester said it was only claptrap, and if he hadn't been a K.C. the magistrate would have pulled him up before he could finish getting it out. I don't know how that was but it sounded very well at the time, only Dr. Slitman looked rather sneering. They say he knows he'll have to 'go down' for two years if not more. It all depends on the judge who tries the case, but everyone seems to think that Nina'll be got out of it. Chester's got them all talking as though it's all a mistake as far as she's concerned, like someone going in at the wrong door in the dark, and they seemed to want to apologize to her all the time. I think Nina got to think that was how it was before we got away, or would have done but for Gifford Smith, who's the downright kind. I think he knows Nina about as well as we do, and he means to marry her, which shows his sense. He's trying to get special leave so that he needn't sail, and can marry her right away. I can't see what difference that makes to the facts, but everyone seems to think it will, and Mr. Blades said that if they didn't get any more evidence than they've got now it ought to about trump the trick. He says he didn't think any jury would convict, but what he'll have to try to do is to make the magistrate think the same, so that it won't go to trial at all.

"They say even in cases like Dr. Slitman's, when they are proved so that there's no doubt at all, you can't always be sure of the juries now, and that's about all the chance he's got.

"Alwyn's staying till the morning, as it will save him coming up again. He's been to the office, and he asks me to let you know that he's got the Petworth cheque, and he's posting it to the works, so you'll find it there if you need to go in in the morning, which I hope you won't.

"I can't write any more now. We're all in Nina's flat, all the people I mentioned before, we're supposed to be celebrating her engagement, and two or three others have come in, and we're filling it till the walls bulge. I want to enclose a letter for you to give to Elsie about things that baby will need done as I'm not back. Alwyn's writing Joyce, but he said he'd leave it to me to tell you the events of the day. I'll tell you all about it when I get back. I don't think we need worry overmuch.

"Usual love,

"Frida."

So much for that. Frida with a pen in her hand had some fluency of a discursive narrative, but her idea that she would be more detailed or descriptive when she got back was a mistake. She was one of those numerous people who are more economical with the spoken than the written word, and more exact in its use.

# CHAPTER THIRTY

IF we look at a human baby with dispassionate eyes, we may observe that it lacks beauty, though it is not a fact to be mentioned obtrusively in its mother's presence. Beauty will come in six months or twelve, as the child takes intelligent control of the strange body into which it has been introduced—from where? If we knew that, we should know a number of hidden things.

But we must observe what we can. We may observe that the attributes of beauty and intelligent control are not as separate as we might think them to be. The young fawn, rising on unsteady legs, will run tomorrow at its mother's side. It will be a pleasure to see. So will be the chicken, when its down has dried in the darkness, and it pushes out from its mother's feathers to face the strange new light with bright unwinking eyes. But the young pigeon, lying blind and helpless in the nest, is uglier even than the human child. Its beauty is to come when its feathers grow, and the soft beak contracts and hardens, and it moves to the nest's edge with a needless flutter of unused wings, and gazes round on a new world. A world which is so much more than the branch of slowly-largening leaves which it has watched since its sight came, as it has lain with no more movement than a lifted neck and a flapping of half-fledged wings when its hunger stirred.

There is ugliness also in the process of human birth. Ugliness and discomfort at the best. Pain and danger as familiar things. It is a problem which the birds have solved (or it has been solved for them) better than we. There is no ugliness in the laid egg, or the chipped shell. This is not less true because we may see that it is a necessity of the air. The embryo must finish growth outside its mother's body. What of that? The birds sought first the kingdom of light and air, and this thing has been added unto them. We cannot tell what they are. We think ourselves to be more than they. They may know themselves to be more than we. Or they may understand us no better than we understand them. But we may think that they have chosen the better part.

We may judge something of what we are, and to what we go, when we consider the other creatures that have found a way of life on the same planet as we. We may look at the ants with humility, though a doubt may follow. They have founded a civilization a thousand times more stable, as it may be a thousand times older, than ours. There must once have been ants that thought and planned, that experimented and blundered in their search for communism, as men do today. A social order so complicated, a subordination so absolute, did not grow of itself. But they may have come at last to a life which is little more than a dead thing. They have the physical fact of life, but if they have more than that, it is something that we cannot see.

When the red ants go out to war, and the front line knows that it marches to certain death, it may be seen that this line changes from time to time, so that it is an equal chance who shall be there when the battle joins. This must have been done for a first time. There is nothing surer than that. It may have been found that none would go in the first line, if they must stay there till their deaths came. Or there may have been one that ruled in a far day who saw that this would be a fairer plan, even though all were willing to die for the common good. We see that there must have been a first time, ordered by thought and will; but who orders now when the line shall change? Is there fear in the hearts of those who lead? Is there the exaltation of sacrifice? Is there only the lust of battle? Or the hope that they may advance in peace till the moment when they may fall back to a safer rear?

We cannot tell, but it is likely that they are much as we. It may be that one of another planet would say that there is no difference worth a word. But we see that they walk by an ordered plan from the egg-cell to the veil of death. They have no freedom at all. And every restrictive law we make is a clumsy stumbling step to the same end.

These may be wandering thoughts, but they are such as it is easy to have when another comes through the gates of birth, as Joyce's baby has come. It lies, dimly conscious of life, vaguely aware of light and colour and shadowy movement of surrounding forms, dimly disturbed by the first sensations of hunger and cold and pain, in the cradle at Joyce's side—and Joyce will never tell anyone to her life's end, not even Alwyn, how she had hoped it would be a boy.

But she did not grieve about that. She would have a boy before long. Frida's first two had been girls. There was nothing in that. She was very happy as she looked at this two-day-old specimen which she had contributed to her race. She did not think of its birth as an event that each moment duplicates. She thought she had done a very important thing. She did not think much of the experiences of the last three days. Had they been exceptional to her, had they been outside the recognized proprieties of life, they would have terrified her. They would have overwhelmed her with shame. But she was the heroine of the hour. Everyone was very kind. They said she had been very brave. What more would you have?

As to health, she had never felt better in her life. She would have liked to get up now, only that they told her she must not think of doing more than being propped up with pillows for the next few days. Very well. She was the centre of the scene. She would act the part. You could trust Joyce for that.

Possibly she was not as strong as she thought. If she talked for a time, she would feel that she had talked enough. She needed a good deal of sleep. Also, she needed food, of which they would not give her all for which she asked. She was really cross about that. She wanted solid food. She had always hated slops from a child. The only other cloud in the sky was that she disliked the nurse. She was a capable woman, but not of the best type. At times her talk would be coarse, in a lewd way. She repeated things which she said that she had seen, or which may have arisen from the dark places of her own mind. If they were true, they should have been left unsaid. Her talk implied that childbirth was a penalty which women paid for their own physical pleasure, and for the lust of men. To the impure all things are impure. That which had been to Joyce a very intimate, a very sacred thing—was she not like the Madonna herself?—became soiled by the woman's speech.

After two or three days Joyce said something of this to Alwyn. She said the woman made her feel sick. Alwyn must have said something to the nurse, for after that the talk ceased. But its effect did not entirely pass. Joyce was too sensitive to atmosphere. Things that she had thought sacred, things of which she had thought as single to Alwyn and her (if she had thought at all), would always afterwards be vulgarized in her mind, with a faint shadow of the obscene. There was another matter which occasioned greater difference, and with more serious consequence.

Joyce wanted to feed her child. She had heard it said that it was the best way, for such mothers as could do it; as most could, but not all. Was her baby to have a disadvantage at the start? Not it. Was she a defective mother? Not she.

The nurse thought differently. She said Joyce was not strong enough to undertake it. She was too small. She was not the right shape. She may have been right or wrong. The opinion may have been better than some of the reasons given in its support. She appealed to Dr. Wightman. Was the poor lamb to be starved for a stubborn whim? Dr. Wightman was not new to such differences. He was not a very bold man when women warred with the tongue. He would be inclined to go with the tide, which doesn't go far either way. He suggested a compromise. Let Joyce try what she could do twice a day. Let it have bottles between.

It was a controversy which we are not bound to decide. If it were impossible to feed a baby except with its mother's milk, we may guess that the number that would die of starvation would not be large. As it is, the human mother loses one child in every ten or twelve, showing herself inferior to the average cow. But the effort to combine the two methods of nutrition can be very rarely successful, even with the utmost co-operation between nurse and mother. When that is absent, any slender possibility; of such an arrangement succeeding is not worth consideration. The baby was fretful. It did not thrive on its mixed diet. The nurse was not over-much concerned about that. Every nurse expects that the baby that is in her charge will have functional derangements, for which she comes prepared with an arsenal of drugs. Train up a child in the way it should go. How would it find its way to the chemist's shop in its later years, if it swallowed nothing but good food when it was young? Joyce was fretful also, and this may have reacted on the child's health. She could not always have it regularly, even at the agreed times. It was asleep, and must not be waked. It had been necessary to feed it an hour ago. Joyce was in less haste to get up than she had been a week before. She had pain in her left breast. It was hot and throbbed. There was a place that was very hard. Dr. Wightman said she must give up feeding the baby at once. It was a pity she had tried it at all. She could see now that the nurse had been right. She did not see it. She thought she could have succeeded if she had had her own way from the first. Yet she saw she must give way.

Now she was on a meagre diet again. She lay tightly bandaged. The milk must be stopped. There were fomentations for the throbbing breast, in which the pain did not cease. Finally, when milder efforts had failed, it had to be lanced. She would never be able to feed a child now.

She had no quarrel with Dr. Wightman. He had been skilful and kind, though, perhaps, rather late in the day. But if she had known that a lifted finger would mean that the nurse would die, it would not have lain flat very long. Joyce found, not for the first time in her life, that she could hate well.

At this time she lay watching the sun and cloud of the April days, and wondered what she had done wrong that God should punish her thus. Had He done it because she had been nasty to Elsie in subtle ways, of which only they two knew? Was it because she had made it difficult for Nina to come home? (Though she was not sure that she had.) Besides. Nina was married now, and everything was going well with her. (The prosecution had applied to the magistrate for permission to withdraw the case against her for lack of evidence, which he had allowed them to do.) Besides, Nina had done something wrong herself, though she wasn't very clear what. God would have to take account of that. No, she didn't think He could have a grudge against her on Nina's account.

But suppose He were really angry? She knew that she had not been nice to Alwyn yesterday morning. He ought not to be in London so much when she wanted him here. But suppose God were *really* angry? *Suppose baby should die.* Panic waked at the thought. It had been taken into the next room, so that it should not disturb her when it cried. How did she know that it was not dead now? She reached for the bell at her bedside, and rang it till the nurse came. She wanted baby to lie beside her. Only just gone off, and mustn't be disturbed now? Never mind that. She was her mother. Very well, she would go on ringing. The nurse gave way, calling her a crazy woman under her breath as she went out.

Soon she lay kissing the tiny hands. She cried quietly and happily, thinking of various appropriate saints to whom she could make appeal. Even if God wouldn't listen to her, He wouldn't treat them in the same way.

As she prayed, she heard the door open softly. She looked up and saw that Frida was in the room.

For some time she could not talk for her tears. Then she said: "Oh, Frida, send her away. I'll manage baby myself. I'll get up. I'm really strong. She wants her mother. She'll be all right with me. Tell Alwyn he must send her away."

Frida said: "She'll go as soon as Alwyn comes home. She's packing now." (Alwyn says that you should pray to God direct, and that the saints don't hear anything. Baptists may be Christians of a kind, and some of them are dreadfully good, but they haven't the wisdom of the True Church. It just shows.)

"Oh, Frida, you won't go?"

No. Frida had come to stay. She had come the first minute she could. She had brought baby with her, and Chester was looking after Christine and Peter at night. Of course, Mrs. Potter would be coming in every day. They would be all right.

Joyce asked why Chester and the elder children had not come with her, as they usually did.

Frida did not answer that, and Joyce went on talking without noticing her silence. Was baby as big as John had been at the same age? No (hurriedly), John was a boy. Boys were bigger. Was she as big as Peter? (Joyce had heard that Peter had been rather small at her birth.)

Frida lied, as she was expected to do. They both knew that she lied. Joyce had never loved Frida better than she did then. They admitted their common knowledge of the lie when they talked of the expediency of trying a change of food.

Joyce felt safe now. Frida's babies lived. If God had had any hostile designs on hers, He would not have let Frida come.

Alwyn came into the room. He looked anxious and tired. "I just caught it," he said, "with a rush." He had promised to try to come on the early train.

Joyce looked at him with eyes that were shining softly. He had not seen that look in her eyes since they had been apart, though there had been times when she had held on to his hands, and begged him to stay at home for that day, or to delay leaving her when he came in to say good night, "the nights seemed so long alone".

"Come and look at her." she said. Moving the clothes away, she could dream that she was the Madonna again, in spite of herself.

Why didn't Alwyn kiss her at once? Not herself—he was quick enough to do that—but the child? Of course, he did it when he was asked. But he ought to have done it at once. Men are queer about babies. You have to get used to that.

Frida said: "I expect you'll like to sleep with her tonight now that Nurse is going?" (How Frida understood!) "Nurse going?" Alwyn exclaimed. He did not sound troubled at the news. "I thought she wasn't...."

"We talked things over," Frida said, "and we agreed that, as I should be here, she wouldn't be needed longer. She's packing now. I expect she's only waiting to be paid. You needn't pay her beyond today. I arranged that."

Frida saw the anxious look come back to his face at the mention of paying her, and then lift slightly at the last words. Then it passed entirely as he looked at Joyce to say: "That's a good riddance. We'll soon have you up now." But Joyce had seen it as well as Frida. She was in a mood to be good, now that God had shown so plainly that He was disposed to let the past go. Being good with Joyce meant thinking a little more of others, and a little less of herself. She said: "There's some money in my bag in the wardrobe. There's nearly thirty pounds from what Uncle sent me." (She had had the usual fifty pounds on the first day of the quarter, and before she could do more than settle one or two of her private bills, she had been lying here.) "You'd better pay her from that." She felt under the pillow. "I've got the keys here."

"No," he said; "I can manage without that." But there was hesitation in his voice.

"Just to please me," she pleaded. "I want to do this myself."

"Well," he gave way, "I must let you have it back. I expect she'd rather be paid in cash."

# CHAPTER THIRTY-ONE

ALWYN had no difficulty with the nurse. She had only been anxious to have it clear that she was not going through any fault on her side. She gave herself fluent testimonials. She hinted that she went to save them further expense because she could "see how things are as well as the next". There may have been some truth in this. Human motives are complex. Also, she was quite clear that she did not want any criticism to reach Dr. Wightman, on whose recommendations she largely depended.

Alwyn reassured her on that. Otherwise he listened in silence. He ignored the suggestions as to how things were. It must be common talk now. Joyce was the only one in the house who had no idea of the truth.

He went up to sit with her. She had heard the nurse's departure, and was in a happy mood, weakness rendering her more than normally excitable. She lay stroking his hand. "You'll come back to me tonight?" she said. "We won't be apart again. I don't believe you've missed me at all!"

Had he not? He had longed for her night and day, even amid the urgent worries of the last fortnight. She knew that well enough, but gave a low contented laugh on being told. "But you can't love me tonight," she added, lest he should expect too much. "Not *really*, you know, I'm—" she left the sentence unfinished. He said of course he understood. In fact, he understood very little. It was all new to him. But he knew that they would be together again. Had he not been counting the days till the nurse would go?

Joyce forgot herself again, looking at Alwyn.

She said: "But how tired you look! I don't believe it suits either of us not being together. You haven't been worrying about me, have you? There isn't anything else?"

It was awkward to avoid a direct question like that. How much should he say? He could see that she was still far from strong. He answered vaguely that business had been rather worrying lately. She said quickly: "You mean your father's?" She had noticed yesterday, when he had come in to see her, that he had avoided answering a similar question. Alwyn admitted that that was so.

She had an impulse to help. "If I wrote to Uncle?" she said. "He's got lots."

Alwyn didn't think there was any need to do that. But she insisted that he should take the remainder of her money from the wardrobe. Suppose he hadn't money to get lunch when he was in Town? Shortness of money interpreted itself to her mind as an inability to buy some needed personal thing. Her financial crisis was to get on to a bus and find that her purse was bare.

Baby was not with her now. Frida had taken it away. She had said that she would have it with her own during the night. Joyce would need sleep. Joyce had agreed easily. Baby would be safe with her. It was fixed in Joyce's mind that Frida's babies did not die.

Alwyn noticed (and none too soon) that she was exhausted with the emotions of the last hours. Her eyes were dark with fatigue. He said: "Isn't it time for you to have something to eat?" He was conscious that he had had nothing himself since he came in.

She said: "No, I think I'd rather sleep. Frida'll get me something later. But don't go. There's a newspaper on the chair, if you'd like to read."

The next moment she was asleep. He waited till he was sure of this, and then went quietly out of the room

## CHAPTER THIRTY-TWO

IT was a month earlier that John Oakley had gone over his morning's letters, finding them to be a better post than usual, both in orders and remittances, till he had opened one to which he had not given the earliest attention because it had the appearance of having originated in a solicitor's office.

He had grown somewhat accustomed to such communications during the last two years, and knew the meaning of the formal writing, and the more expensive envelope than it is customary to use for commercial purposes. He knew that such letters usually contained a request for payment with a hint that if he could not pay twenty shillings today he would be required to pay twenty-five or thirty shillings tomorrow. But he was not perturbed on this occasion. He had his major liabilities well in hand. Last month's turnover had shown some improvement. He had not put the letter down as a thing he feared. He had simply opened others first as being of a greater potential interest.

When this letter had its turn, it conveyed the news of his ruin in a particularly colourless and inoffensive way.

What it said was this:

Dear Sir,

We have been consulted by Messrs. J. J. Winterton & Co., Ltd., in reference to their affairs.

Would you kindly attend a meeting of Creditors which will be held on Wednesday next, the 21$^{st}$ inst., at 3 P.M., at these offices, and oblige,

Yours faithfully,

DUNCAN, FROST, & WINSTOW

It had always been his custom to open the letters himself. As he did so he would put the orders into one tray, the remittances into another, invoices and statements into a third, and other miscellaneous matter into their appropriate piles, so that they should be distributed among the staff, retaining only those which would require his personal attention or answer.

Now he went quietly over these ordered letters again, as his habit was after the first distribution. When he came to the remittances he took up all but two of the smaller cheques, opened a drawer, and locked them into his desk. He dealt with the letter of Duncan, Frost, & Winstow in the same way. Then he rang for the boy who would come in and convey the letter-trays to their destinations.

"Perks," he said, "tell Mr. Sanders that I want to see him."

"Sanders," he said, quietly, when the manager entered the room, "I've heard this morning that Winterton's have failed. There's a meeting of creditors called for the 21$^{st}$."

"I'm sorry to hear that, sir. I heard a rumour yesterday, but I hoped there was nothing in it."

"Well, there is. You'd better have the swarf weighed up today instead of next week, and phone Booth's to call for it this afternoon. I shall be out for about an hour. Of course, you won't mention anything about Winterton's. You can deny any rumour that they have failed. They haven't yet. They may only be asking for time."

He smiled slightly at the idea. Sanders thought that the guv'nor was taking it very well. He seemed rather more cheerful than he usually was at that time of day. He wondered what he would do. He had a great confidence in Mr. Oakley's capacity, and though he knew enough to be aware of the seriousness of this new difficulty, he had not the knowledge which would tell him definitely that it was a knock-out blow.

But John Oakley knew. Had known instantly, as he read the letter, that it was the end. He had known for twelve months past that if Winterton's failed there was no more to be done. They owed him over £3,000, besides the account for the current quarter—£3,000 (it had been a larger figure a year ago) in bills which were discounted at his bank, or had been endorsed over to some of his own creditors.

For a year past he had been fighting against time. Very slowly, he had advanced. His position had improved. By economy and reorganization he had made it possible to show a profit even on the reduced prices and unrestricted foreign competition which he had had to face. But as his line of battle slowly advanced he had known that if it should break at any point, it would be the end. He had no reserves which could be thrown into the gap. He had no securities left. The bank held the deeds of the works. They held the deeds of Birstall House. They held every investment he had which it had been worth their while to take. They had made it clear that they would do no more. There would be no help from them.

He walked over to the café where he usually went at midday for a light lunch, and perhaps a game at chess in the smoke-room if time allowed. At that time there would be others there whom he had met for many years in the same way, with a curiously limited friendliness confined to that time and place. But it would be too early for them. He wanted a place in which he could sit and think undisturbed.

Somewhat to his surprise, Mr. Richard Hayward was there, with a man who did not look to be of his own type. Probably someone who had asked him there for a business deal.

Hayward looked up and spoke, and had a genial response. He thought that John Oakley, whom he liked, looked more cheerful than usual. Had he heard the rumour about Winterton's? It would hit him hard if they went down. He liked John Oakley, but he wondered how soon his premises would be on the market and available for an extension of the Collett Hayward works, which could do with them very well.

John Oakley was conscious that he did not feel as depressed as he ought to have done. He knew that he was ruined. He supposed himself to be disgraced. But there was, subconsciously, the enormous relief of knowing that the fight was done. He felt now that he had known it to be hopeless, ever since the slump came. As a fact, he had almost made it a victory—would have done so, had Winterton's had an equal to himself at its head. But there was nothing now to be done but to surrender his sword. While there was hope, he had fought on. Now that he knew what the end would be, there should be no delay. He would file his own petition before any adverse steps could be taken against him. But there were some things to be done first. There was a rear-guard action to be fought, while the sword was still in his own hand. His mind rose almost gaily to this last need. It was abnormally alert and clear. With the resolution that he would force the issue in his own way, a feeling of freedom and power had come, such as he had not experienced since the days when he could sign a cheque for anything he was likely to desire without a thought of its effect upon an ample balance.

He made rapid notes, thinking of many things that must be done to protect those who would need it most from the blind and cruel equities of the law.

When he went back, he summoned Sanders into his office again. "Sanders," he said, "I'm going to throw up the sponge. We couldn't carry on now that Winterton's are going down."

Consternation was on the manager's face. He was a man born to serve. He was married. In a few weeks he might be out of a job.

"Of course, you'll say nothing of this, but I want you to understand, so that orders go intelligently, and not let the wrong questions be asked. How much is there outstanding on that I.O.U?"

Two or three years ago, when Sanders had been confronted with a private trouble, he had lent him £100. He had received an I.O.U., but had not put the loan through the business books. This omission had been with no other intention than to prevent the transaction being known to the bookkeeping clerks. He had considered Sanders's feelings, and charged the amount to his own drawings. At times a few pounds had been paid off. The amount outstanding now was £73. He went to the safe, took out the I.O.U., and dropped it into the fire.

"I'm not going to risk having your home sold up for that, Sanders. If the time comes when you're better off than I, I may ask you to remember it. You can forget it till then."

Mr. Sanders saw the paper blacken and shrivel with confused emotions. It was a relief for which he expressed his gratitude; but it showed the finality of Mr. Oakley's decision that the business could not go on. Up to that moment he had hoped the guv'nor would find a way.

Mr. Oakley went on: "When you get the money for that swarf this afternoon, I want you to pay Jackson £15 on account, and give the balance to Miss Withers. Tell her to put it all through the books in the usual way, but it's not to go into the bank. But I'll speak to her." He went on to give instructions upon orders in hand; upon the purchasing of needed goods to complete them; upon certain returns which could be made with sufficient pretexts, and to the advantage of creditors; of numerous matters, which we must avoid. Jackson was an outworker who was paid monthly. His money was practically wages, but he was not legally preferential in the same way. The reason for giving him money in the middle month would be sufficiently evident. John Oakley did not know whether it could be held to constitute a fraudulent preference. Probably not. It was extremely unlikely that the question would ever be raised. Besides, there is a proverb about getting butter out of a dog's mouth.

Then he gave instructions to get him through on the telephone to Alwyn's London office. "If he's out, he's to ring me up at once when he comes in. They're to tell him it's very important, and I shall wait here till he does."

He must protect Alwyn as far as possible. Alwyn was now doing well. He had enlarged his office. He had a staff of three competent assistants. The old typewriter was a forgotten thing. He owed Alwyn about £200. The amount was relatively small, but to Alwyn it would be a very serious loss. That couldn't be helped now. But that was not all. There was Alwyn's commission account for the last quarter. It had been made up and the cheque drawn and issued in the usual way, but Alwyn had been holding it back till his father should tell him the right moment had come to pay it in. There were other things.

Would there be time to go to the bank before lunch? He looked at his watch for the first time since he had opened his letters. It was only 10:48. It is astonishing how slowly time will go when the unusual confronts us. We lose our lives in routine.

At about 11:15 the call came through. "That you, Alwyn? I want you to pay in that commission cheque today. Tell your bank to present it specially so that it will be here tomorrow. Tell them you don't want to draw on it till it's cleared. How will it look to them? That won't matter at all. No, but I want a word with you tonight, after Joyce has gone up. Not before. You'd better come to my room. No, nothing at all." He went on to the discussion of details of London business.

After that, he went over to see the bank.

# CHAPTER THIRTY-THREE

WHEN John Oakley got home that evening, the inevitable reaction came. He looked round that which he supposed he was about to lose, and there was a new strangeness in the familiar things. The home which he and the now-dead Frida had built up together, which had been the centre of his life, at least when his life relaxed from the civil war of commerce in which its more active hours were passed, had become a part of himself, but a subconscious part, of which he became aware with a new and very painful acuteness. Here would be explanations and adjustments, perhaps troubles and tears, which would be harder to meet than any business hostility.

He wondered how Joyce would take it. He knew that, to women more than to men, success or failure carry their own verdict, and their causes are of a less account. He supposed that most of the furniture would have to go. It had not been protected in any legal way. He regretted that, now that it was too late. It should have been done when Frida was alive in the old prosperous days. There was the question about Joyce's rooms—about the furniture that he had sold to Alwyn. It had been paid for at the time. All, he thought, had been done in a legal way. But he knew that there was some provision in the bankruptcy law about ostensible possession. He had once had a difficult case on that point in regard to goods that had been on sale in the hands of a man when he had failed. He had got over that on some point of trade custom, and his lawyer had expressed the opinion that he was rather lucky to get the O.R. to accept the view. He must clear that point up further. Would it be better to tell Alwyn to move out tomorrow? How could he, Joyce being as she was? Was his decision a mistake? Would it be better to make a long, slow, hopeless fight, bluffing here, begging there, using excuse and evasion to delay that which he could not meet? Seeing the inevitable "costs" adding themselves to amounts already beyond his resources of settlement?

Had he had a wife, she must have seen that there was some unusual disturbance that vexed his mind. Joyce did see it vaguely, and gave it a natural misinterpretation. It was the day that the nurse had come. She thought her baby might be born any day now. She was filled with a half-frightened, half-wondering excitement, too great for the shadow of a coming trouble to have much place in her mind, though she confided it at the evening meal. She did not like the nurse. She was happier with Mrs. Case, who had seen Alwyn born in the same house, and who was now in a suppressed excitement hardly less than her own. Mrs. Case had said that Joyce should get Alwyn to stay in London. At these times men were best out of the way.

Joyce had not agreed to that. An event of such importance required, to her mind, that the boxes should be full. But if the effect were to make them as her father-in-law was now, so that you had to repeat everything twice, well, perhaps Mrs. Case was right!

Yet she was not cross, for when he spoke to her he was even kinder than usual, and apologetic for his wandering mind. Still, it was depressing. And why was Alwyn so late, when he really oughtn't to be in London at all? She thought she would go to bed.

Alwyn came later. He was upstairs with Joyce a long while, as was natural enough. Then he had a meal. It was a late hour when he could talk with his father in quietness. He heard the news without great surprise. The difficulties with Winterton's bills had been familiar incidents for several months. But he protested against throwing up the sponge. He had his father's fighting spirit, with less coolness of judgement when feeling was strong. There must be same way out. At least, there was no need for any sudden decision. Why not wait till the 21$^{st}$? Winterton's might have an offer to make which would be acceptable. Why not, at the worst, offer a composition ourselves? That would almost certainly be accepted, especially if the last instalment were guaranteed? Couldn't he do that? It might be a large amount for which to accept his name, but he was doing well— was likely to do better in future. Anyway, the name of bankruptcy might be avoided. He was sensitive about the "disgrace" in a youthful way.

He shook his father's resolution, though he did not change it. He said that he had no intention of taking any decisive step before the 21$^{st}$. He was still technically solvent, certainly as a going concern, till he had knowledge of how much he would lose through Winterton's default. As to that, he expected nothing. There were debentures. But, in theory, they might only be asking for time. Till the 21$^{st}$ he would only be preparing for that which he would then do.

He went on: "I told Riddle, in confidence, when I went into the bank before lunch. He was rather upset, but he didn't say I was wrong. He knows what the last two years have been."

"I paid in that cheque, as you said," Alwyn interrupted. "I suppose there'll be no trouble about it. I could have managed without for this week.

"I took over £84 in this morning myself, and paid it in specifically to cover that cheque, and one or two other smaller ones that were out. Riddle quite understands about that.

"He was very decent. He'll see that the wages are right on Saturday. I've promised to assign him some book-debts if enough money doesn't come in before them, but I expect it will."

He remembered that there were other payments that it would have been vital to make before the week ended, if his credit were to be maintained. They wouldn't matter—wouldn't even be attempted—now. No, he wouldn't start it again. The fight was done.

He rose, conscious of age, and of the pain that came at times from the wound that he never mentioned, and which was consequently to others a forgotten thing.

"Well," he said, "I'll think it over again between now and morning. I'll let you know if I change my mind. But I don't think I shall. Good night, Alwyn. I shouldn't say anything to Joyce about this. Not yet, anyway."

"No, Father. We mustn't bother her. Good night."

At an impulse, Alwyn kissed his father, as he had done so often in earlier years. They were both rather ashamed of that, even though no one saw.

## CHAPTER THIRTY-FOUR

JOHN OAKLEY went to his room, but he did not sleep. It was some hours before he took off his clothes. April came, and the night was not warm. A large moon rose in the east: the sky showed hurrying cloud. He knew that he must avoid cold, or he would have a heavier price to pay than would have been the case when his body was undamaged, and his muscles were young. But he did not regard this. He stood and looked at the moon.

The moon had risen so, shining on the same April wall, when he had been young, and they had first lived here, Frida and he. He remembered one night very well. This was his romance, or, at least, his romance had brought him here. He looked at the moon, as romance will.

I should have written "when his body had been young", for men do not change as the young think. They live in bodies that become damaged and worn, and that are soon tired, but they are themselves still. As the years pass, the blinds fall; they become hidden from those around them: but they are still there.

All his life had been centred in that room, which he supposed that he must soon leave. Leave, as he thought, a disgraced and defeated man. There are those who will destroy themselves (though they are not many of our race) when such a crisis comes. There are many more to whom the thought will come, to be thrust aside as a cowardly thing, or as one which himself fears. It is such an easy way out. But the thought did not enter John Oakley's mind. He thought of a hundred consequences that his failure would surely bring, but they were to others rather than to himself. Of Elsie. Of Alwyn, and the minor financial complications in which he had involved his son. Of Mrs. Case, who had become a part of the house itself. Of many business matters and people at which we must not glance. He didn't worry about how Frida would feel, as he did about Elsie. She was too much like himself. Her quietness, her courage, and her help were sure. He was not aware that his thought was of others rather than of himself. He would not have seen any merit in that. It was such a natural thing. It becomes the habit of all who rule, if they are fit to do so, whether in house or business or realm. If he thought of any personal thing, it was for a moment only. He would find some means of keeping the birds.

Yet the thought of the many lives of his own family and of humbler sorts who "found shelter underneath his shield", and who would find that shelter fail in this sudden bewildering way was very bitter in the night hours. He looked up, as so many have done before him—so many countless more—appealing to the dumb heaven against the disasters of life. Is there any pitying, even any regarding, God? Professor Huxley, an honest, unimaginative man, is quite sure there is not. He finds law and order wherever he looks, and it appears conclusive evidence to him that there is no Lawmaker. The bed is neatly made. Then there was no one to make it. What can be clearer than that? But Professor Huxley's mind appears to have been curiously warped by the crudity of his early teaching. God to him means a Deity of a very improbable and paltry pattern. Otherwise, there can be none at all. Jesus Christ thought differently. We may observe the possibility that He may have been right, and Professor Huxley wrong. But if John Oakley doubted God, it was only on the troubled surface of his mind. The deeper places were undisturbed. We prove ourselves, not God, when we look up in the night. In the end, he saw this thing as small as it really was. He gained courage, if not hope. Yet he thought of the dead woman who had shared his life, and of the hopes of the earlier years, and though it did not enter his mind to destroy his own life, he knew that he would be glad to die.

And, very curiously, as it may seem to some, though he thought of his children, he did not see where he had gone wrong. He wondered how this trouble would affect Elsie among her friends, and whether she would have to turn quickly to support herself, and what grief she would have that he could not help, and it did not cross his mind that she was the real cause that he was troubled at all. Each of his children must have cost at least £2,000 since their births. Probably much more. It would have been very useful now. Even without the interest. It was rather dense of him not to have seen that. But a man who can actually trust his God may be foolish in other ways.

John Oakley did not doubt that he was disgraced. He was even surer on the next day when a little incident occurred at the café where he had taken his midday lunch for so many years.

It was a trivial thing. Only that a man he knew acted as though he did not see him, though there had been a second when he knew that he did, and passed on to a further table. It showed how quickly rumour spreads, so that such things may be known to others almost before we are aware of them ourselves. The line came to his mind, "*I am a tainted wether of the flock*", but he was more contemptuous than annoyed in the mood of the midday hours.

He was to see more of such attitudes (and of very different ones) in the weeks that followed. He had occasion to observe that some even of those who were not unfriendly were uncomfortable in his society. It was like health withdrawing from disease. An instinctive antipathy. Some of them would have been puzzled to explain why they behaved as they did.

And during these days of crisis before Joyce's baby came, everything must be kept from her. He must only talk to Alwyn of urgent things when she was not within hearing. Tone and manner must change as she approached. It was the tyranny of the child in another form—the child which so obviously should not be there. Born in a home which was scarcely that of its parents. Which they might so soon have to leave. But it is too late for wisdom now. Even the abortionist would hesitate to destroy it, though it is still moving under its mother's heart, and the casuist may still argue as to whether it has a separate life. Next week it will be lying against its mother's side, and the last chance will be gone.

The day of Winterton's meeting came, and with it went any flicker of remaining hope, and any doubt of the finality of decision. A receiver for the Debenture-holders was in possession. There would probably be a compulsory winding-up. Voluntary liquidation was the only alternative. There might be no dividend at all. It was that evening that John Oakley sold his car.

It had stood idle in the garage for some months—since he had dispensed with the chauffeur's services at the conclusion of Elsie's Christmas vacation, and his neighbour, Mr. Swadson, had hinted more than once that he would be a probable purchaser should Mr. Oakley be buying a new one.

Geoffrey Swadson was a somewhat overfed man of florid aspect, to whom his liver allowed an intermittent jocularity. His occupation was not certainly known. He was spoken of as a bookmaker, as a money-lender, and as being possibly of less reputable calling. He was known to attend race-meetings. He had once given his gardener a most valuable tip, by which that cautious individual had failed to profit, though some of his friends had been more adventurous. He was visited at times by men of pugilistic appearance. He had more money than a man needs. Beyond that nothing was known.

He was on friendly though not familiar terms with John Oakley. They were both interested in poultry. Swadson farmed about twenty acres of pasture, and lost more money upon it than would seem to be easily possible on so restricted an area. He sometimes sought his neighbour's advice regarding his cattle and hay. He respected Mr. Oakley's opinion, as that of one who also had a few acres, and who lost less. A man who seeks your advice cannot be wholly bad.

Now Mr. Oakley called upon Mr. Swadson and said he was prepared to discuss the sale of the car. Mr. Swadson offered drinks. He offered cigars. He was unruffled in temper when these courtesies were declined. He took them himself. He offered the list-price for the car—forty pounds.

Mr. Oakley declined. He mentioned decarbonizing, and the new tyres.

Mr. Swadson said that that made no difference to the second-hand price, but he did not say it with a tone of finality. He ended with "Well, that's my price; what's yours?" Mr. Oakley said it was worth a hundred, but he would take sixty. Mr. Swadson said: "Well, between neighbours, that's near enough." He moved from the fireside chair to a littered desk. He rummaged in a drawer, pulling out an assortment of bank and Treasury notes. He pulled a cheque-book from his breast-pocket, where it probably lived. He seemed to hesitate between these. He said, "I suppose my cheque's good enough?"

There was a second's hesitation in the expected affirmative. Mr. Swadson did not appear to notice this, but he paused with the pen in his hand. When he passed the cheque over, the figure beside the sprawling signature was for forty pounds only. He said, "I'll pay the sixty as between friends, but I'm not going to have that go through my books. Not for more than it's listed. I don't want Jennie to think I'm a mug." Jennie was his wife. She is outside this tale.

He sorted the Treasury notes, making up twenty, with some help from the crumpled contents of an ample pocket.

John Oakley was worried about that twenty pounds. They held an implication that he could not miss. How much did Swadson suppose or know? He did not think that there had been any generosity. The car was worth sixty. It was worth more. Anyway, he would not have sold it for less. But the implication was clear. The price was to be forty pounds. It was for that sum that he had signed the receipt which Mr. Swadson had scrawled. He would tell his friends that he had bought the car for that price. He might tell his wife the same thing. But John did not think that he had done it in that way lest he might appear a mug to her. It was so that twenty pounds of the price might be his without restriction or record in whatever difficulty he might be placed. And he did not like the idea.

During the last few days he had done several things which would be adversely criticized if they should be subsequently exposed. Matters which he must avoid mentioning in the public examination which he now regarded as inevitable. One or two which he knew to be definitely illegal. But he had thought these to be right. He might have done them even though he had known that exposure and penalty would fall on himself, had he also known that they could not be upset.

But they hat not been quite of that kind. Without analysing the difference he disliked the way in which that twenty pounds had come into his hands.

It happened that Chester was with him that night.

He had been on some journalistic visit to the north, and stopped on the way back. He would be glad to have a few hours of Chester's company. He would be sympathetic, but not tragic. You could trust Chester not to look at anything in the conventional way.

He told Chester this tale, almost as soon as he got back to the house. Chester said Swadson wasn't such a bad sort. After a pause, he said: "Any tradesmen to pay?" No, it appeared that they had been brought close up to date.

The question reminded his father-in-law that he owed Chester twenty-three pounds. Had owed it ever since there had been a settlement of the costs incurred in Nina's defence. Chester had told him not to vex himself about that. He didn't want it at the time. He had had some lucky sales with his fiction. "Utter tripe," he had said, "but it goes better than it did. I'll ask fast enough if I get short." So it had been left. It might be repaid now, or its chance was not good. Chester shook his head. "I'm doing well enough now." Then he altered his mind. He took the notes, and pushed them into his pocket-book. He said, "that's the best address for those. What about the balance? I could do with a good pen of Hamburg's. Frida's been worrying me to patch up that other pen at the bottom of the garden, and have a few more fowl."

John Oakley was quite willing for that, though he didn't think that three pounds would go far in the purchase of such fowl as his. Chester differed. "You've got a wrong idea of the value of those birds. There aren't many hens that are worth more than half-a-crown if you boil them down."

His father-in-law differed about that. He did not want them boiled down. He could not conscientiously value them at no higher than two-and-sixpence each. But he finally agreed that Chester should take possession of a breeding-pen of six of his best birds which he had separately shut up, as against the three pounds he owed. When Chester left next morning he had them put on the train with him.

## CHAPTER THIRTY-FIVE

JOHN OAKLEY called on the Official Receiver, which (unless under compulsion) is an unusual proceeding. He faced a wide and highly-polished mahogany counter, and was informed by a half-grown youth that that gentleman was engaged. Would somebody else do?

The boy was new to the office. He did not know how to distinguish callers as he would later. And this one might have puzzled an experienced clerk. But he knew that there were two standards of reception for the two classes of the population who were their most frequent visitors. He asked doubtfully: "Are you a solicitor or a debtor?"

John Oakley controlled an inclination to turn away. He said: "I'm not a solicitor."

During the conversation, several clerks had been working at the high desks in the room. Now one of them looked up, and said: "Better tell Mr. Draper."

The boy went, and returned. He said: "Come this way, sir," and led out through the door by which Mr. Oakley had entered, and across the passage to another office where a young man of a quiet and pleasant aspect was working alone.

He rose and shook hands, indicating a chair, saying: "I suppose you have called to see me about the Hudson matter?"

Mr. Oakley said he had not. Mr. Draper apologized. He had thought his visitor to be Mr. Keatley, of Cross & Keatley.

Mr. Oakley explained why he had called. There was a slight—a very slight—change in Mr. Draper's manner. But he approved Mr. Oakley's action. It would be better if it were more general. If those in difficulties would face the position with the first knowledge of insolvency, and while there were still substantial assets to be realized. That was partly true, although realized is little more than a euphonious word. Slaughtered or destroyed would often be more appropriate, though it may sometimes be a necessary destruction. But we must not expect the impossible. The department of the Board of Trade over which Official Receivers preside is an abattoir, not a hospital. Official Givers are unknown. To the present barbarism of commercial ethics the idea would be foolish. An expert to whom the heads of a business in difficulty might appeal, and who could order at least a temporary moratorium, would save millions of waste and destruction, arresting the first downward step on the slippery path of difficult finance and failing credit, at the sight of which the vultures swoop to the feast. But that time is not yet. The accountancy profession is doing something toward it, and may do more if it should prove great enough for its possible destiny.

Mr. Draper approved Mr. Oakley's attitude, but he explained that there were formalities to be observed. The O.R. could do nothing without the authority of a Registrar of the High Court. Mr. Oakley must present a Petition in Bankruptcy. Incidentally, he must find ten pounds. The Law's benevolent intervention in these commercial adjustments is not given away.

He assumed that Mr. Oakley had a solicitor. Mills and Booth? A good firm. Better go to them. Mr. Oakley wished to avoid needless expense. Mr. Draper almost asked why. Anyway, that wasn't needless, it was absolutely necessary. There could be no bankruptcy for Mr. Oakley unless he could find ten pounds. Mr. Tranter, of Mills and Booth, would (quite reasonably) call it fifteen.

Mr. Draper inquired whether there were any special urgency to protect the assets. "Sheriff in?" he inquired laconically. He most often was. Or the High Bailiff? Or the Landlord? Or the Rates? Or a plurality of these visitors?

Mr. Oakley said they were not.

"Oh, well, Tranter'll know what to do." Mr. Draper held out a hand that had hesitated for a second. The position was a little unusual. But he was gentleman by instinct, and a butcher's assistant by his ability to pass civil service examinations. Also, he was a very busy man. He must get on with his work. There were three meetings of creditors that afternoon—at two of which he would be required to preside.

As Mr. Oakley made for the door, a small fussy man bustled in, whom Mr. Draper addressed with a respectful "sir". He explained the position briefly. The O.R. fussed approval, asked if the figures were ready in the Woodward case, and bustled out without waiting for a reply.

In explaining the position to his chief, Mr. Draper realized it imaginatively as he had not done till that moment. People became bankrupt continually. It was part of his routine duty to examine the claims which were almost always made for the furniture by wives and sisters, fathers and children, under such circumstances, and to decide whether it would be legally possible to smash their homes. In this work he was scrupulously fair, even lenient in a cold-blooded official way. But the most sensitive butcher cannot wipe his eyes for every throat that he cuts, especially on a busy day. And the commercial wreckage that drifted continually before his view was not always of an attractive kind...

But he remembered that Mr. Oakley had had a good name in Hunnerton for many years. He knew (how should anyone know better?) how difficult business conditions had been in the last two years. And it was Winterton's failure that had done this. And Mr. Oakley was facing the position in an unusually straightforward way. There was a note of human sympathy in his voice as he said good afternoon for the second time.

## CHAPTER THIRTY-SIX

THE next morning Mr. Oakley found the ten pounds. With due formality, without haste and without delay, a Receiving Order was made against him, and he was Adjudicated Bankrupt on his own Petition.

He faced the position with courage and energy, accepting without haggling the allowance which was offered to him that he should continue to manage the business, till the orders on hand had been completed, or, at least, till the meeting of creditors should appoint their own trustee, taking the direction out of the Official Receiver's hands, in which case that gentleman's remaining duty would be to bait the debtor in a routine way, at the creditors' expense. Of course, if any serious irregularity were discovered in the course of that bait-ing, the dull routine might be transformed into a slow-moving but no less sinister menace. Otherwise, the investigations were rather boring to all except the man whose depleted resources actually paid for the show.

Mr. Sanders was dismissed at once.

I have said that the bankrupt faced the position with courage and energy. So he did; taking on Sanders's work was well as his own, and being hampered by the narrow limits of the authority which was left in his hands, and the necessity of preparing elaborate and intricate accounts at which no one but the routine examiner would ever look. But though he faced the position bravely enough, he walked with the feeling that he was a disgraced and tainted man.

As a fact, he was no more disgraced than is a swimmer who is caught in some unexpected current, against which no human strength could prevail. Being so caught, he had struggled hard and well. From the moment when he had put down the plant which the War Office has asked him to do, his business had been a doomed thing.

When the War came, the Government of that day took an action which confiscated half the real property of the country, or, rather, which transferred it into the hands of the trading community. It is of the nature of a paper currency that it can adjust the relative wealth of different sections of the population in ways which they are powerless to resist or avoid. If it be doubled, its purchasing power is halved. A mortgage worth £800 yesterday is worth £400 today, though its arithmetic is the same. Had the paper currency been reduced in the same proportion, the £400 would be £1,600.

From this and other causes when the War came, the manufacturer found himself suddenly in a condition of bewildering prosperity. There was a man in the Midlands who papered his bedroom with Treasury notes. That is a fact, not a tale.

As the years passed, there were gradual adjustments. That which had been hard at first had become easier. The original inflation may have been expedient, may even have been a necessary form of taxation of the non-productive elements of the community, but, right or wrong, having been done, it could not be undone ten or fifteen years afterwards without new iniquities resulting; and the plea of necessity was no longer possible.

But the English Government thought differently. It struck straight and hard. By reducing the paper currency, it doubled the real burden of the national debt. It doubled the wealth of the holders of property or mortgages. It paralysed agriculture. It swept the means of finance out of the control of those who directed the industrial output. Though democratic governments have seldom in the world's history been famous for justice or honour, they have usually been faithful to the shrine of expediency. But even if expediency be the only god, we may doubt whether it was a very wise thing to do.

An industrial community which was already misdirecting a large part of its energy to the pursuit of perpetual motion staggered at the blow. It understood what had happened no better than a fish which gasps at the bottom of a drained pond. But with the stubborn obstinacy of the English character, it set to work to overcome the difficulties that had been laid upon it.

But, to many individual circumstances, that was an impossible thing.

John Oakley's business before the War had been well-established, well-managed, and of a satisfactory prosperity. Under War Office urgency, he had added much additional machinery. He had been encouraged to extend his works; to incur capital expenditure in an inflated currency. His profits before the War had been no more than a comfortable income, and under the grotesque incidence of the levying of Excess Profits Duty, he was forbidden to make a more substantial profit.

The imposition of Excess Profit Duty had been first intended to persuade the Trade Unions that manufacturers would not be allowed to become rich. It was imposed by a government which thought the War would be over in six months. It pledged itself (but what has such a pledge ever been worth?) that it should not be imposed for a longer period. Its actual effect was to make the manufacturer who had been rich before the War richer beyond his wildest dreams. The manufacturer who had made losses in the pre-War years had a simple choice. He could falsify his returns, or he could face an impossible burden of taxation which would still be unpaid when the War ceased, and which he would afterwards be invited to pay twice over in the adjusted currency of the later years.

When a man who is doubling his output, enlarging his premises, and laying down new plant, with no more than his original capital and his present profits from which to do all these things, is invited to pay over sixty or eighty percent of those profits in cash, there is only one possible reply. It cannot be done. The larger the profits are, the more impossible it may become.

John Oakley's accounts were accurately rendered. His E.P.D. remained unpaid. No one troubled him about that while the War lasted. Particularly not when he was himself at the Front. (But that was not for long.) It was five years after the Armistice when he signed the last cheque in settlement of that imposition. At that time his works were twice as large as they had been before the War. His plant was twice as great. For much of it he had to seek new uses in trades which he did not profess to know, and when a hundred others similarly situated had been on the same quest. Taxation was oppressively heavy. Rates, doubled in the amount of the levy, and doubled again for the enlargement of his premises, were literally four times what they had been originally. And most of his capital was gone. Orders became increasingly difficult to obtain, prices were lower, bad debts increasingly numerous. Old customers, such as Winterton's, would make payments that scarcely equalled their purchases, so that credits grew. Facing such conditions, the wonder was not that John Oakley's line of battle broke, but that it had endured so long.

## CHAPTER THIRTY-SEVEN

ELSIE walked in, unannounced.

She found Frida in the nursery with the two babies.

"Well," she said, "I've come. I couldn't stand it there." As a fact, she had had little to stand. As to her father's failure, few even knew. None cared. She may have imagined sympathies or slights that were not meant. She may have come home because she thought it the thing to do. But she was not the one to put it that way. Against hostile circumstances, they closed their ranks, with few words, as English families do.

She kissed her sister in a casual way. She threw off her hat. "I suppose," she said, "there'll be something to do?"

"Yes. There's the front step."

"Meaning Ada's gone?"

"Yes. She left last week."

"Mrs. Case here?"

"Yes, she's staying on till the sale. She's doing all she can, but she can't scrub. There's some trouble with her knee."

"How's Joyce going on?"

"She's much better than she was. She'll be down tomorrow. She's wanted to come down since Sunday, but we've tried to keep her up. She'll have to know when she comes down."

"You mean she doesn't know yet?"

"No. Alwyn didn't like telling her till she got better, and then you know she got worse instead."

"Well, she ought to have been told, more or less. It wouldn't have done any harm. How's Father?"

"He's all right if he's left alone. He'll be glad you've come."

"I suppose you ought to be going back?"

"I shall stay till the sale. Mrs. Potter seems to be managing very well."

"Everything being sold?"

"No. Alwyn's able to claim a good deal. They've allowed that. And Chester's been coming up and down, and he's taken a good many of Mother's things. I did what I could till they took the inventory." Frida thought the inventory had been taken too soon. She added: "Father doesn't know all that Chester's taken. It seemed to worry him." She smiled a little at the childish follies of men.

"What about my pictures? I'm not going to let them take them."

"They're not trying. I've locked all your personal things in the clothes-closet in the end room. I told the man that took the inventory what they were, and he said: 'Right you are, ma'am. They wouldn't fetch five shillin', whether or not,' and he didn't put them down."

"Five shillings! Why, the—"

"I expect it was the proper thing to say. Oh, and Swadson's got the black cow."

"You mean he's bought it?"

"No. It's on a visit. It's rather a funny tale. They wouldn't take Father's word for what livestock there was; they said they'd better see for themselves. So Father told them he'd leave it to them. You know how the black cow's always finding a fresh place to break through the hedge into Swadson's field. They say the grass is better on that side. Tommy found it had got through earlier. Tommy was going to fetch it back, but Mr. Swadson was in the field and he told him it would do very well where it was. After that the man came, and Tommy took him round. Tommy says that the man couldn't get the pigeons right, and when he told him he was putting too many down, he told him that he could see for himself, and he didn't want so much of his lip. He says he tried to tell him about the black cow after that, and he wouldn't listen.

"I don't suppose he tried very hard. Why should he? But there was something of the sort. Mrs. Case overheard."

"Tommy must be a sharp boy."

"He's a good boy. He worships Joyce. He'd do anything for her. Joyce made a pet of the black cow."

"I suppose Swadson'll let us have it back?"

"Oh, yes. He's the sort you could trust better than if you'd got a receipt. It's just sport to him. I spoke to him over the hedge, and he said the milk she's giving more than pays for her keep. I said I could understand that better if he wasn't sending us in about three gallons a day. He said she gave more than that. I said she must be a changed cow if she did. And he said it must be the change of grass."

"Does Father know?"

"Not a word. He never goes down the fields now. He can't be responsible, if he doesn't know."

"She is rather a dear, if she has come at the wrong time." The change of subject was due to Joyce's baby, roused from sleep by the voices, and now on Elsie's lap.

"You'd better not say that where Joyce can hear. She thinks that baby's the world, and the rest's leavings. She'd be quite likely to kill you if she heard you say it was one too many."

"She doesn't love me overmuch now," Elsie said carelessly. "It's a bit on the small side. isn't it? I suppose I can say that."

"Not when Joyce is about. I tell lies twice a day about her catching up John, and I'm in a hole now that I don't know how to get out of. Chester promised to get me a pair a scales that weigh wrong. He says most grocers would have a spare set. But she's really been coming on well for the last week. It was only the trouble about the food."

"What's her name?"

"It's to be Frida, if it's a saint's name, about which we're not sure. If it isn't, they'll have to add Mary, or Cecilia, or something worse. Joyce says she's got to have a saint's name. It's a law of the Church."

"They seem to have plenty of laws in her Church. I hope they've got one that'll make her come up smiling when she hears of the smash. I can't see Joyce doing the front step."

Frida didn't say anything to that. There was incongruity in the idea. It would be Joyce's nature to rely upon her eyelashes rather than upon her hands. For her baby's sake—yes, she might even do that. But for Alwyn's, Frida was less sure. Joyce would be more likely to expect him to clean steps for her. But did the question arise?

She said: "I don't think she'll have much need to worry. She's got £200 a year coming to her; and Alwyn's doing well enough. Father owed him a good deal, and there's some trouble over a bill that was discounted at his bank, and that won't be met now, but he says he'll get over that. They'll have to leave here, of course. The bank thinks they've got a purchaser for the house. But they'd have to do that, anyway. They couldn't well stay after the sale, and that's ten days from now."

"And Joyce doesn't know yet? How can they find anywhere where to go in the time?"

"Alwyn's fixing that up. He didn't want Joyce worried till he could tell her it was all fixed up."

"That's silly."

"So I said. But he ought to know Joyce better than we do."

"You forget he married her. The evidence is the other way. But there's one safe bet—if she doesn't like it, it won't last many hours. Where does he propose to go?"

"London. Aunt Muriel's offered him one of her flats that's been empty since Christmas."

"Oh, well—we shall see. What's Father doing now?"

"He's managing the business, but that ends on Saturday. Someone's bought it all as it stands, except the premises. They're taking over this week, and moving the stock to their own works. Father says it's a wretched price, but an auction might have been worse."

"What's he going to do after that?"

"There's nothing settled, but he may take over some of Alwyn's travelling for Collett Hayward's. They're seeing Mr. Hayward about it together tomorrow."

"Poor Father! Still, I don't know. But I'm not doing much good sitting here. She's gone off now. I'll put her down, and do something more active, if you'll tell me what.... Chester coming this afternoon? That's good news. Any time you get tired of married life, you'll know where to pass him on. What's he smuggling away this time?"

## CHAPTER THIRTY-EIGHT

ELSIE, had she been introspective, might have been surprised to observe how far she was from being acutely miserable. But she was unlikely to occupy her mind with such considerations while her health continued at its present robust level, and there were so many exterior interests to engage her thoughts.

She contrived to read the *Daily Dispatch* while she assisted preparations for the evening meal, and a paragraph concerning the fate of a woman whose life might have been saved by blood transfusion had the arteries of her husband, who volunteered a supply, possessed a liquid of the right vintage, caused her to wander into speculations as to whether racial ancestry might not be finally demonstrated by variety of blood, whether children always had that of the mother, and further ones which we need not follow, such as the possible establishment of castes, by this test, on an impregnable basis.

Even the ancient custom of tracing descent through the mother might be re-established.

She mentioned this idea to Frida, who received it with little comment. She was not uninterested. She might even joke about it to Chester at a leisured time, which meant when they were alone together and when she was her ultimate self, but she knew that if you let the milk boil over while you talk about blood transfusion (which is not your job) you are a proved fool.

Elsie decided that she would suggest the idea to Chester when he arrived. One idea leads to another, and you talk all supper-time, while you almost forget to eat, which may be more important than whether you live in Birstall House, or back of 7a Springfield Gardens.

But when she put the idea to Chester he did not show any disposition to develop it in unexpected ways, as he would be likely to do. He did suggest one or two interesting possibilities, such as might occur to anyone, but it was in the tone of one who completes a paragraph. He had something else on his mind.

He turned to Frida to say: "There was a rather funny development about Basil's affairs yesterday. I don't know that it's important, but it's certainly queer.

"A man came to see me when I was at the Shoe Lane office, and brought some papers and a passbook. He said he bought the large desk at Basil's office, when it was sold up, and gave it to his managing clerk—he's a stock-broker. This clerk had been going abroad on some business, and had cleared out his desk before handing it over to his successor. He'd pulled out the drawers to dust it in a thorough way, and found these papers fallen down at the back, as papers often do."

Chester paused at this point. He had gained the attention of the table. Papers in a desk may mean money. A passbook is suggestive of the same thing. It was remembered that there had always been an impression that Basil Lawson was better off than had been proved at his death. It was a moment when a discovered fortune would be a very opportune thing. Almost too good to be—false.

"I thought at first that I was in for a good thing. There were share-certificates for about £1,500. Face value. But he put me right about those. He said that they were shares that weren't worth claiming, even if they were Basil's property. They were only paid up to 10/-, and there's a call on them now that no one wants to pay. I'd better give them a miss. They weren't in Basil's name. They appeared to belong to someone named Dobson—Edward Dobson—at an address in Nottingham. Of course, there was no proof in that that they weren't Basil's. He might have bought shares through a nominee. But the passbook was Dobson's too. I thought at first that that settled the whole thing. I didn't know how long Basil had had the desk. It must have belonged to this Dobson before then, and the things were nothing to do with me.

"The stockbroker said he'd thought the same at first, but, he said, look at the date. And that did make me sit up. The passbook was made up to about a week before Basil was killed."

Alwyn said: "Was there anything in it? That seems to be rather important."

"There was about £37 to credit. Of course, it may have been drawn out afterwards."

"Was there a large turnover?" Mr. Oakley asked. "If it looked like a business account "

"Not in the least. But I've got it here. You can see what it is."

It passed round the table. It contained a record of the transactions of two months only, the account having been brought forward from an earlier book. From the commencing figures it appeared that the turnover was about £600 a year. just a little private account.

"No," Chester went on, "if it looked like another business, I wouldn't touch it with gloves. I've had enough of the one. And the shares seem to me to be of the same kind. I don't want any more fortunes of Basil Lawson's variety. Anyway, it doesn't seem to be anything to do with us. But I'm just about sufficiently curious to go to Nottingham to find out, if I've nothing better to do."

He put the passbook back in his pocket, and the subject dropped. For those whose home was being sold up next week, it was a prospect of fortune too visionary for the satisfaction of the most sanguine mind.

## CHAPTER THIRTY-NINE

FOR successful and happy marriage, there are three vital necessities, besides the obvious one of being able to fulfil its fundamental purpose. They do not include godliness (which may bring a sword rather than peace) nor cleanliness (which is desirable, but not necessary). They are courage, loyalty, and a sense of humour.

To these three, there is nothing that may not be added; without any of them, even the two that remain may prove indifferent armour.

Joyce was of a natural loyalty, an untested courage, and with a sense of humour which was not negligible, but which had its limits and its defects.

She took the news of her father-in-law's bankruptcy well, and yet in a very difficult way. She showed no lack of courage, no lack of sympathy. She was anxious to help. But she stubbornly declined to admit the extent of the financial disaster of which she was told. Birstall House must not be given up. Emphatically, its furniture must not be sold. It would be too great a shame. She had grown to love it herself, which she appeared to consider a fact of decisive importance. She expressed a flattering but embarrassing confidence in both father and husband. She was sure that they had sufficient ability, if they had sufficient determination, to avert the catastrophe. She said this to Alwyn, who replied that he was doing all that he could. He went into details of business efforts and successes, to which he felt that she did not give the closest attention. She said it to Frida, who was discouraging in her replies. She said it to Elsie, who was rude.

Beyond that, she seemed to feel most keenly the need of someone to hate. There must be a villain of the piece. She even attempted to cast Sanders for that part, on the doubtful suggestion that he had once been seen to leave the works before the end of the day. She was sure that there was no fault in the men of her own house. They had done wonders. Unfortunately for their own peace, she relied upon them to do wonders again.

Besides, there was her uncle. She said he had plenty of money, and at such a need it could not be handed over too soon. Also, he had hers. She would write to him at once. If necessary, she would go. She was strong enough for that.

But she found that she was not as strong as she wished to be. She was of a nature that depends upon happiness for its health. The nervous friction with the nurse, and her baffled efforts to feed the child, coming when they did, had left her without the strength which she thought to have. Weakness had its share in her reactions now. That is fair to observe.

The letter to her uncle was a pencilled thing, rather incoherent in places, and she was exhausted when it was done. For three days there was no reply. Then she wired. It was a wire of about seventy words, and that was after Frida's help had reduced it to about half its original length. A reply came the next day.

Mr. Corchester wrote in some detail, and with an emphasis which equalled her own. He had no money to send. He was inexplicably, damnably (she must excuse the word) embarrassed himself. He mentioned the state of agriculture, taxation, the death duties, the Government, and the state of agriculture again. He also mentioned a bank-manager of regrettably plebeian birth. That brought him to his point that Joyce should not so hurriedly have married a tradesman's son. He had always feared how it would turn out. As to her own money, he had no right to send it to her (beyond the quarterly fifty) if he would, till she was twenty-five, and he would not if he could. Did she think he would allow her to lose it in that damned business at Hunnerton (she must excuse the word)? He was thankful that it was tied up at it was. Hadn't he once told her that his father's cousin lost £15,000 in some Spanish mines? But there would always be a welcome for her at Treswick. Probably she had better come at once. He enclosed five pounds.

Joyce read this letter with tears. Tears of anger as well as of disappointment. She had meant to help. Vanity was hurt, as were more generous instincts. She had been sure that money would come quickly after that wire. She was vague as to amount, but she had made it clear that she wanted a large sum. Enough to stop the sale. And when the letter came the sale was only two days away. Five pounds!

With the suddenness which had been one of her most bewildering characteristics from childhood, her mind changed. She not only reconciled herself to the sale, she began to regard it as an almost pleasantly exciting thing. She bestirred herself also to increased activities. She had already made things easier for everyone by getting Ada back. She said she would pay for her herself. It would be so much cheaper than for anyone to fall ill from overwork. You can see that. So Elsie did not clean the front step. Not yet, anyway. That she was grateful to Joyce is more than it would be safe to say.

Joyce said she would begin to bath baby herself. She did this with Frida's help. It took about twice as long as if Frida had done it alone. There were intervals for baby-worship. There was much needless talk. But if you think Joyce was a fool you are miles out. She would bath baby tomorrow (if she must) and would make no omission and no mistake in that elaborate ritual. If babies choose their own parents (which we must regard as a possible rather than a probable supposition), the third Frida had shown exceptionally good judgement.

Regarding her baby during the ceremony hardened another resolution in Joyce's mind. Uncle had got to behave differently from that. She was not interested in death duties, or the state of agriculture. It was her uncle's conduct which concerned her, and she concentrated upon its reformation. It had been a rule of her life never to send a letter if a wire would do. Now she wrote one which she did not invite Frida to edit. If Ada said that she had paid nearly ten shillings for its despatch, and there was some natural comment on

Joyce's extravagance at a time when her father-in-law was walking into Hunnerton (on the fine days) to save the bus-fares, it did not come to her knowledge; and had it done so, she would have only said that it seemed a silly thing for him to do. Also, the time would have been short for the post, and the laugh was hers when there came a registered letter on the morning of the sale, and, when Alwyn came to say that she really must get up now, there were five ten-pound notes lying on the bed.

It is true that it was no more than a forestalling of her next quarter's allowance that her importunity had secured. But it was today it was wanted, and today it was here. Alwyn could make plenty of money for her future needs. What are men for?

When she got down to breakfast the others had finished, and were discussing the catalogue, and the things for which they could afford to bid. Elsie and her father had taken some unfurnished rooms in Hunnerton, and the few available pounds were to be used for the retention of such things as would be most useful there. They spoke of the suite in the lounge, which would not be too large (at least, they didn't want to think that it would be too large) for the new room. But it was unlikely that they could manage that. How much would it fetch? Chester thought £20. The dealers would go that far. If a private buyer meant to have it, it might be twice as much. Alwyn was more sanguine. It might go for £12. Neither of them was near the truth.

Elsie wanted to do the bidding. She knew what she wanted— what it would be most vital to have. She would watch how the money went. So it was agreed.

It cannot be said that Elsie bought very well. She bid too soon, and she repeated her bids too quickly. She was new to the game. She was the kind of buyer that an auctioneer sees in his dreams.

Meeting in the door of the crowded lounge, Joyce asked: "You're going to buy the suite?" Elsie shook her head. The pencilled figures on the margins of the catalogue mounted in a ghastly way. There were still the kitchen things to be got. They were a more urgent necessity.

The auctioneer paused a moment when he came to the suite to draw attention to its quality and preservation. It was the kind of lot for which the trade should give him a good price.

"Now, ladies and gentlemen, give it a start. Anywhere you like. It's not where we start that matters, it's where we stop." The crowd laughed slightly at the joke that he was known to make about three times a week. Twenty pounds to start? Ten pounds? Five pounds? Anywhere you like, so that we get on."

"*Yes, I want that.*" It was an urgent appeal rather than a bid, with the underlying plaintiveness that came so easily into Joyce's voice when she pleaded for what she would. It silenced the room. Everyone turned to look.

"Five guineas bid. Now, gentlemen, get on please." But no one spoke. In the end, the auctioneer let it go, as he must. There are no reserves at the sale of a bankrupt's goods. "Well, gentlemen, I'm in your hands. You know it's no money for this lot."

"Let the lady have it, and get on," a burly dealer, who was one of his best customers, called from the back of the room. The hammer fell. "Name, please?" The suite was hers.

Elsie kissed her later for that. You will agree (if you are a woman) that it was a rather generous thing for Elsie to do.

## CHAPTER FORTY

THE flat that Aunt Muriel let to Alwyn for £110 a year, making some merit of the fact that it had previously fetched £130 (but it had been empty since Christmas—flats were not letting in London as they had done a few years earlier), was about three minutes' walk from Gloucester Road Station. It had two living-rooms, two bed-rooms, and a small kitchen. It was on the first floor, and self-contained. Aunt Muriel had a similar flat for her own use on the floor above. It might have been a better proposition if she had been farther away.

Joyce thought the rooms horribly small after the more spacious and better-proportioned ones to which she had been accustomed at Birstall House. But she took the change of fortune with a coura-geous gaiety. She made no objection to Alwyn's choice. She had not Frida's passion for the green spaces of the open country. That which she had come to love at Birstall must first be missed before she would know the value of what she left. She knew nothing of Aunt Muriel. She was in a mood to accept what Alwyn had arranged.

As a fact, she liked the excitement of change. She liked to su-perintend the transfer of the furniture, and its settlement in the new home. It was the first home she had really made. The first that was *hers*. She was happy in that thought, and in the buying of new things.

For some new things there must be, and Alwyn was slow to say how difficult it was to meet all her demands. He felt it hard to re-fuse. She had given up so much. She had been so loyal, so brave. Even Elsie owned that Joyce had faced the position well.

There had been the episode on the train. Alwyn, Chester, and Joyce had got into the London express at Hunnerton, as Joyce came south to her new home. As the train passed the back of the empty premises which had once been John Oakley's, a man at the farther end of the compartment pointed them out to a companion with a jocularly contemptuous reference to their bankrupt owner.

Chester and Alwyn might have passed it in silence had it gone no farther, but Joyce forgot her natural nervousness in a sudden intensity of anger that declined to be placated by the awkward attempt at apology which was offered when she disclosed her identity. When they came to Covington the men changed to another compartment. There was no doubt of Joyce's loyalty to the family which she had entered.

It was agreed that she was not yet strong enough to have the baby at night. A young woman, Myra Cotrill, with all the credentials and some of the qualifications of a nurse, was installed in the second bedroom. A cook was engaged to come in daily. Alwyn was to discover that the cost of a flat and a cottage such as that of which Frida had made a home may not be greatly different, though there is so wide a disparity in what they give. Neither was Joyce of a steadily economical habit. There were efforts, earnest and brief, and extremely uncomfortable in some of their minor details. There was a quick realization that they were not worthwhile. Alwyn saw that. Joyce saw it very clearly indeed. The best way was to kiss Alwyn and tell him how sure she was that he would he clever enough to supply her needs. He was very fortunate to have such a wife, and a special effort should naturally follow. They both saw that.

On the whole, things started well enough, and Joyce was of a decided happiness till the afternoon when Aunt Muriel (who had been having a rather prolonged holiday in Switzerland) called to be sure that her new tenants were comfortable, and to make the acquaintance of Alwyn's wife.

Muriel Coates was a kindly, good-natured, self-indulgent woman of about fifty, a half-sister of Alwyn's mother. She had strong "modernist" opinions, as destitute of originality as were the arguments that supported them. She believed honestly that all Victorian families had consisted of at least twelve children, the mothers of whom had died at the birth of the fourth, if not earlier. She believed with equal honesty that Nature had made English women so deplorably that they have a natural physical tendency to produce such families, with an inevitable penalty of debility, disease, and premature dissolution as its reward. She did not require any facts or reasons to support these improbabilities, having found confident assertion a satisfactory substitute. In their expression she had as much originality as a mirror, and as much variety as a gramophone record.

It is difficult to generalize with accuracy in comparing or contrasting women and men, and it may be allowed that there are many men of no higher intellectual level than Miss Muriel Coates. It is more difficult to imagine such a man spending his time in the active propaganda of the idea which he has adopted. It is impossible to imagine that he would be influential among his fellows.

Miss Coates had found popularity for many years as an advocate of "birth control", which she represented as in some way essential to something else of which she spoke with an equal vagueness as the emancipation of women. She repeated the stock arguments of the advocates of this new gospel in all their crudity, and was assisted by all the weakness, selfishness, and credulity of the women to whom she spoke. She was assisted also by the economic hardship of the post-War years which had failed to reach their expected prosperity by the policy of developing their pleasures and letting their necessities take their chance.

Do we labour in a sea of financial difficulty? Let us jettison some of the cargo. Should not the useless troublesome children be the first to go?

Are the children really no part of a nation's wealth? We need not answer this question with an awkward directness. We can talk of the "rights" of a child to go to a more expensive school than do those in the next street; of the "rights" of the mother to "have a good time". We need not mention duty, or any of the old-fashioned unpleasant ideas on which the strength of the nation grew.

We can talk of the disadvantages of the slum-reared child. It is obviously harder to clear away the slums than the children that infest them. (Infest is a good word.)

We can talk with a less base appeal of the overworked life of the unassisted mother of a large family, whose elder children we have kept at school so that they cannot give her the willing help that they once did. Let them buy the rather doubtful (for most of them) class-room advantages with their brothers' and sisters' lives. We do not mention the half-million young female idlers now drawing doles, who might be giving the needed help.

We can't help people sometimes asking if emigration would not be a better solution, but we can answer that there are no picture-houses in Australian wilds. A baby on her lap is a poor substitute to offer a woman who might sit with an artificially-barren womb, gazing at a Hollywood film. Besides, we are told that "birth control" is practised in Australia as much as here, if not more. We are not clear what that proves (if anything), but it's a quite useful reply.

Perhaps, if we did think what it means....

But if we turn our eyes to the Southern Continent, we may observe that birth restriction seems insufficient to produce prosperity, even in a new land.

## CHAPTER FORTY-ONE

IT was a bright July afternoon when Miss Coates called, and was received by Joyce with a little inward reluctance, due to the fact that it was Myra's afternoon out, and the cook was always off duty from three to five-thirty, during which time she went to her own home in the Earl's Court Road.

The third Frida was asleep at the time, but it was a peace that might be broken at any second, and Joyce would have preferred that this call should have been on another day. No, she said, Alwyn would not be in till evening. They were very comfortable in the flat. The little room looked its best that afternoon. The sun came through the open window. The window-boxes were bright with flowers.

Aunt Muriel looked round with audible approval at the furnishing of the room. She said it contrasted with that of the previous tenant.

Joyce was pleased at that. Would her visitor excuse her a moment? She went to the kitchen to put a match under the kettle, and to add a second cup to the tray which was already laid. When she came back Miss Coates remarked that she had seen some of the furniture at Birstall House. Was not the table the one that had stood against the wall in the breakfast-room? At least, it had been there years ago. She had not (she said) been asked much to Birstall House since "poor Frida" died.

"Yes," Joyce said, "we had to sell the other table. It would have been too large for this room."

"Yes, I suppose almost everything went. It did seem such dreadful news. I didn't think poor John would have got everything into a mess like that. And you just married, too! I couldn't help thinking Alwyn would have been wiser to wait. I always say it isn't fair to the girl. A man shouldn't marry till he's quite sure. You do hear such dreadful things."

Joyce's answer hesitated. There was nothing here that she could specifically resent. It occurred to her to say that Alwyn's business had always been separate from that of his father, but put in that way it sounded like a reflection on her father-in-law, which she would not make.

She said only: "Alwyn's doing quite well."

"How fortunate! He always was a dear boy. And I hear there's a baby, too. My dear, what a risk you took! But, of course, you'll be more careful now. And you so young, too. I often say that if men knew what it meant they'd be more considerate than they are. Though I don't know, even then. My dear, I don't think any woman ought to be *asked* to take such a risk before she's twenty-five *at the least*. They're too young to understand all it means. I always say if a man really cared for a girl he wouldn't *allow* her to risk her life in such ways. He'd exercise more self-control. And, of course, there's no excuse now, in these enlightened days."

"I don't think," Joyce said, "I quite understand. I'll see if the kettle's boiling." She went out.

Aunt Muriel had time to think. She believed herself to be as tactful as she knew herself to be wise. She knew that young wives are sometimes absurdly touchy at any remark which appears to reflect upon their husbands. Probably Joyce had realized how inconsiderate Alwyn had been, but she would not like to hear it said, even by his own aunt. She would speak plainly to him. He must have *known* how precarious poor John's position had become. It was criminal to have married at all. But the poor girl must be talked to in a more tactful way.

"My dear," she said, when Joyce came back with the tea-tray in her hand, "you mustn't mind anything that an old woman says, and one that's known the dear boy since he was born."

"But you're not an old woman," Joyce said, lying pleasantly. Is fifty old? That depends on our own age. It is old to nineteen, let us dress it as we may. "You're not old at all."

Miss Coates was pleased at that. It was a compliment coming from Joyce's youth, and in Joyce's caressing voice. She began to like Alwyn's wife better than she had done at first sight. Joyce had a pleasant sense of having said the right thing in the right way.

In an atmosphere of concord Miss Coates went on: "Oh, yes, my dear, I am. No, no sugar, please. I'm old enough to have seen how the world goes, and the dreadful risk young people take when they've got no one to advise them. I'm not blaming dear Alwyn. I don't suppose John said a *word*. And your own mother dead, too. But you must be firm now, for your child's sake, as well as your own. I should tell him not for three or four years *at the least*. You'll need all your strength to look after the one you've got."

If we stop at that point, it is not because Miss Coates did the same. It is because she went on with a fluency which the infant Frida did not interrupt for nearly half an hour, and when that happened at last, she had said much more than there is any need for recording here.

Joyce had said little, and what she had said was destitute of any certain significance. There had been sudden lightnings once or twice when a word had seemed to reflect on Alwyn, or to make too light of the miracle in the cradle in the next room, but Miss Coates had been quick to recognize the signs of approaching storm, and adroit to divert its course. Joyce had said little, because her mind was puzzled and disturbed by a new thing. She needed time to think. She needed to talk to Alwyn. She was glad when Frida waked, and Aunt Muriel went, without having made the mistake of failing to admire the baby that was already there.

Miss Coates felt that she had done good, where there had appeared to be an unusual need. It was criminal that girls should be allowed to marry so ignorant, and so young.

She did not doubt her power to secure converts to the strange gospel she preached. In fact, she overvalued the influence she had exerted in the last ten industrious years. Such ideas, such arguments, could seldom take root except in the minds of those who already desired to believe them. But she might have fairly claimed that she had direct responsibilities for the fact that four or five English children were unborn, and four or five potential mothers reduced by unnatural practices to an uncertain future fertility.

At this time the physical intimacies on which their happiness, and, to some extent, their physical health, was based, had established an approximate routine, pivoted upon the fact that Joyce liked to be loved in earnest before getting up in the comparative leisure of Sunday mornings. Twice a week was the rule, and if Alwyn would leave her alone till Wednesday night (which it was not always easy to do), it would not be so desperately difficult for them to go quietly to sleep on Saturday with no more than a gripped hand, and avoid the spoiling of the pleasure of the morning hours.

It was Wednesday now, and Alwyn should nurse her before they went to bed, and she would tell him these new ideas that Aunt Muriel said that everyone believed today. She was confused and worried, and a little frightened. It was not easy for her to discredit that which was spoken with confidence, nor to go contrary to anything that "everyone" around her believed or practised. Suppose she…were already pregnant again. She knew it could not be more than a fortnight ago. But it might be so today. And people would think it *strange*. They would not think it a beautiful thing. They would not envy her that she had such babies. They would think it *strange*. That had been Aunt Muriel's word. She did not like to do unusual things, at which people joked or laughed. And they would think Alwyn "inconsiderate". They would say he did not love her as he should. A dreadful thought. And she would grow old all at once, and lose her hair and her teeth, and her figure, even if she didn't die. And it would be all Alwyn's fault, and he couldn't really care, or he wouldn't let her get old like that.

And if she had a baby it would be sickly, and most likely die, because children should be "spaced" for their own sake, as well as that of their parents. And suppose she died, and baby were left for anyone to look after or neglect. (But that shouldn't happen. She would write to Frida tomorrow. She would tell her that she might be pregnant, and how very frightened she was.) Her first duty was to the child she had. Alwyn ought to have told her that. Alwyn hadn't told her *anything*. All he wanted was—what had Aunt Muriel said all men did?—to "gratify his selfish lust". That was it. It would not have occurred to Joyce to put it quite like that, but she saw the point. Alwyn ought to have thought of her first. There was no shadow of doubt about *that*.

## CHAPTER FORTY-TWO

JOYCE had her talk with Alwyn that night. It left them both troubled and puzzled, and each having an inarticulate dissatisfaction with the attitude of the other. Joyce lay unloved that night, and was kissed next morning with an unusual coldness. She was restless and dissatisfied all day, and in the evening she went out, as she had promised to do, to consult a priest of her own Church.

Alwyn had proved to be less than a fount of wisdom on the subject. He had been contemptuous of much that his aunt had said, and on one or two points he had exposed inconsistency or exaggeration. But the question that seemed to Joyce to be of the most vital importance—what was the general practice of their neighbours?—could be no common ground of decision between them.

One thing Miss Coates had made clear. She could not have a second baby in that flat. Such a proceeding would be scandalous to all the more intelligent neighbours. Well, Joyce admitted to herself, it was small. Alwyn said, don't worry till the question arises. If necessary, they could move. Yes, but could they? There had been something almost approaching a quarrel over some expenditure yesterday. She didn't say it wasn't rather needless, but it had been only a matter of three pounds. And he had got cheap tickets for the theatre next Monday. That didn't look like moving to a larger house. And Aunt Muriel had said that the cost of a baby is *dreadful* if you're in town. "Quite out of the question", had been her expression. It was no use Alwyn looking sulky, or saying that they'd got to let things take their chance. They'd got to find a way out. Or at least he had.

But he had made one point that she had been obliged to take seriously. He had said that, though he didn't profess to know much about it, he was sure that her Church taught that what Aunt Muriel advocated was a mortal sin. She had agreed to clear that up, with an inward thought that a priest would tell her some way out of the mess.

So she tried to put this sudden trouble out of her thoughts till evening, but she did not send out for the oak stain which she had decided to use for the renovation of the dining-room floor. She had lost much of her pleasure and interest in the flat now that its limitations had been explained. She didn't mean to move. She didn't mean to have another baby that would make people joke and stare, and ruin her own health, and be no good when it came (beside all the expense), but, all the same, she had lost interest in the flat.

## CHAPTER FORTY-THREE

JOYCE got no help from the priest. She heard something about the curse of Eve, in which she was not greatly interested. If she understood it, she thought it grossly unfair. She was told that childbearing was a sin-bred curse. That having married she must submit herself to her husband. If she refused to fulfil her vows he might be led to sin with other women, and the fault would lie at her door. If she were physically unfit for marriage, she should appeal to her husband's generosity. If she took any illicit steps to prevent pregnancy it would be no less than a mortal sin. She found that Alwyn had been right in that. But the other ideas were new. The idea of Alwyn leaving her for other women was rather dreadful, or would have been so had she been able to take it seriously. But she felt sure that he wouldn't do it. She was shrewd enough to see that he wasn't of that kind. And the idea of her meek submission to an unwelcome brutality stirred her to some inward amusement. She knew (if Alwyn didn't) that the times when she was *really* loved depended about fifty times more upon her inclination than his. She expected him to want her always, and to have her at her own times. But it was a horrible mess, and it would have to be Alwyn's business to find a way out.

She made this clear to Alwyn when she told him what the priest had said, which she did with a frank simplicity, including the picture of himself as a brutal or unfaithful husband. He said little to that. He knew that he walked thin ice. Joyce might see humour in a priest's words, or she might show resentment, or even declare an occasional defiance, but it did not follow that she would like to hear it from others. Besides, he recognized that he had support to his own idea, which was, as he put it straightly to Joyce, that they should let Aunt Muriel "go hang", and be happy once again in a natural way. But Joyce would not agree to that. They argued for hours with an increasing friction. Alwyn thought her unreasonable, as, in fact, she was; for now there was an idea in her mind which she dare not speak. She thought that, if she were obstinate long enough, she could see a way out. Alwyn, developing arguments against Aunt Muriel's contentions with what he felt to be an increasing weight as he dwelt longer upon them, found her unwilling to give them more than a formal hearing. He thought that if she really loved him she would be more willing to listen to the other side of the case. Had he been frank with himself, he would have called her attitude that of a cold-blooded cowardice.

Joyce said: "Men wouldn't go through it themselves. If a man had a baby *once*, he wouldn't have it again as long as he lived, not for *anything*."

"I suppose that's from Aunt Muriel?"

"Well, if it is, it's quite true. You know that."

"I know it's utter rot. If you're willing to listen to nonsense like that...."

"I don't think it's nonsense at all."

Alwyn restrained an inclination to answer impatiently. He had found himself sometimes short of a ready reply to the specious arguments which Joyce had passed on as she had received them. But though he was less acquainted with the terms of the controversy, and at a disadvantage in attempting an instant answer to his aunt's stock arguments, he had the advantage of a logical faculty that she certainly did not possess. Now he restrained himself to answer patiently.

"I doubt whether that's true at all, and, of course, it's impossible to prove it, one way or other. You can't say that men don't take their share (or a bit more) of the pains and dangers that are open to both, but I don't see that it's any argument, if it were true. If men can't bear children, there doesn't seem to be any particular reason why they should have the right qualities for doing so; but if Nature's made it a woman's job, and women haven't got the pluck, or the right-shaped bodies, or whatever they need, she's made a bad break."

"You've got no right to say I hadn't the pluck. Everyone said I was very brave. You know you said it yourself."

There were tears from Joyce at this thought. Alwyn startled Joyce by saying: "Oh, hell!" She couldn't remember hearing him speak like that before. Besides, she was crying, and she was not looking to him for comfort, and he was not offering to comfort her. The last was the most incredible thing.

Alwyn walked irritably across the room. He was farther away now. He said: "Damn Aunt Muriel."

Deep in Joyce's heart there was an echo of that oath. Was it worthwhile? All this trouble for a doubtful gain, if gain it were. But deeper still was the lurking thought that had come half an hour ago. If she held out long enough....

## CHAPTER FORTY-FOUR

AUNT MURIEL did not leave the good work incomplete. She wrote Joyce a little private note. She enclosed books. Joyce read the books, and felt rather sick. But she was not insensitive to their reiterated assurance that a new hope had come to the world. The constant representation of child-bearing, not as the glory of womanhood, but as a curse which was being removed, could not fail to affect her mind. From a very different angle, it was the attitude of her own Church. Joyce had no use for curses of which she was to be the victim.

When Miss Coates looked in again, she gave her her books back, rather to that lady's surprise. But Joyce did not want them lying about. She felt instinctively that they were unclean. Yet she could not reject the poison which had entered her mind. She was not going to be different from other women. She was not going to have pain and discomfort which (this was the great point) other women had found a way to avoid. But she hated Aunt Muriel with an intensity of which she was hardly conscious herself. It did not prevent the smile with which she thanked her for the books as she handed them back, explaining that, as she was a Catholic, she could not take their advice.

"Yes," Miss Coates answered, "but Alwyn can, and he ought to see where his duty lies."

That was the thought that had lain in the darkness of her own mind. If she said that to Alwyn, it might be a mortal sin. She was not sure, but it's the sort of risk that you don't run if you are a wise girl. But why couldn't he think of it himself? If she held out, it would be almost certain to end in that.

Miss Coates went on to suggest that the Catholic Church was not always quite as obdurate as Joyce supposed. Why did she not see one of the Jesuit fathers at—?

Joyce would not admit that her Church could fail to speak with one voice, but she decided to take the advice. Matters could not go on as they were between Alwyn and her. There were hours when they scarcely spoke. If his hand touched her in the night, he would withdraw it as though he had touched a snake. Did he think he could tire her out? He would find that two could play at that game. Had she not left the books lying about before she handed them back, and had she not *known* that they had been moved, and (of course) read?

The Jesuit priest was a man of more culture and learning than the one she had seen previously. He put her at ease at once with a gentle impersonal courtesy. He had a wider range of language, and could express himself with greater subtlety, and superior exactness. She found herself understood better, while she was required to say less.

She had a sense of being received with sympathy and consideration which made the interview very pleasant while it lasted, but she realized as she came away that she had made very moderate gains.

She had ascertained clearly that, being married to a non-Catholic, if he insisted on the use of illicit means of birth-prevention, she did not therefore sin in her intercourse with him; but she had received a disconcerting warning that if she encouraged or condoned such practices, even by a passive attitude, she would share the guilt. Had he read that thought in the dark rear of her mind? She did not like the idea. She had been told that if she were really unfit for child-bearing she should propose a mutual continence. She considered that advice without gratitude. She was practising continence now, and she did not like it at all. But she had learnt one thing more. Conception was held to be unlikely to take place at certain times, and if marriage relations were confined by mutual consent to such periods the Church did not necessarily condemn.

Beside that, the conversation had the effect of somewhat lessening the effect of Miss Coates's propaganda. It had been gently suggested to her mind that the views to which she had listened were not of a very reputable kind, and were by no means universally held.

She had been invited to analyse the motives in her own mind, which she was not over-willing to do. It is a difficult world.

Events might have proceeded by a somewhat different path, though to the same end, had she not happened to meet Miss Coates as she re-entered the house, and been asked a direct question as to whether she had yet consulted the Jesuit oracle. She answered frankly and fully, and alarmed Aunt Muriel into supplying her instantly with a book containing a marked passage which emphasized the uncertainty of any theories as to the times at which conception can occur. The *only* certain and harmless method was to purchase the goods that the author advocated. Who shall decide such differences? Joyce certainly had no knowledge that would enable her to do so. But (as we said once before) she was very far from being a fool, and she did have a passing wonder why all these books protested the harmlessness of the practices they advocated, and the goods they recommended. If they were so harmless, why was it necessary that it should be said so frequently? She felt that they protested too much.

But on the whole, she decided, she would take the risk. It was just the time that she had been told was comparatively safe, or perhaps a bit later than that. Unless she were to hold Alwyn off for the next three weeks or more, there would be no gain by delay. She would be a good Catholic and a good wife tonight, and (incidentally) she would follow her own inclination, making a very good combination, indeed. As to going on like this for another three or four weeks—well, she had no confidence that she would be able to do so, even though to give way would mean almost certain twins! Joyce had learnt that if she wanted anything seriously, its self-denial was a very difficult thing. No, she would be good tonight, let the consequences be what they would.

## CHAPTER FORTY-FIVE

ALWYN had struck her. There was no doubt of that. Startling to himself in a second's time, on an impulse of indignation, he had struck a single, hard, deliberate blow.

And up to that point they had been so passionately loving in their recovered union. And then, at the last moment of surrender, the very last, she had had a revulsion of fear. All Aunt Muriel's warnings had come back to her mind. *She couldn't have a child in that flat.* She had drawn away with a sudden: "No, I won't! You wouldn't if you really cared!" And his answer, instant to her own words, had been that deliberate blow.

"Alwyn, how dare you!" she exclaimed in an anger that was the greater for the sense of guilt in her own mind. "I'll never love you again now. Never till you've said you're sorry for that."

"I'm sorry it wasn't harder."

"And just because I— You don't care what happens to me. I think it's hateful of you not to give in. And you know I can't. It isn't as if you'd got any religion. Not that really matters. I didn't think men were such brutes. I'll never speak to you again till...."

"Well, you shouldn't have led me on, and then acted like that."

"I didn't mean to at first. Really, I didn't. But you don't know how frightened I am. Besides, you ought to be able to make me give in. You would, if you really cared. You wouldn't want me to, if you really cared. You'd think more about me being dead. I never thought you'd have acted like that. It's like—like navvies! To hit the mother of your child." (Joyce thought that was rather good.) "You've made me quite *sore*. If you don't say you're sorry I'll never speak to you...."

"I'm not asking you to, am I?"

Silence ended the skirmish. Silence and angry thoughts, and then sleep.

In the morning Alwyn waked first. Joyce looked adorable. The cares of life did not appear to press heavily upon her. Even this difference with Alwyn would not easily disturb the gentle regular breathing of her dreamless rest.

Alwyn, looking at her as he dressed, could not be sure even of his own feelings. Was it a brutal primitive instinct in him that strove to make her—behave properly? Was he really careless of her life and happiness for the sake of his own gratification? Was he wrong to obey the instinct of repulsion. by which he shrank from the devices which had developed a sudden front of respectability? Was it a lack of manhood in himself that could not subdue her to her natural end—even with all the love she had for him, and with all the primitive passion that her nature held? Was it a proof of the poorness of his own love, of his undisciplined selfishness, that they should have come to this pass? Should he strike her again at the same issue—and not desist so easily? Using his physical strength till she should give way, and there should be again the old happiness, and the old peace? Was he quite sure that she would yield to the argument of physical pain? Suppose she quarrelled in earnest? Suppose she left him, or drove him into leaving her? Cruelty and desertion. Couldn't she get a divorce for that? But, no, being a Catholic, she had not that remedy! Joyce had mentioned the unfairness of that position more than once. Not that she ever thought of divorce, except as a jest, but it *was* unfair that she wouldn't be as free as Alwyn, if she did want it. A most inconvenient religion. Somehow, with less than perfect logic, this distinction seemed to lay a heavier obligation upon him to make her marriage happy. Actually, he was less of the kind to seek such a course even than she. You might search the records of his family backward for several generations, and there would be no instance of any married unhappiness that had found such an outlet. There are many of such families. They have differences and disappointments and defects to meet or to forgive. We can know that without inquiry into private things. But they meet them in a different way. And they are of the families that are seldom childless.

But Alwyn looked at her as she lay, and thought of the recovered heaven that would follow if she would love him in the old manner, with the old abandon, which had gradually conquered the uncertain pruderies of the first weeks. But he saw that no coercion could bring that—not quite. If there were still the fear in her mind, there would be a reservation in her surrender which would spoil it all. Curse Aunt Muriel and all her kind! Forcing their lying poison upon those who would otherwise have been happy in a natural way. Yet was it poison, or was the fault in himself? Suppose she did give way, under pressure or threat? Suppose she had another baby, as she had become sure that she would immediately? Suppose she—*died*? In imagination Joyce looked at him from her death-bed with reproachful eyes. Worse than that, she forgave. Killed by his brutal lust! Killed because he was too stupid, too pig-headed to do what *everyone* else did now. He heard Joyce's intonation in the stress of that *everyone*. It would always be a strong argument with her.

Yet he did not make the world, or the portals of childbirth. He had enough sense to see that. To come back to the point. Was he going to tell her he was sorry? Not unless he meant it. Did he feel sorry? Not he. He was not sure whether he ought to have felt sorry or not, but it was a fact that he didn't.

Should he kiss her before he went? Yes, of course. But he would not wake her. He was going early, and getting breakfast on the Hunnerton train. There was still no sound from the next room, where baby slept in Myra's charge.

He bent over her. She was adorable as she slept. Made to be loved. He wished that he had hit twice as hard. He kissed her lightly. She did not appear to wake, but she drew away, and turned over. He saw that he had offended her so deeply that she shrank from him, even in sleep. He was not so sure that he wasn't sorry, as he went downstairs

Joyce had been watching him for some time. Long lashes have other uses than the cajoling of men. She thought he looked almost as miserable as he should, though, perhaps, not quite. Never mind. She hadn't finished with him yet. And he deserved it, too. Why couldn't he be sensible? He wasn't a Catholic. It didn't *really* matter if he did things that were wrong. And, anyway, if he really loved her as he pretended, he'd do it for her, whether it were a sin or not. And she wouldn't have any sin on herself at all. She imagined herself going to confession and asking if it were wrong to be childless when your husband *made* you do it, and the consolation she would receive. Joyce's conscience could creep through a very small hole when her inclinations called it. But the hole it must have. And now Alwyn was selfishly blocking it up. He couldn't love her at all.

She stood before the glass at this stage of her thoughts, and twisted round to get a glimpse of the effects of the punishment she had received. One of them was certainly rather pinker than usual. And Alwyn always said they had such beautiful curves. So they had. It was a subject on which she was quite sure. If he had really wanted her, he would have hit harder than that! It was a contemptible blow. Looked at properly, it was an insult that he had not hit harder than that. Why, she could scarcely feel it at all. Of course, he would have her, if he really wanted. He would *take* her. Well, he should pay for it when he came home. He shouldn't have her at all now, not for ever and—at least a week. Or say, till Sunday.

But she mustn't stand like this. She could hear baby now. If she didn't hurry she wouldn't be in time to bathe her. And it was no use Myra saying that she could do it. She wasn't nearly as careful as she might be about the water, and—other things. (Myra knew a simple way of telling the temperature of the water, which should be familiar to every mother. If it is too hot, the baby goes red; and if it is too cold, it goes blue.) She would always bathe baby herself. She was a very good mother. One of the best. Far too good to die having another, while the one she had was so small, and no one else knew how to take care of it. Fancy Alwyn trying to bathe it, if she were dead! He ought to see that. But men think of nothing but themselves. They don't really love their children, nor their wives. They only think of themselves. And so they have to pay for it when they come home at night. Joyce felt quite capable of superintending that part of the programme. She smiled happily at the thought.

Half an hour later, looking at Frida in the bath, she considered that she produced babies of a quite exceptional quality. Obviously, a factory capable of such output ought to work full time. If she had become pregnant last night, as she might have done, she would have had a baby in May. An excellent month. It was all Alwyn's fault. He didn't deserve such a wife. Would people think she was defective, if things went on like this? Could they call her a barren woman? She didn't think that would be quite the right word, but she had heard her uncle explain that a heifer is still a heifer till after she had had her first calf. They called it a heifer calf. Was Frida a heifer calf? It didn't sound nice at all. She must ask Dr. Fordyce. Or the priest. Perhaps it would be better to ask the priest at confession, because he isn't supposed to laugh. (It isn't usual to ask such questions at confession? No, but Joyce wasn't usual either.) Myra, we want the soap. No, it is the other side. How stupid Myra can be! But we are in good spirits ourselves though it is still a little sore on one side, which would have been both if Alwyn had really cared. But we must think out how we can make him pay when he comes home at night.

# CHAPTER FORTY-SIX

ALWYN travelled to Hunnerton that morning on a special appointment to meet Mr. Richard Hayward, and with a little latent anxiety as to what the subject of the interview might be.

Prior to his father's bankruptcy, he had been getting on very good terms with Richard Hayward, who had asked him out to lunch about once a month, when they had been able to discuss business on an intimate and friendly footing. It could not be said truly that the disaster to the family fortunes had made any immediate difference. Rather, Mr. Hayward had shown a prompt and practical sympathy. He had offered Alwyn an extension of his ground to the East Coast. Not the most profitable ground, nor the easiest to work, as Alwyn knew. Mr. Hayward was no sentimentalist. He considered his firm's interests. But it had made it much easier for Alwyn to find an adequate position for his father, without too serious encroachment on his own income.

But recently, from whatever cause, these invitations had ceased. Business relations had appeared to be as friendly as ever, but they had been conducted in Mr. Hayward's office. Now he had been first asked if he would come to the usual restaurant in the old way, and then Hayward had said: "But, perhaps, better not," as though thinking aloud. "Come down on the early train if you can, and I'll see you here."

What could this proposed interview be about, and what did this attitude mean? He knew of no business matter of such urgency or importance that he should be asked to make a special appointment to discuss it. Certainly none that should make it reasonable to ask him to come down by the early train.

He was shown straight into Mr. Hayward's office when he arrived, and found him not alone, but with a man of rather doubtful respectability, whom his father would have recognized as being the one whom he had seen at the café on the morning when he had received the news of Winterton's failure, and his own doom.

Mr. Hayward mentioned that the name of this man was Rufus Gordon. Alwyn nodded across the table. He said: "How do you do?" He did not really care how the man did. He disliked his looks. There are some good things that do not blend well. Some Scottish men, both Highland and Lowland, are of excellent quality. They may run by the side of the tram till their breath fails, to reduce the ultimate fare, but most of them have too much sense to choose a tram that is going the wrong way. The Scot who was asked, when he returned home, how he liked the English, and replied that he hadn't met any, as he only interviewed heads of departments, had some truth in his jest. But Scots have even better qualities than industry and appreciation of the value of money. It is equally true that there are very generous Jews. But a combination of these two races is not necessarily of an equal pattern.

Mr. Rufus Gordon had an undersized body, and a furtive foxy face, but his character does not concern us. We have neither to give him a medical nor a moral certificate, and the result of his association with the firm of Collett, Hayward & Co. may be interesting, as all things are, but is outside the survey of this narrative. We must avoid looking over any more hedges. Alwyn felt that he was out of place in that office, and was the more puzzled as to what his own part in the interview was likely to be. Mr. Hayward came to his point at once. "I want it to be understood that anything that's said here this morning will go no further. I can trust you for that, Gordon, because, if there is, the deal's off; and I know you wouldn't give us away, Mr. Oakley, even if it mayn't ultimately seem equally to your advantage to keep it quiet, as I hope it will. The point's this. We're thinking of a large extension to our business by undertaking some classes of goods that are being made in Germany now, and if we do this we shall want new works, and the premises your father used to have are about the only ones that are vacant that are about the right size, and they adjoin ours. I don't want any idea to get about that we're willing to buy, for reasons that are easy to guess. Gordon here knows what's needed as well as I do myself—if not better. He's been in the best German factory for this class of goods—that is, the best in the world—for the last three years, and he's kept his eyes wide. If we do what we intend, he's to have a five years' agreement with us; and after that if he likes to do us one in the eye by going over to another firm, well, it's up to him. Yes, of course, I understand that. I'm only joking. But I want you to tell us just what accommodation there is, and what kind, so that I can estimate what changes we should have to make, and how long they would take before we could get the output we want."

Everything's interesting in this world, and the more you understand it, the more so it becomes. If we turn aside from the conversation of the next hour, it is only because there are other matters that concern us more. At the end of that time, Gordon went, and Richard Hayward came to the most important part of the interview.

"I'm having lunch sent in here," he began. "I don't want us to be seen together too much. It's a hundred to one it wouldn't make any difference, but it wouldn't be the first time that this firm's come a cropper on the long odds. What I want to say is that I'll give you £7,000 for those works, and anything less than that you can get the bank to take is your profit on the deal."

Alwyn took this quietly. It sounded good. His business experience had taught him to think first and speak afterwards. He said: "You've had this in mind for some time."

Richard Hayward was as quick as he. "You mean because I've stopped us lunching together? Yes, of course. If the bank gets the least idea of what's on foot, the price is nine thousand, not seven or six, and there's nothing for you, and a lot more for us to pay. More than I could afford to allocate to that."

"Why do you want to do it through me?"

"Because if we put any agent on it they'll know there's a chance of business, and the price stiffens at once. It's so with all property deals, but it's most so with business premises. They're often the devil to sell at all, but when a buyer turns up he's usually keen if he's willing to deal, and the trumps are yours.

"But you might naturally be interested in your father's affairs, and if you say you might find them a customer if you got a month's option at £6,800, or whatever you like to try, well, they might be persuaded to give it, even if they didn't think there was much chance. They might even give it more readily for that, especially if you put up a deposit, as you'd probably have to do."

Alwyn demurred to that. The bank manager was still very friendly. He did not think he would wish to see him lose a deposit, even for the bank's gain.

"Well, you know him. I don't. But you're the best one to approach him in the way we want, and if you make a bit for yourself, it couldn't go to a better address."

Alwyn thanked him. He would do what he could. It did not appear to be a case for any expression of gratitude which went beyond an ordinary courtesy. It was a shrewd idea. Besides, it risked nothing. He was not sure that he would not have preferred a settled fee or a commission on the deal. He was less sure that he could get an option within the required limit. Still he would try.

Hayward, used to Alwyn's quiet way, left the subject readily. In subsequent conversation he got as near to being confidential as he often did, for he was a shy man.

Talking of the position which Alwyn had made for himself, he said: "You know you had a better father than I. My governor meant well enough, but suppose this business had gone five years ago in the way your father's did last year. I was just through college, and he was just dying. If the business pulled through the slump, it was no thanks to him. He'd built it up, and made it what it was. I can thank him for that. But he'd made me what I was too. A young man just through college, who knew nothing about business, nor anything useful, and thought that five or six hundred a year was the smallest sum on which a man could live, even with no one but himself to keep. I'd been taught and trained to think that. If I'd been thrown on my own resources, I'd have been worth three pounds a week, if that. I'd been trained to be parasitic, just as those young people are now who prefer doles to domestic service. It's the same thing at both ends, and it's hardest of all on those who think it's giving them a good time.

"Well, the business flourished. It was in Lampson's hands, and he was just the right man for such a time. I don't say he's much good now. There's a time to go slow, and another when you must let the furnace roar."

He grew silent, thinking of that of which he would not speak. He had recently offered marriage to a young woman of a "county" family to whom he had been strongly drawn, and who had shown him more than a casual favour, to find himself rejected when it was learnt that his income from the business was only a thousand a year, on which he had proposed to live. He had not been refused because he was a businessman. That would have been a foolish (because an obsolete) snobbery. He had been refused on the even more contemptible ground that he had a limited income. He had not emphasized the fact that it would be far larger when his mother should die. He did not want her to die. It was not a thing to anticipate or discuss. He did not mention that his income might have been higher, but that he had been fighting against the amounts which others had been drawing out, and could not ask for a different treatment. He wanted the capital kept in the business, even to the reduction of the usual dividends. And so he had been refused. With a hint that he might return if he could offer a more adequate prospect. Return? Not he. His infatuation was not such that he could not see the worthlessness of a woman who sought victory without battle, and who was to be bought with a long purse.

He knew that he had lost nothing, but the repulse had been unexpected, and was still bitter.

He turned the conversation to Alwyn's own circumstances.

He said: "You owe your father a lot for the way he kept that business going. The War gave it its death-wound, or I suppose I ought to say that the government did that. It wasn't only that they taxed it to death, it was the extra plant that they made him lay down, and the premises they made him build—all to come out of the profit that they took away. And I don't suppose that he kept anything back. I wouldn't like to say it was the same here, though I don't know. But I remember my father saying that old Tommy Dibber got drunk at the club in 1918, and boasted of the false returns he made for the E.P.D., and when someone tried to pull him up, he told them they were all doing the same thing, but they hadn't the pluck to say so. He challenged any man to say that he paid taxes on what he really made. He said they all knew that nobody could, unless he'd been making a fortune before the War, and they all looked uncomfortable, but no one spoke.

"But it was right enough for us. We'd made our record year in 1913, and the law was that we were to have that profit duty-free every year as long as the War lasted, and as much more as we could get. It was velvet for us.

"But your father carried on for another five or ten years, more or less, and he'd given you the sort of start that made it matter less to you when the trouble came. If he'd sent you to college, you might have been on the pavement now. Though I wouldn't say that. There's a lot in what we are ourselves that our parents can't alter or help. We're apt to blame them for too much, and not thank them enough. But I'm afraid your sister's not having a very gay time. She's a fine girl. Yes, I met her at the tennis-club last Saturday. How's your father keeping?"

Alwyn was concerned about that. He thought his father seemed older. There was more change than had been observable in the difficult years. He was doing well enough, covering as much ground, and getting through as much work as a younger man. He was like a horse that will try to break into a gallop toward the crest of the hill. Some horses are like that to their life's end. Others will throw the collar-work on their team-mates, if they are harnessed together, even in the strength of their youth. The difference is not physical, but of the spirit, the existence of which some modernists are disposed to doubt.

"Well, it's not my business, but if you clear a round sum out of this property deal, as I hope you may, I should let a lump of it go to the old man. He may need it later, and he'll like to feel it's his own. I don't mind telling you that I should have offered him the chance, but I thought the O.R. might claim it, if it were known that he'd made a haul."

Alwyn said yes to that, but with reserve. Without quite understanding his own feeling, he resented the implication that his father was one to be helped or pitied, or that anyone, even Richard Hayward, should intrude advice into the family finances. He may also have preferred that he should decide his own generosities. That it is more blessed to give than to receive is universally true, but of nothing more so than advice.

He decided to see his father before proceeding in the matter. It was right he should know of a proposal which, though it might be personally advantageous to Alwyn, might be detrimental to the interests of his own creditors. Alwyn was not even certain that he would approve. He was far from confident that he could handle the matter as well as his father would have been able to do. He must see him. But seeing him tonight meant staying till the late train. He considered staying the night in Hunnerton. But he could not do that without expense to himself. His father and Elsie had no spare room to offer in their present quarters.

He thought also of Joyce, and of the cloud that had come between them. It had been a shadow at the rear of his mind all day. Joyce would think he was staying away on purpose. That might do her no harm. He saw that with his intellect, but his feelings rebelled. He had a restless desire to return to her, though it should be only to quarrel. He could not forget that she would be waiting miserably for him.

He would stay to see his father, but he would return on the late train.

He went to 54 Elston Road, which was his father's new address, in the latter part of the afternoon. He had no other business in Hunnerton. Elsie would give him some tea, and he would be there when his father should arrive, and no time would be lost. As he approached the gate he saw Chester enter. When he rang, Elsie and Chester were still in the hall. Elsie said: "I didn't know Chester had asked you to come too." What did that mean?

They went into the living-room, where tea had been laid for three. Elsie said: "Father may be here any minute now." She fetched another cup and plate for Alwyn. She answered to his natural question; "Chester wrote that he was coming, and asked Father to be home early to meet him. He's got something interesting to tell us."

"It's no use trying to draw me out," Chester interrupted. "I'm not going to talk twice."

"It wouldn't make any difference," Elsie retorted, "considering you never stop. It's always talk with you, or those silly verses. I believe you could make them up in your sleep."

"So I do. I dreamt a beautiful sonnet last night, and tried to remember it when I woke, but I couldn't get beyond the first two lines. I got a headache trying to recover the rest. I felt sure it would be something new in English poetry."

"No doubt. How did it start?"

"It seems to have been a bit shaky just at the beginning. But after that it improved with every line. It began

We love suet, and all full things.
As full as the Universe.

"There's rhythmic originality there, whatever you say, and the second line doesn't do itself justice, because it went on further than that, but I can't get what it was."

"You're sure you can't remember any more?" Elsie inquired anxiously. "It's a lot better than anything I've heard you do when you're awake. More substance, somehow. It's the sort of poem that makes you wonder what's coming next."

"I can't remember anything more, except that 'things' rhymed with 'swings', and I can't be sure whether it was a noun or a verb. But it's a sound rhyme. It shows how well-constructed the whole thing must have been...and the queer thing is that I don't like suet at all."

"I don't see anything queer in that. That's the obvious complex. You've been suppressing the thought that you don't like suet all these years, and it comes out in a dream. Freud could explain a little thing like that even when he's awake. It's probably why you married Frida."

"I expect you're right. I believe I've spent whole weeks before now without once allowing myself to think about not liking suet. The complex must have got mad. And Frida helped me to forget. Why only yesterday…."

But the door-bell rang again, and Elsie went to the door without waiting to listen further.

A few minutes later they were all seated at the table, and Elsie said: "Now for the news." Her eyes were on Chester, but Alwyn had been thinking that there was no need for him to be on the last train, after all, if he could get away in twenty minutes, and there was no reason that he shouldn't speak freely in that company. He said: "There's one thing I want to tell you about first, if I may. I want to catch the 5:45."

"Something important?"

"Yes, rather." Chester said. "Mine can wait."

"He's naturally a silent man," Elsie admitted.

Alwyn turned to his father.

"I've got a chance of selling the works, and perhaps making a margin for ourselves out of the deal." He narrated the morning's conversation.

His father said: "How much did you think of offering?" Alwyn said: "I thought of trying to get £500 out of it. Of course, I might have to be satisfied with less, if the bank won't budge."

John Oakley thought silently for a few moments. Then he said: "I think you could get more than that. At least, I could. I think you'd better leave seeing Riddle to me.

"But it cuts both ways. It means the bank'll lose more, and I always told Riddle I'd see him right. They want £9,000 for the works, to bring them out on the right side."

"They may want," Alwyn said, "but they can't hope to get."

"They might, if they wait their chance. But a bank usually likes to get a thing like this closed. Besides, I don't quite know how they will come out. They've sold the house rather well. And banks aren't quite like other creditors. They can prove for the gross amount, whatever securities they hold. There's something of that, anyway, though there may be exceptions. You'd better leave this to me. Of course, I'll get the option in your name. But there'll have to be a deposit. It has no legal value without that."

"It needn't be for a large amount."

"I suppose you're sure that the bank hasn't got any idea of what's afoot? They don't miss much. You or I approaching them might put the idea into their heads."

"I don't think it will. Hayward said that they'd approached his firm to know if they would be possible buyers, and Lampson answered the letter. He told them not in a million years, or something like that. He knew nothing about this project, and he's against any expansion, so he got the right tone into what he said."

"All the same, it would be awkward if Riddle asked a direct question. I've always been frank with him. And he'd have to know in the end."

"Why not let me do this?" Chester interposed. "You're neither of you any good at a downright lie, and I'd rather tell one than not. Besides, I can't if I want to. No journalist can. You can't tell lies unless you think people believe what you say.

"I don't see that," Elsie objected.

"Oh, shut up, Elsie," Alwyn interposed hastily. "Don't start arguing now. I've nearly missed my train, as it is. Chester's the best one for this, and he won't need to tell any lies, for the bank won't think of any connection. I'll leave a cheque you can fill in for the deposit. But don't make it too much. I shall have to get Hayward's to cover it, anyway. I meant Father and I to go fifty-fifty on this, if Father thinks that would be fair, but Chester can have something out of my half. We shan't quarrel about that."

"Oh, I expect we shall," Chester answered hopefully. "But you needn't trouble about the cheque, if you're in a hurry to bolt. What's the usual deposit?"

John Oakley answered that. "Ten percent is usual in an actual contract to purchase. On a mere option, it's a bargain of the smallest amount the owner'll take."

"Ten percent on £5,000?—I don't intend to offer more. Everyone knows that you can't sell business premises these days. That's £500. I can manage that."

Alwyn stared at his brother-in-law. Was Chester serious? It wasn't always easy to tell. "I'd rather leave a cheque." He had his cheque-book out now, and was standing impatient for departure.

"You can leave it, if you like; but if you'd sit down for half-an-hour instead of rushing off to watch the tail-end of a train that's just left the platform, you'll understand why I shan't use it, if you do."

Alwyn hesitated. "You know it's too late now."

Elsie urged. "And you've scarcely had any tea."

"I think you'd better stay if you can. I don't want this matter decided hastily," his father said, and turned the scale. He sat down to listen to the tale that Chester had come to tell.

## CHAPTER FORTY-SEVEN

"IT'S that Edward Dobson business," Chester began, "that I told you something about when I was here at the time of the sale.

"I didn't really take it very seriously, because what was there, at the most, beyond some shares in someone else's name, that I didn't want even if I could claim them, and the fact that there had been £37 in the name of Edward Dobson in a Nottingham bank a year or two ago? But I did mean to follow it up when I got the chance, and it happened that I had to go to Peterborough about four or five weeks ago, and I managed to get a few hours in Nottingham on the way back.

"I went to the bank first, as I'd planned to do after looking up the manager's name in a directory at the hotel where I had lunch, and if he'd been in, I expect I should have done more than I did. I asked to see him, without saying what for, but I found that he was on holiday, and the man who was taking his place was at lunch, and in the end I had to tell a clerk at the counter that I'd called to make some inquiries about a Mr. Edward Dobson who had an account with them. He went to speak to some others at the back, and, after some talk, he came back and said that inquiry must be made through another bank.

"So I turned away at that, without giving my name, thinking I'd try again when someone in authority was in, and went on to 30 Bennet Street, which was Edward Dobson's address.

"The place looked like a boarding-house, as it was, but I got no reply when I rang, and was turning away when a neighbour told me that Mrs. Stevenson was out, but wouldn't be more than half-an-hour, so I walked round for a time, and then rang again. I saw the woman then, and got a door-step reception. She said Mr. Dobson had left a long while ago. She gave me a feeling that the sooner I did the same the better she would be pleased, but I did get her to give me the date when he left, and I remembered, as I walked away, that that was about the time that my cousin was killed, which seemed queer, but it was too late to call at the bank again, as I had half-intended to do, and so I came away without having learnt anything worth knowing.

"After that, I did make an inquiry through my own bank, and got a reply that meant nothing, and I was more than half inclined to give it up.

"I might have been keener, and found out more, if I hadn't been half afraid all the time as to what it would be. But I'd been bitten once, and those shares seemed to be a warning of what I might get again if I inquired into what wasn't my business if I hadn't the sense to leave it alone. Anyway, I didn't mean to go to the expense of another journey to Nottingham.

"But I did have one more try. I posted the passbook to the bank, putting an unsigned slip into it with a request that it should be made up to date and returned to my address. I didn't feel sure that I should see it again, but it came back by the return post. It showed that £50 had been paid in a day or two after it had been made up before, and two small cheques had been paid about the same time. These cheques were in the pocket of the book, and when I looked at them I sat up. They were signed Edward Dobson, but the writing was my cousin's. There was no doubt of that. Edward Dobson was he, beyond a doubt, and there was about eighty pounds to be picked up, if there were any legal way in which it could be done."

"So you went to Nottingham by the next train?" Elsie suggested, as Chester paused at this point, to pass his cup to her for some more tea.

"No, I didn't. I wrote the bank-manager a full statement of the position, and said that I thought I had a legal claim to the balance, and what steps did he require me to take?

"I got no answer to that for three days, and then there came a request to call at their head-office in Leadenhall Street. When I did that, I was questioned by the manager for about twenty minutes, and then I got the real shock, when he said that it appeared to be his duty to inform me that they held securities for Mr. Edward Dobson, which he valued at £4,730. He was so precise that I wondered he didn't mention the pence."

"You mean all that money's yours?"

"It's not only that, but it seems that it's to be mine without any trouble at all. They asked to be put in touch with my own lawyer, and to have a properly authenticated photograph of Basil, and some other things that we've just finished doing, and I heard yesterday that they've formally admitted the claim, and I can draw against the securities if I want."

"And you've known all this for weeks, and haven't said a word?" Elsie asked.

"I didn't want to raise any hopes till I was sure, after all that happened before."

"There didn't seem to be much doubt."

"Oh, yes, there was. How did I know that I shouldn't find that he'd got a wife in Nottingham, and perhaps six or eight children?"

"That wouldn't have altered the will."

"It would have altered the destination of the money. And he might even have made a later will."

"And now you're sure that there isn't?"

"Yes, I think I can say that. I went to 30 Bennet Street a second time, and I got inside. I gave the constable on the beat a shilling to stand outside while I knocked, and you know how silly women are about anything that seems to threaten them with the law. And she had a bad conscience, too.

"She was shaking like a jelly as she took me up to his room, which she said she'd kept just as it was. She claimed that she was entitled to rent for the whole time, and I suppose she would have been if she'd run straight. I found that half his things had been scattered about the house, and there is evidence that there was £120 in notes in his desk. If she hadn't taken that, somebody else had. And I found out a lot besides, that I needn't trouble to tell. It wasn't worth words, as long as I got his papers and could find out what he'd been doing there in another name, and I told her she could just keep the furniture against the rent she claimed, if I were satisfied that I'd got all his papers, and she'd held nothing back. More or less, I suppose I have."

"And there wasn't any woman in it at all?"

"No, I can't say that. There were letters showing he'd got mixed up with a Bertha Jeeves, but that didn't seem to be the reason that he'd taken the room in that name. It began later. I suppose we shall never know all the truth. But there'll be no trouble with the Jeeves woman. She's a haberdasher's wife now, and in mortal fear that he'll get to hear of her relations with Edward Dobson, and some less creditable things that the police know. No, I've got to the bottom of all that, as far as I ever shall, and the money seems safely mine."

"I suppose Frida's glad?"

"She isn't exactly in tears. We've arranged that she's to have all she can spend, and there are a few debts of that infernal business of Basil's that are still owing that I can clear up now, and there'll be about £3,000 left, that we don't want." He turned to John Oakley as he continued rather awkwardly, "we thought—if it would be enough to give things a new start—to straighten things out a bit—here? We've no use for it ourselves."

John Oakley had rather thought that was coming. He said quietly: "That was a kind thought. What did Frida say?"

Chester remembered that Frida wrote letters. He saw no use in a lie. "Frida's willing, but not over keen. Not on paying the business debts, I mean. Women don't understand how men feel about these things."

"Frida's quite right." There was the clear decisive tone in the voice characteristic of the John Oakley of an earlier time. "It was a kind thought, but I couldn't think of it being used in that way. But you can try to get this option on the works tomorrow, and I'll share what profit there is equally, Alwyn and I. If it's a good sum, there are some things I should like to pay—but not through the Court. If you tell Riddle about this money that's come to you, and tell him you'd like to try what you can do with a month's option on the works, he won't think anything except that you're doing something rather silly. I should say you've got to see some profit for yourself if it comes off, and you'll give him a deposit for a month's option at £5,000, but not more."

He relapsed into thought, and the look of weakness and age came back to his face. Of course, Frida was right. Six months ago such a sum properly used, held in the background of the position, might not have enabled the business to be continued, but it might have saved him from what he felt to be the stigma of bankruptcy. It would have saved his home. He would have taken it then. Now it would do no good. It would not be enough to cover the deficiency, and get the order rescinded. It would mean some pleasant words if he should hand over such a sum for the creditors' benefit. But it would be a kind of falsehood. It would not have been due to any exertion of his. There was no reason why this money should be taken from Frida, and Frida's children, to be given to his own creditors. As he saw it, such a transaction would increase the severity of his defeat. Six months ago it would have done so much! It was a kind of mockery now. There were debts that he was resolved should be settled in full. He was working hard and spending little. He would pay them all if he could. It was a question of time and health. Elsie was managing well, controlling everything with an effortless, well-judged economy, and keeping up her own work. She had proved a good daughter to him. He would never have known what she could be had this trouble not come. But what was lost was lost, and no £3,000 could ever bring it back. He looked round the room which was furnished mainly with things which had been bought at the sale, or which had reappeared mysteriously after Chester had called. He often wished he had let them all go. He remembered too much. It was useless thinking of the dead things. His mind returned to consciousness of the conversation around him. Alwyn was teasing Elsie about something that Richard Hayward had said about her this morning, and she was replying with off-hand words, but without power to control the blush that came so easily to the faces of his fair-skinned daughters.

Chester caught his eye, and asked whether it was all over now—the fuss at the County Court?

Yes, he said, wondering a little that the subject should be brought up. The examination was closed. He had signed the notes last Tuesday. He remembered the dreary ordeal in the almost empty Court. There had been first the long wait while he listened to the examination of a bankrupt butcher who had been mysteriously robbed of £800 of paper money a week before his failure occurred, as bankrupt butchers are apt to be.

The Registrar had watched the butcher with a slightly amused expression, his chin in his hand, leaning a little forward upon his desk, while the O.R. and the solicitor of an outraged creditor had questioned and ridiculed the tale. Once or twice he had interposed in a gentle voice to protect the witness from an unfairness of assumption or interrogation. "I don't see how you can take it farther than that," he said to the O.R. at last, with his quiet smile, and the baffled official sat down. Then his tone had changed to an incisive curtness as he had said that it was an unsatisfactory case. He was sorry to have to say that he did not believe a word of the bankrupt's evidence. The examination would be adjourned *sine die*.

After that John Oakley's turn had come. The butcher had gone out with his friends. The few scattered people in the well of the Court had risen and left. There had been about twenty minutes of question and answer. A reiteration of familiar figures. The quiet watchful control of the Registrar, ending with a word of courteous regret for the position in which he had found himself that day. The examination, he said, was closed, except for the signing of the notes. But why was Chester asking about it now?

The answer came in his next words. "Because, if so, Frida said I could tell you about the black cow."

This had been a trouble on Chester's mind ever since the day of the sale. There had been a day when a throaty voice had called to Frida as she had alighted from a taxi outside Hunnerton station, and she had turned to see Mr. Swadson standing beside the car which had once been theirs, and he had asked her for the address to which she was going.

The next day there had been a registered envelope for her at Birchett's Wood, containing twenty-five one-pound notes, and with a crude drawing of a black cow on the flap of the envelope. That had been plain enough.

Chester's trouble was that this money, with the twenty pounds that had originated from the same pocket, had been used for Elsie's purchases at the sale, and had been supposed to have been provided by his own generosity. Frida said, what did that matter? Chester felt unwilling to be thanked for that which he had not done. It had been agreed that the truth should be told when the knowledge could no longer embarrass her father in any evidence that he might have to give.

Now it was told, not without laughter, and the sense of a skirmish won.

After that they went on to talk of the fowl. Chester had some Black Hamburg chickens now that were well-grown, all old enough to leave the hen. Elsie said the new pen would be ready on Saturday. For a small extra weekly sum they had bought the rights of the neglected garden. Her father said, do not bring many of the chickens. Hamburgs—particularly the young—do not thrive in a confined space.

The pigeons? Yes, Sanders was looking after them. (They had been knocked down at the sale for eight pence each, to John Oakley's mingled relief and indignation. There had been no difficulty about buying *them* in.)

Alwyn rose, saying that it was time to go.

In the train, on the way home, he thought over his quarrel with Joyce, which had receded somewhat, altering its significance and proportions before the excitements of the day. But he was going back to face it now, and it reasserted itself accordingly. He saw that, if Joyce were genuinely fearful of their financial future, he might be able to give her some assurance from the news he brought. He did not look for any direct benefit from Chester's good fortune, but the opportunity to make a substantial profit on the purchase of the works was a different matter. It would relieve a bank account that was overdrawn, and provide the capital which he was urgently needing. Apart from the shortness of funds to finance his office and home expenses till the commission cheques should come in, he had no need for anxiety. He was doing well, and with less risk of heavy losses than must be taken by the manufacturers and the merchants and retailers between whom he dealt. He had characteristic dreams of developing into a selling organization employing many travellers, and becoming a power in many trades. But he would say nothing to

Joyce, he decided, closing his lips with the quiet obstinacy that Joyce had observed, and of which she had a little secret dread.

She was his wife, and it was her part to believe in him, and that he would find means to support whatever children might be theirs. It was a monstrous thing to propose to break off their marriage on such a pretext as that. Suppose the Rat weren't large enough (which he was unwilling to see), they could move, couldn't they?—they could move, couldn't they, *if and when*. It was absurd to make themselves unhappy over such a question when there wasn't any sign that she was pregnant at all. Of course, if she were really unwell, they ought to agree to wait. He couldn't object to that. But was she? Anyway, she hadn't gone about it in the right way. He knew that if he had felt that he must fail her from his side—in any physical or financial way—he would have said how sorry he was. He would only have failed because he *couldn't help it*; not because he felt it would be best for himself. And, first and last in his mind, she had had no right to lead him on as she had last night, and then play that trick at the last. She had deserved all she had got, and a good deal more. He would never say he was sorry for that, and he would tell her nothing about his business prospects till she was behaving as a wife should.

This was the mood in which he came home to the wife who had expected him some hours earlier, and had resolved so confidently in the morning that she would make him pay when he returned. But when does anything happen as we have planned it shall?

"Oh, Alwyn," Joyce's voice reached him as he turned to hang his hat in the narrow hall. "I'm so glad you've come! I thought baby was dead."

## CHAPTER FORTY-EIGHT

I CANNOT say that Alwyn was greatly disturbed by that rather startling announcement. He knew Joyce well enough to know that it was not in that voice that she would communicate any urgent trouble. As for Joyce, she had given some thought to the morning's quarrel, even after the events of the middle day. In fact, the last two hours had been a period of restless worry as she contemplated the possibility—horrible, though remote—that Alwyn might not return. But she had a tale to tell, and as she heard the latch-key turn, everything else left her mind.

It was a tale soon told, and without any possibility, now that it was over, of dramatic suspense in its single incident. She had thought, on what seemed conclusive evidence, that baby had swallowed a pin. She had been mistaken. While in the distraction of that belief she had sent for Dr. Crowder from over the road. He had said several nice things about the baby, proving himself to be a sound man.

Alwyn was suitably sympathetic, suitably concerned. The morning incident was forgotten. It is one of the difficulties of those who are closely married that a quarrel is hard to sustain, because so many things of common interest interfere.

But Joyce had more to tell, and she was not one to keep silent now that Alwyn had kissed her again in the right way. She was not one to lose opportunities of asking advice or help. If her own mind were troubled, should other minds be at peace? It wouldn't be at all fair.

When Dr. Crowder had asked the question that had located the pin, he had been asked in turn to give his views on birth-prevention as applied to the race in general, and in particular (very much in particular) to Mrs. Alwyn Oakley.

"Alwyn," Joyce said demurely, "Dr. Crowder thinks that we ought to adopt a child."

To understand this rather surprising proposition we must glance at the conversation that had produced it. Dr. Crowder had established a reputation among the women of South Kensington, to whom, and to whose none-too-numerous children, his ministrations were given, by a habit which was emphasized in the written instructions which he would leave for his *locum tenens* when he went for his annual holiday. These instructions would always end with a reference to the book of Proverbs, and when the young doctor to whom it was addressed had the curiosity to look it up (as he always did), he would be informed that *Even a fool is counted wise when he openeth not his mouth.*

He received the shrewd naïveté of Joyce's pointed questions in a weighty silence, and when his mouth opened at last it was not to answer, but to ask. By this means he learnt much and committed himself not at all. When he left he had pronounced no more contentious verdict than that some modern women were of unsound health, and that such women could not be expected to bear children with the frequency or of the quality of their more robust sisters. He gave Joyce a vague feeling of disquiet, as though she had accused herself of some disparaging inferiority. That had not been her idea at all. He told her of a sad case within his own experience of a woman patient to whom he had been obliged to break the news, after the birth of her first child, that she would be unlikely ever to bear a second, and how she and her husband had met the position by adopting another of about the same age, so that their child should not have the disadvantage of solitude.

"Of course," he said, "my dear lady" (which was a method of address that he used to all his feminine patients of sufficient years), "I am not suggesting that you are likely to be faced with a similar problem." He rose with some difficulty from the low and comfortable chair in which he had deposited a bulky frame. He left Joyce in some doubt as to whether she had received any advice, and if so, what it was, but with a somewhat altered perspective. She saw that the idea that it was a mother's duty to a first child not to bear a second might not be universally held. Then she thought mischievously of the way in which she could present the conversation to Alwyn, and was in a very happy mood till the hour of his expected return had passed, and a fretful anxiety supervened.

"Alwyn," she said, when the topic of Dr. Crowder's call had been exhausted in all its aspects, "I'm sorry about last night. I didn't mean to be such a pig."

Alwyn said: "No, dear, I know that. It was all that damned woman upstairs."

But how Joyce meant to behave in future was a thing that she did not say.

## CHAPTER FORTY-NINE

JOYCE could not have said what she meant to do, for she did not know her own mind. She wished she could see Frida, to talk it over with her. She felt that Frida would understand. She thought of proposing to Alwyn that she could go there for the weekend. Not with Alwyn. Alone. How should she put it to him? She commenced a letter to Frida, which she tore up when she remembered that there would always be time to wire.

During Friday she gave her thoughts to consideration of the women around her. Had each of them a large family? If not, why? She asked the greengrocer's wife, who confessed to seven. But one of them had St. Vitus's dance. You couldn't take an example from that. She felt sure that the young woman on the ground floor flat had not got any. That was a clear case. (How wicked some women are!) She assumed that every married woman either produced an annual child, or prevented its birth by some illicit method. She did not originate that unsound proposition. It had been given to her. She was sure, in any event, of her own potential fecundity—"I should leave babies all over the place," she said to herself, in her vivid way.

She looked at the married women around her, attributing every visible defect, every sign of advancing years, to the adverse influence of child-bearing. She did not attempt comparison between them and unmarried women of the same ages, which would have been illuminating.

When she had been producing the third Frida, she had read one of the medical books which are written for the guidance of women in such circumstances. Such a book must contain references to every possible discomfort, every disability or illness, that may be incidental to such a period. At the time, she had thought little of it. Now she recalled its accumulated horrors as though they were united in every normal experience.

If a childless wife appeared to be robust and comely, she looked at her with a curious blend of contempt, and envy, and hatred. Was she to find the path of wickedness flowery, while she (Joyce) *lost her looks*? If a woman had two children, it showed that she had birth-prevented a third. If she had three, it showed that she had taken the same action to avert a fourth.

Saturday morning came, and she had still said nothing about going to Birchett's Wood End. In any case, she couldn't go till evening, because Myra had got a day off, and baby was on her hands. She had been very loving to Alwyn during these two days, as though to atone for the infidelity of any thought which she knew he would not approve. But something must be done to make up her mind. Sunday morning would come, and he would want to love her again. And (this was the worst of it) she would want to be loved, which would make resistance a very unhappy thing. But she didn't want to lose her hair, and her teeth, and her looks, and leave babies all over the place. She thought again that it was a very difficult world

But, as Myra was out, she had to do everything for baby herself, and doing that does make you think what precious things they are (especially yours), and you feel that perhaps after all. Yes, it is a very difficult world.

And then on Saturday afternoon something unexpected happened, as it so often does. Myra wired to say that she had found that there was measles in her own home, and ought she to return? An hour later Frida received a wire that said: *Myra away illness coming with baby tonight not Alwyn hope not inconvenient ask Chester meet eighty thirty train Joyce.*

# CHAPTER FIFTY

ALWYN, suddenly left alone at the flat for the weekend (with the cook who didn't live in), might be excused if he were in some confusion of mind. In the too-hurried explanations which had taken place in the brief interval between his arrival home and Joyce's starting for the train, it had been clear that she had had to make an instant decision in his absence, and that she had done wisely in wiring to Myra not to return. That this had necessitated her also wiring to Frida that she would take the baby there might be less easy to understand, but it was a fact that the wire had been sent, and that it had included the statement that Alwyn would not go. Probably that had been right. There must be consideration for Frida in the numbers of this sudden invasion. The one point that was clear was that the wire had gone, the decision been taken, and that there was no time to talk if Joyce were to catch the train. It is so easy to forget one of baby's needs when you are in such a hurry as this. Alwyn must help her to pack, and she would write to him tomorrow. She really would. She would tell him what train to meet.

Write she actually did, but it was to say that Frida agreed that it would be best for her to stay at the cottage till a new nurse could be secured. Would Alwyn be *sure* to insert the enclosed advertisement in the *Morning Post*? Would he be *sure* to call at Belland's Registry, and ask them to send her particulars of any suitable nurses on their books. She did hope he wasn't too miserable. She missed him *dreadfully*. She hoped he missed her. The sooner a nurse was secured, the sooner she would be home. Would he be *sure* not to forget, etc.? There was a message for cook about his meals. An exclamation as to Christine's growth since she had seen her last. Altogether a very long letter for Joyce to write. Alwyn realized that. His answer showed that he did not think there was any shadow of misunderstanding between them, though Joyce had gone off as she did.

It was on Sunday, before the letter was written, that Frida said there was no reason that Alwyn should not come too, and that Joyce had been confidential in her sudden way as to why she did not want him to come. At the back of her mind she thought she knew what Frida would say. She did not expect to be encouraged in Aunt Muriel's views. It was the wrong house for that. But the fact was that Joyce felt the forces of righteousness to be too strong for her to resist them successfully. There was the very awkward fact that her Church was against her. There was the further fact, very fortunate for her peace, that Dr. Crowder had not given the new views the support which she had half expected to hear. There was the traitorous weakness of her own heart. No, she could not look to Aunt Muriel for any strength to defeat such a combination as these, with the risk that Alwyn would be really cross to be thrown into the already-loaded scale. What she wanted were assurances from Frida that her fears were vain. She wanted Frida to take verbal responsibility that all would be well with her, even though she should leave babies all over the place, as she felt that she would be likely to do.

But she found that Frida would not do this. She was sympathetic. She laughed at some of her fears. But she told her she must decide for herself. If she felt that she was too weak for further motherhood she must tell Alwyn, and they must agree to act accordingly. Joyce took no pleasure in that idea. She knew she wasn't weak in the least. Besides, she liked being married, as most wives do. It was a rotten idea. She mentioned the size of the flat. The financial questions which Aunt Muriel had thought so serious. "I don't think I should worry about that," Frida said definitely. "Alwyn isn't doing so badly that he can't buy a baby's food."

She came at last to her real fear. Would she be certain to lose her looks if she had another baby in less than three years, as she had been told?

Frida might have asked if she had lost her own, but she took a different line. She said bluntly: "Do you mean that you wouldn't have another baby if you thought it would be bad for your health or looks?"

The question disconcerted Joyce for a moment. Aunt Muriel had assumed that if a baby were liable to be detrimental to its mother's health, the baby must not be born. As she had talked, it had seemed an obvious thing.

Frida said: "If Chester found that it would be better for his health to go to sleep under a hedge rather than writing books—?"

"I don't see that that's the same, if the babies aren't born at all."

Frida looked puzzled. "Of course," she said, "they have to be born first. I might never have had Peter if I'd listened to those kind of ideas." That seemed final to Frida. Peter might never have been born.

Joyce gurgled into inconsequent laughter. She couldn't imagine Peter not being born if her own wishes pointed in that direction.

With her usual honesty, she went on to tell Frida what Dr. Crowder had said. Did she really think that every baby needed another about its own age? Frida certainly did. She was sorry for the solitary child. She thought three years apart was too great a gap, if it could be helped, but, of course, you couldn't make children come. She instanced the gap between Peter and John.

Joyce still thought it to be a very difficult world, but the thought didn't depress her as much as it had done two or three days ago.

She thought that she would stay with Frida till the new nurse should be found, and then go back to Alwyn. By that time she knew from experience that they would want each other very badly indeed. She would please herself in giving way, and feel that she was doing right at the same time—a combination that she approved. So the letter was written.

But things didn't happen quite as she planned. They never do.

Frida spoke plainly to Chester that night in the privacy of their own room. "If I'd fallen into that trap, I should have had her coming to me for the next twenty years, saying she'd got a grey hair or something equally dreadful, and it was all because she'd listened to me, and I'd let her down."

"You've summed that young woman up about right. I told you at first she was about as soft as a padded cell. Which side of the fence is she coming down?"

"On the right side, of course. There's never been any doubt about that. I couldn't help being fond of her if I tried."

"That's Alwyn's trouble."

"And yours."

"You're not far wrong. She's a little devil that it's easy to like. By the way, I've got that option from the bank, though they didn't consent straight off. I'd been feeling doubtful whether I shouldn't have to bid higher, but it's come through by this evening's post. It means a thousand each for your father and Alwyn. I expect they'll both know what to do with it."

"Father'll be glad. I shan't say anything about it before Joyce. She's always too ready to spend. But I suppose Alwyn'll tell her."

"I suppose he will," Chester answered indifferently. His mind had wandered to another subject of thought. Silence followed, and then sleep.

## CHAPTER FIFTY-ONE

ALWYN visited the Registry Office, and inserted the advertisement, but the week lengthened without the engagement of a suitable nurse. Letters have to be received and answered, references taken up. The engagement of a baby's nurse is not to be rashly concluded. Especially if the baby be of the importance natural to one that Joyce Oakley had originated. On Wednesday she went up to London for a few hours to interview some possible applicants. She had lunch with Alwyn, and wished she were returning home with him. She said she would come for Sunday, whether she had secured a nurse or not. But the change (she said) was doing her good. Yesterday they had spent the day in the woods, gathering faggots to be stored for the winter days. Frida bought no wood, and little coal. Joyce remembered the gardens and fields of Birstall House with a keener regret than when she had left them first. She mentioned some of the economies of country life of which Frida had told. She spoke hopefully of the time when they might have such a house instead of the confinement of the fiat, with which Alwyn concurred.

It was a happy lunch. She went back in an afternoon that was still bright, but the wind had become cold, and she was glad that Frida had a fire when she got in.

The next morning was fine and bright, though the wind was still cold. Joyce took the two babies out in the perambulator in their usual routine. It was built for two, having been used at one time for Christine and Peter. It had a canopy which covered one end completely, but was less satisfactory at the other. The wind grew colder and the sky darker, but Joyce did not notice this, being occupied with her own thoughts. She met a nun from the Convent School at Midcombe, which is about two miles from Birchett's Wood. She had become aware at this time that she had come too far, and was not sure of the best way to return. She stopped the nun, to ask where the lane on the left would lead. There was a moment's admiration of the babies. The nun said that there was rain coming—would she like to shelter at the Convent, which was not more than a quarter of a mile away?

No, Frida would be anxious if she stayed out longer. She would hurry home.

When she got home, she was drenched. So was one of the babies. It was not hers. Their places had been changed since they started. Frida noticed that, though she made no remark. But she did blame Joyce for not watching the weather and going so far. Joyce said she never understood weather. How could she tell that a storm was coming? It might have been going away.

No harm came to Frida's baby, which was well for the peace of Joyce's mind, but the weather was worse next day. The wind was bitter and the sky grey, with occasional chilling rain. It was exceptionally cold for the time of year.

On Friday morning there was a letter from Elsie. Their father was ill. He said it was nothing more than a bad cold, and did not wish a doctor called in. But she was worried. Could Frida come?

Frida hesitated. She had little more experience of adult illness than Elsie. She would be of no particular use. Never one to fuss, she considered that her father might be better able than Elsie to judge of the state of his own health. If she should leave her children and household cares to find him recovered when she arrived, she would look rather silly. Chester was going up to London. He could phone Alwyn. Alwyn was always going to Hunnerton. It was no expense to him. He might find it possible to go today and call at Elston Road to inquire.

She wrote to Elsie to say what she had done, and that she would come tomorrow (though she did not know quite how she could get away) if it were really serious.

Chester came home in the afternoon saying that Alwyn had gone to Hunnerton, and would write tonight. In the evening there was a telegram: *Father seriously ill pneumonia come at once staying here tell joyce alwyn.*

Joyce said: "Of course you'll have to go. I can manage till you get back."

Frida said: "Yes, I must go. You'd better give the boy a reply that we'll be there in the morning." The last remark was to Chester.

It was easy to say that they must go, but how? Joyce might be willing to say that she could manage, but, again, how? Frida could not say how soon she would return, and Margaret Potter's annual holiday was to commence tomorrow. Things were different from when they had been able to close the cottage on such occasions and take the children with them to Birstall House.

Joyce with the four children, and all the cooking and the house on her hands for an indefinite number of days. Frida thought not. Joyce had had time to think also, and had a similar doubt. She seldom lacked expedient in such emergency. She said, what about the Convent? Frida looked doubtful. They did not take small children or babies; it was a boarding school for older girls. Joyce said: "Well, they'll have to begin now." What was the use of being a Catholic if you couldn't get a little thing like that?

Joyce had shown herself to be fertile in emergency before now. It was true that her expedients were always of the nature of commandeering the help of others, but they were no less effective for that. She said she didn't mind the walk; she would go over, and inquire now.

Frida agreed that it would do no harm to inquire. Joyce went.

It was two hours later that she came back, tired but triumphant. The Mother Superior, reluctant at first, had given way to the nervous importunity on which Joyce relied almost as much as her eyelashes for overcoming the oppositions of a difficult world. She was to take the children over herself in the morning, and they would be kept at the Convent School till their mother could return to claim them. She would go home with her own baby, if Alwyn were returning to the flat. If he were remaining in Hunnerton, well, she would decide what she would do when the morning letters had arrived.

Frida did not like this plan overmuch. She did not care to hand her baby over to the charge of others, even for a few days, whatever assurances they might give. She thought Christine would be happy enough. There would be other girls there little older than she. But Peter was so small, so young. She had never been away from her mother's side. She had little sentimentality, but she was perturbed at the thought. Chester said he was, too. He was not worried about Peter, but full of sympathy for the nuns.

Told their fate in the morning, Christine was quietly anxious, but not unwilling to encounter the new experience. Peter took it complaisantly.

Alwyn's letter came, and was disquieting. There was no doubt of the seriousness of his father's illness. The doctors said they should have been consulted earlier. The crisis would not come till tomorrow, but there was heart trouble, and a dangerous weakness. He had asked to see them all, including Joyce. Alwyn was staying in Hunnerton. Elsie had got in a trained nurse before he arrived.

Joyce said she would go, of course. It appeared that she had already discounted the probability, or, at least, that of Alwyn's not returning, in which case she would not have cared to be alone either at the cottage or the flat. She had (it now appeared) arranged for the reception of two babies, not one.

She did not see that the Convent was doing anything extraordinary. Sister Teresa had seen the babies when she had taken them out on the day of the storm. That had been a very fortunate thing. It should be no hardship to childless women to take care of such babies as those! They ought to be very glad.

In the end, Frida decided that she must go with the children. There was so much to arrange, to explain. She trusted Joyce, to a point. But she trusted herself a good deal better. There were things to be said about Peter which might avert trouble, both for the nuns and her. But Peter was unperturbed. She parted with her mother without emotion, even with satisfaction, in the Convent hall.

Frida realized that if she were undemonstrative, her child might be the same. Did she not love Mother at all?

"You can come back," Peter conceded. She dismissed her mother with her happiest smile.

She turned away with smiling lips and grave considering eyes to accept indifferently the worship of adoring nuns.

* * * * * * *

Next Tuesday, Frida called at the Convent again. She was shown into the Mother Superior's presence. She had come to ask (she said) that the children might be kept somewhat longer, if the favour were not too great. Her father was still critically ill, and it would be a convenience to leave them, at any rate till the end of the week, when Mrs. Potter would have returned.

The Reverend Mother made no difficulty about that. They were children the most charming. And so well-trained, so good. There had been trouble but once, and that of a trivial kind. It had been a (very) early morning episode when Peter waked and demanded the instant fetching of a doll which had been left downstairs. Frida could imagine the disturbance of the Convent quiet. She knew what Peter could be like when her demands were unsatisfied.

"I hope," she said, "that Mère Saint-Dieu did not give way.

The Reverend Mother hesitated. Mère Saint-Dieu was, she explained, of an exemplary firmness, of a discipline the most strict, but—with a child so young? It was hard to deny such a request. With gentle firmness she had no doubt.

Perhaps not, but Frida had. She had more than a doubt when she saw the children themselves. They were, sent in to her after the baby-inspection was over, one at a time, where she could see them in a room, alone. She appreciated that.

Christine said she was happy, with tearful eyes. She had much to tell. She had tried to be good (she said) and not to feel lonely. She had made new friends. Frida was well content.

Peter came later. She told the tale of the doll from another angle, and in a single illuminating sentence.

"Mother," she said in a tone of happiest triumph, "I bited Mère Saint-Dieu, *and she never bited me back.*"

# CHAPTER FIFTY-TWO

THERE is no harm in an east wind, even when it blows keen and cold over the East Anglian flats, if it be one that has lately turned from another path, and its burden is that of the North Sea. It is when it blows steadily, day following day, bringing the stale air of the central plain of Europe and the further steppes, that it is a bitter and deadly thing, be the time of year and its own temperature what they may.

Pneumonia is said to be an infectious disease. If it be so, it is a fact of little practical consequence. It may attack those who gather round the bed where one of its victims lies, but its attacks will fail. It must search for the weakened life. It must find the moment of lowered vitality at which it can establish itself in the body that it seeks to kill.

It may be observed that it is when the east wind prevails that cases of pneumonia are the most numerous, and the most fatal. It may be that it brings infection from a far land, of a kind which is hardest to overcome.

But, however deadly the fight may be, in most cases it is soon over. He who lives a week may call it a beaten thing. But there are exceptions to every rule, and a month had gone, and John Oakley lived, but he had lived for that time on the border of death, which he was still near.

The corpuscles of the blood have a highly developed organization and an elaborate technique. They have a curious, but curiously limited, intelligence, without which we could not live for an hour. Their operations are regulated by controls of which we have no knowledge, and which we are unable to influence. We have, indeed, no control over our bodies, except as purveyors to them of the food that they require, and a partial muscular direction. We may use these powers to their advantage or their destruction, but if a meal be digested, or a bruise healed, it is no doing of ours.

The corpuscles of John Oakley's blood fought a vigorous well-directed fight, though the weakened heart-muscle failed to hurry the stream in which they lived at the pace which it could have given in earlier life. To a point, they worked well, and with discretion, and then, suddenly, they began to do an absurd thing. They found a spot under his ribs where they formed a sac of the waste product of the disease of which it was their duty to make a final clearance. It was a temporary expedient which might appear to give momentary relief, but being left to itself, it must have fatal consequence. At least, so the doctors thought. If those hurrying corpuscles or whatever controlled them, had a wild idea of future clearance it was one which the experience of the doctors discredited. It was a case for the knife to save, if any saving could be. They faced with reluctance the necessity of an operation which their patient was too weak to endure. Yet endure it he did, with a quiet confident courage, being resolved to live, if he might, and yet not greatly afraid to die.

They cut away some inches of rib, and removed the source of the trouble. After that, if it did not recur, he might slowly regain strength, and be no worse, or little worse, than before.

So he lay through the slow summer days in the bedroom in the suburban Hunnerton road to which he had withdrawn his defeated life, and one by one the children who had hurried to his side resumed their accustomed duties, and Elsie, helping the nurse as she could, and writing daily letters of little-varying report, wondered whether it was right to be happy in the fact that Richard Hayward was so often finding pretext of call or gift, though her father lay as he did.

And then there was another trouble—trouble with that old ignoble Bethune wound, for which the doctors did what they could with patient, useless skill; and slowly, as the slow days passed, the tide of life ebbed backward, and did not turn.

There came a day when Elsie, her mind distracted between the dawning warmth of her love for Richard Hayward, the doubt of whether she should take the advice in Frida's letter of yesterday, and tell him of the episode in Perrott's cottage how glad she was now that it had gone no further!) and the nearing shadow of death, must write to Alwyn and her sisters that the doctors said the end could not be delayed for many further hours.

## CHAPTER FIFTY-THREE

JOHN OAKLEY, bankrupt, defeated, his debts never to be paid as his last dream had been, withdrawn from the home that he had made to this alien suburban room, lay oblivious of all these things, and his children gathered to see him die.

"Doesn't he know us at all?" Nina asked—last to arrive, through no fault of hers. No, he would not know them again.

He knelt on a piece of sacking (for the grass was damp) planting pansies with a trowel in the stiff soil of the new border that he had made to edge the little lawn at the side of Birstall House.

Was he planting them too far back, not making allowance for the space which would be left when the edge of the grass should be trimmed to the new line, as he had planned it to be? He called, without looking round, to ask what she thought, and Frida—his own Frida—answered that she was putting Nina into the hammock, and would come in a moment. But Frida did not come at once, for the hammock had a twisted cord, and as he went on planting the pansies, his mind wandered and failed...dimly, confusingly, he heard the sound of Nina sobbing beside the bed...but the strangeness faded to a new reality. Frida was beside him again. Side by side, they watched the hurrying moonlit waters, leaning on Llangollen bridge.

* * * * * *

## ABOUT THE AUTHOR

SYDNEY FOWLER WRIGHT (1874-1965) penned over seventy volumes of science fiction, fantasy, classic mysteries, historical novels, poetry, and non-fiction, many of them being published by the Borgo Press Imprint of Wildside Press.

www.ingramcontent.com/pod-product-compliance
Lightning Source LLC
Chambersburg PA
CBHW031419250626
47155CB00004B/1553